Also by the author:

Books

Acid Reign
Einstein's Lament
Lazy English
Spoken English for Chinese Speakers
Ulysses: The Comic Apocalypse
Waterlogged Chopstix
Word Power

Music CD's

Live at the Palace
The Phantom of the Piano

Anthology

Spiritual Modalities:
Religion, Tolerance and Freedom of Conscience
(Ancient Greece to the fall of Rome)

TIME CURRENTS

AREA 51

Fred W. deJavanne

Order this book online at www.trafford.com
or email orders@trafford.com

Most Trafford titles are also available at major online book retailers.

Printed in the United States of America.

ISBN: 978-1-4669-3338-5 (sc)
ISBN: 978-1-4669-3339-2 (e)

Trafford rev. 09/14/2012

www.trafford.com

North America & international
toll-free: 1 888 232 4444 (USA & Canada)
phone: 250 383 6864 ♦ fax: 812 355 4082

Dedicated to the memory of my father,
Frederick Caesar deJavanne, who gave me discipline of mind,
the joy of learning, a relentless curiosity and the gift of writing,
and who, above all, safeguarded my spirit.

CONTENTS

"The only reason for time is so that everything doesn't happen at once."

Albert Einstein

He dwelt upon the summit of timespace,
the dimensionless point of the cone.
Vast was the horizon, broad and powerful his vision,
fusing all into unity.
They named him Conch.
Conch, the captive alien from Sirius C,
home of the gentle Nommo,
whose vanguard had journeyed here from his homeworld
to serve earthkind thousands of years ago,
the alien who coveted our beautiful waterworld
as the future home of his species,
whose own sun was cooling, darkening,
and whose home planet was dying.

Not a single human being on Terra
knew that Armageddon was poised to begin
in a matter of hours.
Only the alien.

He couldn't have that.
Something would have to be done.

Now . . . .

FOREWORD

The fabric of time was rent, and when the draidel of time began spinning counterclockwise, the whirlpool turned centripetal—a temporal vortex.

Erich von Neumann

TO THE READER

This is a true story, a time travel chronicle. I was a minor player in this epic saga, but I've recorded every event, interacted with all the players, and have explained the science and the theories behind it all to the best of my ability. This is also the story of how humanity was nearly rescued from thermonuclear Armageddon, from the mad generals on both sides, from the American nuclear arsenal and the Russian doomsday machine—an extinction level event! Yes, I said *nearly* because it's not over. But hope remains, and we must cling to hope. And we are alive.

I've changed a few names to keep the publisher from being sued and to keep my own name pristine and pure. Hah!! Most of the events are arguably "public domain" anyhow because they happened 100 years ago (though only days ago on *my* timeline)—in 1900—except for what occurred momentarily in 1999 and 2000. The past swallowed up the present and became the *de facto* future, and the currents of Time became a whirlpool, or more properly, a centrifuge. At least for 107 souls in the part of Area 51 that was caught up in it—plus the alien—the one rescued at Roswell in 1947.

In truth, it was the alien who would make all the difference.

NASA, the Air Force and the "intelligence" agencies no longer concern me because they cannot act against me. If they sued or prosecuted me, they would be confirming what they are desperately trying to cover up, and they know I could blow it wide open. Let's just call it an uneasy truce. And if it is true that they're out to get me, then it follows that I'm not really being paranoid, doesn't it? Doesn't it?

But with the White House, and ultimately with their historians, it's another matter: three Presidents were involved, two of them—William McKinley and Teddy Roosevelt—long dead. Bill Clinton knows the whole story, since, at that crucial moment, it was his own vision and forbearance, and, quite surprisingly, the level-headedness of Boris Yeltsin, that jointly pulled us back from catastrophe, at least for the moment. True harlequins of hubris, those two? Perhaps so, but heroes nevertheless.

Then there was the equally improbable hero, the enigmatic Nikola Tesla who straddled the nineteenth and twentieth centuries and almost made it to the twenty-first. If the world is saved, he, too, deserves much of the credit.

The actual story—Time Currents—call it a documentary or call it a novel—follows the Prologue—the "Scientific Fable"—a creation story of three species. Members of the first two, one from the Sirius system, the other from a star system in Orion's Belt, found their way to our Solar System early on, each seeding the earth's oceans with their DNA, which struggled in opposing directions to influence the evolution of life on earth. The third is us.

So there you have it. Remember: facts can be fictional, and conversely, fiction can be factual! And if you're only looking for entertainment, just skip the Prologue and go straight to Part I. The story begins at midnight in Moscow.

Wear your incredulity like a magic cloak, an invisibility cloak! The truth may yet filter through.

Gerhard Terfehr
Narrator

PROLOGUE

A Scientific Fable

i

Triple helix: Birth of two worlds

Nova

Sirius System   The Dark Star   4,000,000,000 BC

*To the majestic Dogon tribe of Mali, Africa, Po Tolo, smallest seed, was Sirius B, the Dark Star, invisible but spirited companion to giant Sirius, brightest star in the heavens, which they had worshiped for thousands of years as Sigu Tolo. They had also known about the dark star's 50 year orbit and its incredible density for several millennia before modern astronomers discovered it, and of the intense hawk-like beings from her fifth planet who had ventured out into the galaxy **en masse** centuries before the cataclysm. Po Tolo was about to make her debut as a brilliant nova, which would be witnessed by every star in the galaxy. A red giant with a mass slightly greater than that of our Sun, she had just run out of hydrogen fuel, which had fused, doubling itself into helium, fused again tripling into carbon and quadrupling into oxygen, then into magnesium, silicon and iron, as pressures swelled within to a raging fury. Within minutes, the stupendous* *explosion would expand in a brilliant fireball which would propel immense jets of pent-up matter and energy billions of miles into space in all directions, engulfing her five planets. Then Po Tolo would contract to a fraction of her size and enter her long earned rest within the darker modality of the Densely Packed.*

When she blew she was at the closest point of her orbital pass with the regal Sirius A, Sigu Tolo, the main sequence star, and a chunk of burning stellar matter 75 times the mass of Jupiter was sundered from the great star as Eve from Adam. It would slingshot to the very edge of the gravitational field of the star system, condensing into a tiny red dwarf star which would draw in for fuel all the available hydrogen from the dense cosmic cloud surrounding it. Now at just over 80 Jupiter masses (84 were needed for thermonuclear ignition) the newborn star was beginning to cool, not quite able to re-ignite, though it seethed mightily as it radiated on the brink.

Billions of years later, the new star—Sirius C—would be venerated as grandmother Emme Ya by the Dogon.

Sirius B, Po Tolo, now an incredibly dense white dwarf, nestled into a healing orbit around the wounded master, Sigu Tolo, knowing that their travails had brought about the nativity of their daughter star, Emme Ya (Sirius C). The three bodies ultimately settled into a complex but stable orbit with a prancing, precessing center of mass all of which inscribed a live triple helix pattern upon the intervening space. Emme Ya assumed a wide elliptical orbit of the triple star system every six years, perpendicular to the long, narrow orbital path of Po Tolo. The emerging star spun off the heavier elements, which agglomerated around it into the form of a single congealing planet, which promptly spun off a moon of its own.

With her new solar system, her royal cortege which included the new planet Oanna Ma and its moon Mana, Emme Ya wove an even more complex helical dance about her mother and father, Po Tolo and Sigu Tolo, cyclewheeling from brilliant, particle-rich summer at its zenith—at aphelion[1]—slowing and cooling, to solitary, crystalline winter at far distant perihelion,[2] seeming to poise, enchanted, for a timeless moment at nadir, preparing for the next pass. Then there was Oanna Ma's own seven month planetary year and 19 hour day, her seasons based upon a gentle 11 degree inclination to her star.

Less than half the diameter of earth, Oanna Ma, Sirius C's sole planet, became a waterworld bathed in reddish golden light from her own star, Emme Ya, enduring an intense bombardment of light and radiation during her nearest passes to her two parent suns, called the Blazing Year. At these crucial times, usually lasting just over a year out of the six year cycle, the planet, Oanna Ma, would be exposed to Sigu Tolo's (Sirius A's) searing light and heat and massive gravitation, and at stepped intervals to superdense Po Tolo's (Sirius B's) relentless pulsations, causing the surrounding oceans, nearly 20 miles deep, to heave mightily and heat up on the surface, and triggering volcanic activity on both the planet and her moon, most pronounced when Sirius B's and Sirius C's orbits coincided in their closest pass to the massive star, Sirius A. Frozen CO_2 at the planetary poles would then sublimate to powerful jets of gas, escaping her gravitation and streaming out into space, immense storms convulsing her entire surface as powerful hurricanes of water vapor, the remaining CO_2, sulfur dioxide, oxygen, nitrogen and ammonia, swept violently across the new planet.

During the Blazing Years, much of the oxygen, O_2, was converted to ozone, O_3, which blanketed the planetary sphere in a dense protective mantle, offering welcome insulation from the periodic assaults of destructive radiation.

As regal Sirius's dazzling thermonuclear furnace blazed unremittingly, three events coalesced into a miracle. First, the intricate triple helix of the orbit of Emme Ya (Sirius C) around Sigu Tolo

---

[1]   Zenith: closest approach to Sirius
[2]   Nadir: farthest distance from Sirius

(Sirius A) and Po Tolo (Sirius B) was woven. Subtle harmonic cycles were superadded by the pulsating tidal rhythms of her moon Mana, the entire sequence of patterns coded in microcosmic structures on the new born planet, all of which created stabilizing conditions for the orderly procession of the life force. Then, the pranic seedwinds from Sigu Tolo, pure potentiality, penetrated the fecund sea-womb of planet Oanna Ma. Finally, the dancing center of mass of the entire triple star system, precessing to the auspicious moment, triumphantly activated the codes, providing the quickening spark.

Life, cycled afresh, had arisen victorious yet again.

Progeny in this placid new waterworld now sprang forth in dizzying profusion. Under siege during each Blazing Year of the system's hexannual near passes to Sigu Tolo, the new life abounding in the oceans would take refuge in deep, cool trenches close to the poles, there to regroup and commune, then re-emerge as the waters cooled.

The growing tip of this life wave ultimately evolved into a magnificent, telepathic race of androgynous, amphibious, dolphin like beings, the singing Nommo, nourished and ministered to by their tiny sun, the gentle, ruby red Emme Ya.

Their mental processes were quantum right down to the lattices. They communicated in tonal harmonics. Their physical brains were not hemispherical but undivided, in perpetual direct contact with the primal, pure tonality of the Mother. Logic and emotions were not cloven apart, but instead bound together in stunning harmonic coherence. Music, sequential and thus time-binding by its nature, defined, dominated and pervaded their lives, their language based upon equal exponential divisions of the octave into even scales of 2 and 108, a prime scale of 23, and a magical prime scale of 137 and a fraction, activated only during Epact, whose tones and miraculous ratios directly conjoined matter and spirit, actual and potential, finite and infinite.

The Nommo reproduced out of themselves at Epact, an astronomical event in which all the major bodies in the Sirius system were perfectly aligned, a master cycle which took place every 1,296 earth years, 216 of their yearly cycles, and was celebrated for the entire orbital year. The vivified Center of Mass served as the transmitter of the seed pattern—the tonal life codes—directly to and through Oanna Ma, to the ritually gathered Clans of Nommo at the base of grand Telesis, the sacred sea mountain, quickening the latent zygotes into burgeoning incarnate life through nearly 150 million beings, 23 to the 6th power.

Cyclically returning to their unmanifest phase within the bosom of Oanna Ma, each Nommo nevertheless retained his/her inviolable identity, and, upon cycling back to the physical, retained perfect, unbroken memories of all previous sojourns, with full access to the planetary mother's collective consciousness.

The Numinous Forge

Orbiting the Galaxy	A Thermonuclear Family	4,000,000,000 BC—Now

Four stars including our own sun formed, in the distant past, a perfect tetrahedron, a shimmering stellar diamond. Sol and Sirius had once been even closer neighbors than they are today, along with two other star systems, Rama, and Rana (epsilon and delta Eridanus). At that magical time they were precisely equidistant from one another at a distance of just over one light year. Now linked in a fiery effusion, the four, during that crucial period of time shone forth as a perfect equilateral simplex (hyper-tetrahedron), an inner crucible which became a numinous forge of proto-mind, stellar consciousness merged and enhanced within the living galactic web. At the precise geometric moment of perfect juncture, a galactic beacon on the causal level of creation, a powerful but ordered spirit explosion surged forth to the next higher order within its living network, linking with the Pleiadian star, Alcyone, 250 light years away.

A growing, cumulative series of orbits, each greater orbit fully inclusive of the lesser, coherently grew, like larger and larger gears in a huge clockwork, all included within the Orbit of Orbits, that of total universe around the Great Attractor, the precessing center of all mass in our universe, still point of the turning world, junction point with the neighboring universe within the multiverse, and entry point of all dark matter and dark energy.

The consciousnesses of the four stars with their respective planetary systems, which were intimately joined in the formation of life as we know it in our sector of the galaxy, remain esoterically connected despite the increased distance between them.

Bantam Astronauts

<u>Sirius System</u>   <u>Planet Oanna Ma</u>   <u>3,500,000,000 BC</u>

In the stages of her earliest life development, at the outermost reaches of her orbit around Po Tolo and Sigu Tolo, a series of powerful sea volcanos at the perfect moment, calibrated at the perihelion of the new planet's six year orbit, sent trillions of hardy myco-spores from the planet's primeval ocean streaming into interstellar space at a leisurely three miles per second, easily breaking free of the light gravity of the planet and that of the triple star system of Sirius.

Within a mere 100,000 years, traveling in a gentle arc, some of the spores were captured by the gravitational net of Sol (at that time, you will recall, much closer to the lead star, Sirius), trillions of miles hence, and those long patient spores, hardy interstellar travelers in deep freeze, coursed into the fertile wombs of the seas—both of Terra and of Mars—who conceived.

By 2,000,000,000 BCE, still on their own planet, the Nommo had become the full manifestation of the collective consciousness of Oanna Ma. They flourished in the winedark seas, their span of physical incarnation nearly 2,600 standard earth years, nearly 450 of their planetary years. By now they had evolved limbs to navigate a newly growing mass of dry land. The globe circling sea had receded to 90% of Oanna Ma's surface.

The planet was bathed in tawny, burnished gold which brightened to dazzling vermeil during the Blazing Year. Protruding mountains with ancient rocky promontories, under the eclipsing chiaroscuro of their three suns, were now divided by lush deep green valleys and iridescent purple plains; wide rivers coursed through them. Banyan like trees, immense single organisms joined by their latticed branches and unified networks of roots covering great expanses of land mass, appeared, evolved and prospered on the incredibly fertile lands, providing a massive umbrella, which, along with the dense layer of ozone, O_3, protected the hardy flora and fauna and the brilliant, day-glo rainbow fungi during each Blazing Year. The profusion of flora began consuming the CO_2, displacing it with molecular oxygen, O_2, which now made up 10% of the atmosphere. The Nommo now ventured out upon the blessed Oanna firma.

The Nommo, the vertical Nommo, the time-binders, never lost touch with their high collective, Emme Ya. Death held no terrors for them, for it was always a conscious merging, and every individual would return at the succeeding Epact.

Powers of the Air

<u>Orion System   Star Bellatrix, Planet Fitru   2,750,000,000 BC</u>

Another class of intelligent life forms, the giant catlike Narashi, had evolved a billion years earlier than complex life forms upon earth. The Narashi, the horizontal Narashi, the space-binders, were warlike, mighty winged beasts with hemispherical brains and double the Nommos' life span, who had grown up on the desert land mass of Fitru, radioactive fourth planet of the Bellatrix system in Orion. With their powerful wings, they easily negotiated the super-dense atmosphere of Fitru, preying upon weaker species and even upon each other. But for most of them, the brain formation had gone wrong. As the creatures evolved, DNA strands assimilated unstable isotopes of crucial elements such as tri-valent phosphorus, which mutated into tetra-valent silicon upon emitting its proton, leaving a single valence gap in the DNA to assimilate pot luck, and causing the helical staircase in most of the creatures to wind around its axis in a left-handed spiral.

The intervening body joining the cloven cerebral hemispheres, analogous to our own corpus callosum, had formed such that its circuitry, calloused and coarse, could not mediate between the elegant multi-dimensional synthetic wholes of the upper hemisphere, tied directly into the planetary collective, and the logic chopping, analytical lower hemisphere, tied to physical survival and winning, which became increasingly isolated, and was, in time, believed to be the only reality.

Great ones were created on Fitru nevertheless, notably Narasimha Ma, Savior of the Narashi, but her efforts to redeem the race and the mother planet were doomed. After only a few generations, her teachings were distorted and corrupted, and turned cynically to the political ends of the corrupt and power hungry elite, the priesthood. Morality quickly degenerated into self-righteousness and false piety, and was used against itself. This ultimately became the prelude to the final destruction of the race and of the motherworld which had brought it forth. Pitted against all others, even their own kind, each and every member of their species subsisted like a tiny fortress besieged on all sides, holding out against a hostile world with every particle of their being. Thus, theirs became the realm of intrigue, of treachery, of total paranoia. *They suspected everything and everyone. They feared death to the point that they had become totally obsessed with it.*

Love, above all, was the most suspect, the supreme weakness. Over time the upper cerebral hemisphere atrophied still further and the species found itself disconnected from, and ultimately at enmity with, the planetary consciousness. Tragically for them and for their motherworld, they had also become the dominant species. They ruthlessly exterminated the two other intelligent species, and destroyed or enslaved all remaining life on the planet. They warred unceasingly with one another, exhausting the resources of their world, and ultimately reverting to cannibalism.

They had raped their mother planet, leaving her to die a burnt out, depleted husk. They needed to find new worlds to plunder. Ultimately, they developed space travel and ventured out in huge, ornate ships.

First they ravaged and despoiled the other planets of Star Bellatrix, and then, ranging outward from their home system, their vanguard, suspended in deep freeze for millennia of interstellar travel, ventured out many light years to surrounding systems, discovering our solar system over 240 light years distant, arriving in the dawning of its evolution.

But they could not fly in Terra's thinner atmosphere, and a large number of them were abandoned on the planet by their peers. They managed to survive, males and females, for a few generations. On Mars, below Cydonia, they survived for millennia living underground, and actually built a primitive civilization, but they ultimately succumbed.

The Narashi finally became extinct, but not before their parasitic spore had attached to, and merged inexorably with, those of Oanna Ma in earth's primeval oceans, the defective DNA forever altering the evolution of its creatures, splitting their evolving brains into two warring hemispheres and their physical bodies into two genders driven ineluctably to seek reunification, however brief, with their estranged counterparts.

But there was hope. Oanna Ma's gentle influence also exerted itself as earth's evolution proceeded. Horizontal was superimposed upon vertical; creating the Cross of Terra

When earth's primeval sea creatures ventured out on the land mass, a new class of life, the mammalia, split basically into two types as it took up the growing tip of the life wave—those of planet Oanna Ma and those of planet Fitru.

With one exception.

Homo sapiens became the dominant land species, and their issue were irrevocably split, individual by individual, tribe by tribe, between the dominance of the spore of Oanna Ma and that of Fitru, whose archetypes warred against one another, like angel and devil in mortal combat, within each and every individual consciousness of this species.

On earth, godlike collective beings, closely analogous to those of the ancient Hindu pantheon, developed from each as their cosmic evolution slowly unfolded towards its zenith, its Omega point: the Devas from the spore of Oanna Ma, the Asuras from Fitru. From the dreaming mind of the Supreme manifest God, the Galactic Imperator, Vishnu, through the spore of Oanna Ma, emerged the first full embodiment of the earth goddess, Gaia: her first Deva Avatar, Matsya, the fish god. In Vedic legend, he vanquished the Asura, Hayagriva, the evil horse god of the spore of Fitru, who had stolen the knowledge of the Vedas to use for his evil purposes.

Nevertheless, the divinely just Vishnu ultimately allowed two of the Asuras to evolve sufficiently to become Avatars. These were Narasimha, Lion Man, male counterpart of the peerless Narasimha Ma of Fitru, who became on earth the fourth Avatar of Vishnu (following Varaha, who had rescued Gaia—mother earth—from the depths), and the sixth, the just Parasurama, who saved the world from the oppression of the arrogant warrior caste, the Kshatriyas.

The Hindus, and later the Tibetan Buddhists, knew the descendants of Oanna Ma and of Fitru by their respective archetypes, the Devas—the high gods, and the Asuras—the jealous gods. In his time, the Persian avatar, Zoroaster, distinguished them as Ahura Mazda and Angrimainyu[1]. Finally, in the faiths of the Levant—Judaism, Christianity and Islam—they were seen as absolute good and absolute evil—God and Satan—or as the warring archangels Michael and Lucifer, take your pick.

Miracle in the Nile Valley

<u>Prehistoric Egypt, North Africa</u>   <u>1,300,000-1,294,000 BC</u>

Time the engulfer, the fleuve, river of rivers, was born of the Dark Ocean toward which all flow and into which all empty, change state and return: cycles within cycles, wheels within wheels, key to time. A seachange. Shades of the gentle seer, Edgar Cayce, "There is a River". Shades of the first great Greek philosopher, Thales, who fashioned the first T.O.E.:[2] "All is water." The furious currents of the River of Time swept everything before it, tumbling down gigantic Niagaras, ineluctably returning to the great Dark Ocean, daughter of Old Night, mother of Time.

Long dry cycles like those of the Kalahari brought us to this, as did annual cycles like the **resaca** pools in the Amazonian backwaters where our equals, our contemporaries, the dolphins, first honed their intelligence, forced, for millennia, to leap with razor sharp precision from pool to pool to pool at the last minute as the water receded with frightening rapidity, lest they be trapped and die. Evolution worked: the fittest, the ablest, the brightest survived. Finally, cycles like those

---

[1]   Also called *Ahriman*.

[2]   Theory of Everything

in the fertile desert west of the Nile valley where our most immediate simian forebears, herbivores, our true link, were isolated for 170 generations.

Unable to migrate, our ancestors were forced to live on fruits and herbs, on cactus pears and rainwater—and on mushrooms—**those** mushrooms, as their triangular valley gradually greened and finally opened to the world around them. It was a long, unbroken period of prosperity. Time and leisure were plentiful and predators were non-existent. Curiosity was born and the rhythms of nature were observed—the river, the tides, the moon, and patterns of the stars, especially Sirius,—whose annual rising signaled the flooding of the Nile, the season of life reborn and recycled, of Nature's great bounty.

There, in the potassium rich Nile riverbeds and surrounding desert, creative evolution shifted into high overdrive. Legs and arms were stretched; spines verged to vertical as they reached on tiptoe for sweet, forbidden fruit in those tall unclimbable trees with marble slick trunks and high branches, until they stood fully erect and did not revert.

Their brains were steeped in the radiant light-bearing nectars of the magical fungi, sparkling with and penetrated by the naturally occurring K-40 positron-emitting isotopes—terrestrial anti-matter. Spindle neurons grew in profusion in the cingulate and fronto-insular cortexes, creating complex and vastly enhanced neural networks. As the mirror neurons flashed their energies, filling the vacuum between them, nascent mind sensed the doppelganger image, caught itself in the act, and in the brief delay felt the passage of time, recognized the self and called it "I", saw the the Other in the mirror of the self, called it "You", seized the fleeting instant and called it "Now", sensed its Center ever in the midst of all that surrounded it and called it "Here". Neural connections proliferated and became infinitely complex. Cognition, imagination and abstract thought, born of those unhurried millennia, were honed to a fine art.

One could say that humanity mushroomed therein!

Advent of the Nommo

<u>Planets Oanna Ma and Earth</u>   <u>Year 15.71E^2</u>   <u>25,000-3,125 BC</u>

The civilization of the Nommo had peaked on their home planet, and their curiosity, as well as their knowledge of the mortality of their mother star, Emme Ya, had led them to explore other worlds in search of a new home. Emme Ya was now the color of dark sorghum and had begun to cool. The waters of their planetary sea had chilled significantly; ice had amassed at the poles and was now edging towards the equator. Her light would not expire for nearly a million years, but the Nommo knew that at the end the star would cool, the music would cease, and their beloved seaworld would congeal into ice. Then Emme Ya would enter the next stage of her life, a sister to Po Tolo. Only Sigu Tolo, the main sequence star Sirius, still young, would blaze his stunning golden-white light forever. Or nearly so.

The Nommo had mastered interdimensional travel and, using sound, had developed stargates which could serve as matter transmitters. They had also developed—actually had grown—organic space ships filled with the Nommos' medium, rich seawater, ships that could carry their physical bodies across interstellar expanses to neighboring star systems.

*It was now the beginning of the 25*th *millennium, BCE, at the heart of our most recent Ice Age. Twenty-three Nommon ships had just entered into earth-space. In the oceans, the Nommo were overjoyed to find creatures, especially the sea mammals, who had grown and evolved predominantly from the original spore of their own beloved Oanna Ma. They were disturbed to discover the extent to which the seed of the long defunct Narashi had influenced the development of life, and knew of the grave risks to the new world they entailed. They foresaw the time, within a few thousand earth years, when they would have to intervene to save this world. They had also begun to envision earth's oceans as the future home of their species.*

They first entered into the Indian Ocean and encountered a wondrous profusion of creatures, then the Aegean and the Mediterranean seas. Succeeding waves of ships arrived and a harmonic trans-global network was created throughout the deeps of Terra. Myths grew up around them, musical myths of mermaids and mermen, of shapeshifters, sirens and other fabled creatures. With the whales and the dolphins, beings most like themselves, they spent the great majority of their time singing, frolicking, communing and celebrating.

For millennia they gathered information on Terra and her life forms in the sea and finally ventured onto the land, first interacting with the Sumerians, who called them Oannes, then the Phoenicians, who worshiped them as their principal deity. The People of the Sea— the Philistines—worshiped them as Dagon.

Tales of fish-gods spread throughout the burgeoning human civilization in North Africa and the Levant. The Egyptians worshiped the great dog-star Sirius, called Sothis (also known as Sept) as the God who upon his annual appearance on the horizon just before sunrise, brought forth the water of life from the annual inundation of the Nile, bringing life and sustenance of its earliest inhabitants. The most fervent worshipers of Sirius, which they later came to call Sigu Tolo, were a tribe who first lived on the northern edge of the Sahara, then migrated to what is now present-day Mali. They were known as the Dogon.

On this halcyon day 3,200 years before the birth of Jesus, having explored inland and observed their chosen tribe, three Nommo materialized in Dogon sacred space, an altar in their temple, through a glowing portal and a pillar of light, to the amazement of the gentle, dark skinned natives they had chosen to visit and teach.

They could not have found a more open and curious group of learners than the Dogon.

ii

Seeds of a new humanity

The Merman and the Princess

Sea of Galilee   10 Nisan 3760, Hebrew Calendar   3-22-1 BC

High above the Sea of Galilee a rippled cirrocumulus cloudscape shimmered as far as the eye could see—a mackerel sky. Cool, gusty winds perturbed the surface, threatening to bring rough waters for the fishermen who had ventured out only this morning for the first time that year. Across the waters of Galilee, rays of sunlight darted and danced in and out of the minutely scalloped cloudscape, highlighting a sail here, a frothy wave there.

Sixteen year old Miriam, a dark beauty with a mass of windblown auburn hair and teal eyes, her white blouse knotted in front, walked serenely along the shoreline on this first day of spring, pondering the intensely vivid dream she had awakened from only hours before, and the august shining Presence who had knelt humbly before her.

*She sat down on a rounded stone on the shore, an old Greek **omphalos**, lulled by the rhythmic surf, reliving the peace and serenity*

of the dream time, and her eyes brimmed with tears—tears of longing, tears of happiness. Never again would she be cynical, selfish and demanding.

The Presence had shown her visions of a devastated earth and of an enslaved and dispersed people, of a rapidly descending blackness which would engulf all in chaos and in pain, and had entreated her aid. The majestic single-horned Presence, a being of land and sea, the color of teal like her eyes, signified benevolence, compassion and forgiveness to Miriam. Would he return tonight in her dreams? What would he ask her?

A ray of sunlight opened in the mottled sky and shone upon her face. She closed her eyes, and suddenly was enveloped by a whirlwind; she was back in the dream, but a dream more real than real. The Presence stood before her, spinning the whirlwind like a draidel. Like a wreathed rainbow, it wound long and narrow above his long, knuckleless finger, and as it spun hypnotically, she saw the silken whirlwind woven with vibrant life forms. It made a faintly discordant musical sound. Then, as it turned, she saw a rip in the fabric and watched a figure jerk and buckle as the rip opened and closed like a wound; it would not heal. Standing in the breach was a winged, catlike being writhing in great pain and great anger as its form was successively ripped apart and put together.

The godlike Presence then blew on his conch shell, and the image changed; she saw herself in the breach and the breach immediately healed; the figure spun effortlessly and smoothly, its radiant colors harmonized. He sounded it again and within the figure starry space expanded to near infinity, and, trumpeting forth a third time, permeated the space with sublime music, which set the entire starry scene in spherical motion. The ray of sunlight intensified and focused like a fine laser, and penetrated her entire being with deepest rapture.

She was being asked to become one with Gaia, the Mother, the spirit of earth, at the Center, and to bring forth a new seed, child of *the starry heavens. She would save the world; she would become the second Eve and bring forth the second Adam.*

*There was never any doubt. She turned to the Presence and said, simply, "**yes.**"*

The Wandering Star

Naqsh-i-Rustam, Persia Year 1737, Zoroastrian Calendar 9-25-1 BC

At the autumnal equinox, a brilliant new star seemed to wink on near Sirius, towards nearby Orion, a few moonwidths from the beginning of the Crab. A Nommon spaceship, just arrived from its orbiting base around Oberon, second moon of Uranus, moved into orbit at the Clarke radius, 22,236 miles above earth at a 33° angle to the equator, and parked.

It was the 1737th year of the Proclamation of Zoroaster, the calendar of the Zend-Avesta. Observing simultaneously at the high ziggurat towers at Naqsh-i-Rustam and Persepolis were the Magi, court astronomers of King Arsaces XXV and the Queen mother, Musa, and their assistants, the keenest-eyed observers, their human telescopes. All saw the star move in a west by northwesterly direction from deep in the southern sky to a point twenty-five moonwidths to their west, then wink off, still far above the horizon. They were elated and disturbed, not knowing what this might portend. The following night, at the same time, it was in exactly the same place, and the following, and the following. Night after night they watched it move visibly, steadily across the sky, thirty moonwidths every hour, vanishing in mid-course well above the western horizon. They first thought it was simply disappearing until, on the eleventh night, one of the observers, faithfully tracing its arc, saw it as a black dot moving across the face of the waxing moon. They named it the Visitor.

Their libraries held a vast store of information on the stars and planets; they had witnessed many celestial wonders, but never a star whose brightness did not wax or wane, which moved steadily, turned on and off, and returned, always at the same time, always to the same place in the sky. It was an astounding astronomical event, the greatest any of them had witnessed.

The Watchers, the hawk-eyed ones whose naked eye visual acuity was so sharp that they could distinguish individual stars within certain far distant subtle binaries, manned the ziggurats nightly. Unlike the distant stars, but like Venus, Jupiter and Saturn, and often Mars, the best of them could discern a tiny disk when they observed the Visitor through clearest night skies.

The astronomers were highly sophisticated; in fact, they were the most advanced on the planet. They had assimilated the stunning scientific advances of the Greek astronomer Hipparchus, a guest of the Magi at Takht-e Jamshid (Persepolis) a century and a half earlier, and had advanced his knowledge still further. They knew of the precession of the equinoxes and how to calculate it, and could cast a star chart at any location complete with cardinal points, house cusps and precise planetary and stellar positions—within a fraction of a degree.

The King's court was in turmoil, and the King himself called a meeting of his Royal Council of Ministers, the Magi, and the high priests of Zoroaster, to interpret this wondrous event, coming exactly at the Magian Year. The news was elating. At Solstice, of course, the long awaited Magian year would begin, a major Epact, the dawning of a new age. This they had known from the beginning. The equinox point had just precessed out of the Ram and back into the Fishes, inaugurating the Age of Pisces. It would take just over 2,000 more years to cross the Fishes, before backpedaling into the constellation of Aquarius, the Water-Bearer.[1]

---

[1] This is the origin of the common expression in speech and in song, "The Age of Aquarius."

But for such a major event to occur precisely at the Magian solstice: that was almost too much to bear. Even the Greek astronomers, philosophers and mathematicians had warned the world not to expect perfection in the alignment of the heavens with events of great import in the human world; there would always be a lag, something just a little late, sometimes a little early—an apparent flaw in the cosmos that depressed some of them in the extreme. Nevertheless, they could count on a portent, integrate the larger patterns, and master the disparate syntax of the star patterns—the language of the gods—the angelic script.

They had already cast the wheel, with the entire planetary Zodiac surprisingly forming into a perfect cross at the cardinal points, Sun and Moon, exactly at the moment of the next winter solstice. The question was, exactly where would it occur, and at what hour would ascendant and midheaven, descendant and nadir, be perfectly equidistant, equiangular, and aligned—in other words, a perfect cross standing straight up? Where, then, would the Visitor be exactly overhead—at midheaven. At exactly what point was it winking off? They refined their calculations further. It all dovetailed into one location. This caused even further excitement.

Egypt! At the very eastern end. Near Gaza. In fact, just over the border into Palestine. Not far from Caeserea on the Mediterranean— Be'ersheba, to be precise. At midnight on the winter solstice, here is where the heavens would move into perfect alignment: Sun exactly on the nadir, Moon exactly on the western horizon, Venus at the precise midpoint between them in the 5th house, the house of love, and the Visitor directly above. A stupendous event! A millennial occurrence.

The wild celebration of this Magian Solstice would not be on Solstice day, nor the next three days when the light was not decreasing but also was not increasing. It would follow the third day, the ancient Natalis Solis Invicti,[1] occurring on the 24th of December, sometimes

---

[1] "Rebirth of the invincible Sun"

the 25th, which was the first day that the day's length was clearly seen to increase—the Return of the Light.

The Royal Council was convened again, and the three Magi with their royal entourage began the 1,200 mile trek across the Arabian desert to the edge of the Eastern Mediterranean.

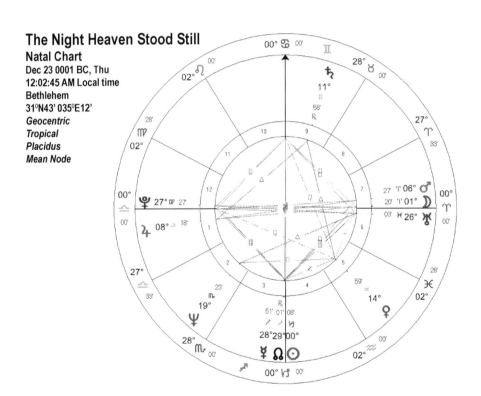

The Night Heaven Stood Still

Natal Chart

Dec 23 0001 BC, Thu
12:02:45 AM Local time
Bethlehem
31°N43' 035°E12'
Geocentric
Tropical
Placidus
Mean Node

The Magi

The Night Heaven Stood Still

Be'ersheba, Palestine   20 Tevet 3761[1]   12-22-0001 BC

Miriam had grown great with child. She and her husband Jossel b'n David (scion of the ancient House of David), an aging man of 35, had gone to temple in Bethlehem to pay their tithe, and were preparing for the day and a half journey back home, when she suddenly entered into labor.

Jossel was sadly reminded of the ridicule he had suffered from the people of Nazareth when he decided to marry this pregnant girl barely half his age. The belly laughs when he repeated Miriam's tale of the fish-god, the merman. Now he half believed it; indeed he nearly did believe it. He also knew well that jealous Herod's henchmen were mercilessly slaughtering all the newborn males, especially those descendants of the royal House of King David like himself, targeted by Herod despite their low estate because many believed that the sons of David were the rightful heirs to the vacant throne of Israel, and Herod was taking no chances.

Miriam found herself deep in thought as they prepared to embark on their journey back to Nazareth. Something was stirring in her; she knew the travails were about to begin. As the first contraction riveted her attention on her body and what was about to happen, she thought back tenderly to the special moment on the beach of Galilee with the Being. **I never even asked him if he was Jewish.**

The sun was setting, and Miriam told her husband in no uncertain terms that she knew that the child would arrive at midnight. They had very little money. They searched for lodgings around the city but it was Solstice time and there were none to be had for the price they

---

[1] Hebrew calendar

could afford. Seeing them in distress after being turned away from the southernmost inn in Bethlehem, Dov, a cartman who was at the inn and preparing to leave for Be'ersheba with a load of hay for his horses, offered them a ride, and told them there were lodgings along the way. Miriam and Jossel clambered into the cart and the three headed south.

Six and one half hours passed as they lumbered and jostled along the crude rock-lined mountain roads. They passed three more hostels, all of them either full or too costly, the last one in Hebron. By now Miriam's contractions were barely a minute apart.

At last Dov arrived at his stables. He ran inside; his wife, son and two daughters, who had been waiting for him, came out and helped Miriam off the cart. She was already dilated and her water had broken. They moved her into a middle stable which was warm and insulated from the chilly air and put out fresh hay and blankets. The oil lamps shone brightly, brighter and softer than they had ever known.

Miriam delivered a beautiful baby boy exactly at midnight. They named him Yeshua.

The Royal Persian astronomers, the Magi, with their entourage of seers, had arrived in Bethlehem on Tuesday, December 14, in time for the New Moon festival, and delivered official greetings on behalf of their king to the Roman Governor of the entire province, Marcus Tullius. The Governor and his staff welcomed them warmly, and found spacious, luxurious accommodations for them at the Megilla, Bethlehem's finest transient complex, which catered to high Roman officials and wealthy travelers.

The Romans, too, some of scientific bent, had noticed the Visitor crossing the sky and then winking off nearly directly overhead; it had caused quite a stir in Palestine. Roman and Greek astrologers also knew of the astounding lineup of stars and planets, sun and moon, that was due to occur exactly at winter solstice, a very rare event. The populace, too, were aroused by these strange portents.

Everyone knew of the fierce reputation of the Persian astronomers and were made even more curious about the nature and significance of this event—which had now brought this eminent group to such a remote place as Bethlehem, complete with royal credentials and seal from Arsaces XXV, King of Persia, the world's most fearsome potentate next to Augustus Caesar himself, and special blessings from the Queen Mother, Musa.

The consensus was that something major would occur at solstice. The Persians kept to themselves and busily prepared for the next evening's New Moon festival, exactly a week earlier. Privately they believed that a royal birth would take place at solstice, and they were curious as to why the alignment of sun, moon and ascendant centered in such an obscure place as Be'ersheba exactly at midnight. They soon learned of the ghastly injunction of King Herod of the slaughter of the innocents laid against every male newborn in the province. They notified the Roman Governor, who sadly informed them that he could not interfere in the affairs of the locals, particularly Herod the Great, so long as they did not threaten Roman sovereignty. Herod was trusted by nobody in Palestine—Jew or Gentile—and was, in fact, viewed as a madman. But he had made special political and fiduciary arrangements with Augustus Caesar—major concessions to Rome concerning Palestinian sovereignty—and he was making the most of it.

*The astronomers found a suitable starwatch point at Mt. Tethos and began their observations the following night. Their seers began the sacred **Jashne** ceremony, which would last for seven days, right up to the moment of the Solstice.*

*By early evening on Solstice Day, their search for the woman about to bear the Anointed One had garnered few leads. They had inquired at each of the hostels, but were mostly met with sullen silence, since they were suspected of being agents of King Herod. Finally they reached the inn by the road to Be'ersheba, and convinced the owners with passionate argument and a generous **backsheesh** that they were by no means connected with, approving of, or cooperating in any way* *with the agents of Herod; in fact, they would probably be able to shield the newborn from harm. Convinced at last, the stableman there told him about his friend, the driver Dov, and of the inns on the road to Hebron and Be'ersheba.*

*In the sky above the Visitor shone ever more brightly as darkness dropped once again over Bethlehem. As the entourage of the three Magi, full of radiant light, neared the home of Dov, the star suddenly intensified. They stopped and turned into the small farmstead, to the astonishment of Dov and his family, to everyone but Miriam, who was in the final travails of childbirth. For a moment, time froze; the light became as the **urlicht**, the divine eternal light. Then, just as they entered the enclosure in the stable they heard the shrill cry of the newborn.*

iii

The Prelude to Y2K

The Nommo and the Millennium Bug

Homburi Mts.   Mali, Africa   January 31, 1933

On this night in far off Mali, the Hogon, the chief of the Dogon priests, initiated the sacred ritual on the highest altar, Amma Na, the Altar of Lebe, and three Nommo once again materialized through the pillar of fire and the sacred door, as they had done ritually every 60 years. Four lights appeared around Sirius on the corners.

The Nommo knew that planet earth was in danger: first that its human natives might destroy themselves and their planet, as the Narashi had done. Their task was to save the world, for its inhabitants, and ultimately for themselves.

Two of the Nommon ships were nestled in their sea base near Cape Verde, in the deep waters off the coast of West Africa; they had arrived in 1899 and had been communing intimately with earth's planetary consciousness during the intervening years.

But today a planetary crisis was coming to a head.

On this day in 1933 the grim chariots of war were set in motion. A ruthless tyrant, scion of the dark brotherhood of the Narashi, had been elected Chancellor of an angry warrior nation the previous day. At enmity with all life and bent upon supreme vengeance, he would steep the world in bloody war and unprecedented destruction. For the Nommo, our protectors, the time had come for extraordinary action

With the special guidance of their extraterrestrial guests, the Dogon inaugurated a world-serving, world-saving ritual, invoking the spirit of Gaia, the soul of the planet, the collective earth consciousness. At great price, it would succeed, but the tides of evil were rising inexorably and would flood the plains of Europe and much of Asia, exacting a terrible toll before they would begin to recede. The Nommo foresaw the advent of the atomic age. In 1943, through mental projection, they helped the military's research in employing sound currents to transmit gross matter to other dimensional points in the omni-directional space-time continuum, a tragically misapplied phenomenon we called the Philadelphia Experiment. Late in 1944, they brought one of their spaceships out of the ocean, resolved to learn to navigate the thin atmosphere, which proved a Gargantuan task. They jettisoned the entire water medium of the ship to lighten it. The broad saucer shape provided a degree of lift, but not at slower speeds, where maneuvering was dicey and their controls were sluggish; earth's mass was several times that of Oanna Ma, and in the thin air, earth's powerful gravity exerted its full force upon the craft. They were seen often, and tales of UFO's began to abound as never before. Their ships had been designed to accelerate to great speeds through thin gaseous atmosphere and directly into space to achieve the modest escape velocity from their own planet, not to fly around it slowly from place to place. They practiced their maneuvers over open waters, frequently making crash dives into the ocean, where gravity was gentler because the water medium displaced the weight of the craft.

Now, as the ultimate event, the first atomic explosion, was about to take place in the New Mexico desert, they needed to fly nearly 1,000 miles inland from their temporary Pacific base at Puerto Peñasco,

Mexico. They visited Los Alamos, nestling at the base of the steep, otherworldly Puyé Cliffs, where they communed with the earth gods, and upon lofty Tunya, the sacred Black Mesa, just to the east, shared by the deeply spiritual Pueblo dwellers, the Santa Clara and the San Ildefonso, whose shamanic rites reached the heart of the anguished spirit of Gaia, helping her to emerge from the dark night of global war into a new era of hope.

Roswell and beyond

In May, 1945, the Nommo witnessed the birth of the atomic age near Roswell—the first atomic explosion. For two more years they visited the Land of Enchantment, investigating, learning, healing the wound in Gaia's side, and finally the inevitable occurred. Their ship crashed in the desert. Three were fatally wounded; the fourth survived with minor injuries.

Radical right wing elements of the United States military leapt into the fray, and the rest of the story is partially known. The ship was secured, and the surviving Nommo was captured and hustled away. A remote base in the Nevada desert, abetted by the infusion of tens of millions of dollars in clandestine capital, evolved into the now open secret of the enigmatic Area 51. The Nommo, an amphibian, required a seawater medium to live in. His first Nevada home was a huge, inflatable pink plastic swimming pool under a canvas canopy, into which truckloads of Instant Ocean were dumped.

A small but renegade element of the military and scientific elite, with the approval and aid of Senator Joseph McCarthy and others of his ilk, were brought to the secret base to reverse-engineer the spacecraft, learn its secrets, and to make the United States of America an invulnerable super power.

They would save the world, first by exterminating the Soviet military machine, and then by deposing all Communist governments around the globe. They hoped ultimately to bring the entire planet under the sway of an American government ruled, of course, by their own. They would create a utopia which would last a thousand years. But the secret got out, the cold war ended, and many of them died off. True scientists—empiricists—truth lovers with open minds and intellectual integrity, by means of a fortuitous default, were now in charge—except for a stubborn remnant of the Old Guard, of the spore of Fitru. These men now needed a new enemy, which emerged manifestly as that bane of free enterprise and rugged individualism, world communism thinly disguised, darling of the knee-jerk liberals, tool of the Trilaterals: the loathed and detested New World Order. The inscrutable Nommo knew this. He deftly guarded the crucial secrets whose revelation might have harmed him or the planet or placed too much power in the hands of the glassy-eyed military types who had captured and confined him, while at the same time carefully parceling out more or less innocuous but useful technical secrets and techniques, which earned his keep.

He made few requests of his original "hosts", who hypocritically addressed him as "honored guest." What he asked for he got, usually first class. First, a viable seawater environment, secondly the right to choose his human and cetacean associates, and third, to be left alone at those times when he requested it. In turn he would assist them in their quest for new technology. He had no possessions save a large, perfectly shaped, brilliantly reflective conch shell which he constantly carried and often blew, earning the nickname "Conch" from his human caretakers and friends.

Most recently among these were three prominent scientists and a physician, and the Nommo's most intimate human friend, the venerable Dogon priest, Puplampu, reputed to be over 120 years old, who had been flown in from Mali in 1948 and had been with him ever since. In 52 years, there had been changings of the guard among the scientists and physicians, but this Nommo continued to exercise his right to choose his associates, while the ageless Puplampu and his ancient Aegean friend, the dolphin Lantos, remained steadfastly by his side.

After the active cold war with the Soviet Union ended in 1989, Conch allowed himself gradually to be integrated into the Area 51 community, and actually began participating in some of their activities, especially music. His human associates were surprised and delighted. He loved the cello most of all and with his four fingers had learned to play it with great skill and unprecedented depths of expression, mastering the twelve tone division of the octave, which was very different from his species' divisions of 2, 23, 108 and 137. The first, only the octave and perfect fifth, contrasted with the last, which provided a near infinite set of combinations and permutations, upon which the deepest subtleties of the Nommon tonal language were overlaid.

The perfectly exponential twelve tone scale, along with India's 24 quarter-tone Sitar scale, taught him both the splendors and the limitations of the cloven brain of the humans. The compromised deviations of the tempered instruments caused him agony and he refused to play with a piano or harpsichord.

Privately, he composed and played hauntingly strange sound combinations on his cello, which, to the surprise of the techies and scientists, frequently registered uncannily powerful patterns on many of their detectors. The string quartet's scales were never tempered; they played in perfect tune. In time, with the help of Dr. Ludmila Ivanova, base physician and violist, specific types of communication—standardized signals and messages in the tone language were created. The dolphin's rhythmic squeaks and chatter were translated by Nommo and found to carry highly specific meanings, some with great depth and subtlety. Dr. Ludmila was taught to respond directly to the dolphin, Lantos, with her own body language and with vocal intonations, an interpretive dance with vocal accompaniment. At times, when she did so both Lantos and Conch made a characteristic *chattering sound, which she later recognized as laughter. Ultimately she learned to laugh long and loud with them and with Puplampu, happy that humor and play helped to define their lives. These were moments of great joy.*

In March, 1997, just before the mysterious lights appeared over Phoenix, Conch the Nommo withdrew into solitude, accompanied only by Puplampu and Lantos. He requested that there be no interference or unscheduled visits until further notice, and for nearly two years, emerging briefly for occasional musical interludes with the string quartet, performed continuous and elaborate rituals with his two companions. The scientists now began to notice that, at predictable intervals, their sensitive detection equipment would register strange energy bursts around the various labs.

During the final weeks of 1999, Conch, his Dogon shaman and Lantos the dolphin engaged in intense, continuous ritual activity. On the last day of the year, they finished, and Conch and the seven foot tall Puplampu emerged from seclusion. Late that afternoon they walked into the main lounge on the top level where three scientists—two violinists and a violist—were rehearsing chamber music for that evening's New Year's celebration. Puplampu, in colorful native dress, was carrying the cello and the Nommo was wearing a specially tailored tuxedo. The scientists were overjoyed. They began rehearsing two of their favorite string quartets, the Death and the Maiden and the Quartettzatz of Franz Schubert. Puplampu sat down and listened, smiling, radiating intense joy.

Lights over Phoenix

To the northwest of the Valley of the Sun, an evenly spaced series of brilliant amber-white lights, locked in a gentle arc pattern, began to appear one by one. As amazed witnesses watched and videotaped, the lights, with no variation in their V pattern, began slowly moving southeasterly over Phoenix, then reversed direction and moved, at that same leisurely pace, to the northwest, ultimately disappearing over the Hualapai reservation just south of Kingman, nearly two hundred miles north. The switchboards of the police and sheriff's departments were flooded with calls reporting the incident.

At nearby Luke Air Force Base, F-15's were scrambled and streaked northward. As they approached the area near the lights, they suddenly began evasive maneuvers, launched into a steep climb, and disappeared from radar.

At the Sky Harbor control tower, pilots began urgently calling in reports of the sighting. No blips showed up on the radar at the site, even though the lights were clearly visible all over the Valley of the Sun. At 10:28 PM a second series of lights appeared in the sky over the mountains to the southwest, then gradually disappeared behind the mountains.

The Dilettoso commission, later convened, performed a thorough analysis of the nature of the light and found no similarity to any known light generation. Each of the primary pure laser-like frequencies of red, green and blue had blazed with invariant singularity and precise harmonics.

A brilliant amber light was then seen just below Sirius, the brightest star in the sky, eclipsing its brightness for a moment, then gradually fading out.

Another Nommon ship had just arrived from the Sirius system.

Lights over Timbuctu

At the same moment, the Dogon Sirius watchers, observing the light around their sacred star, knew they were being summoned. The shamans and priests assembled and began the intense Sigui Dance by firelight at the Altar of Lebe. Since the time was out of the 60 year cycle, they knew it must be of crucial importance.

Shortly before dawn, a few minutes after the light appeared around Sirius, the intricately carved sacred door began to glow, and two round points of light appeared in the right center of the door, growing to fill the two circles of darkness, growing into a tall pillar of brilliant, shimmering greenish-white light. The Hogon, chanting continuously, poured honey on the sacred Altar of Lebe and scattered millet over it. The two Nommo who had visited during the 1994 ritual walked through the light doorway. At their instruction, a new world saving ceremony began.

Their brother Nommo was imprisoned deep within the concrete bunker at Area 51, yet his form, too, emerged through the pillar of light. The three merged ultra-dimensionally before the sacred altar as the Hogon, the smiling high priest, stretched out his arms and legs upon the ornate, carved door, chanting in longing, clear tones, whose vibrato echoed eerily through darkest Africa, from the tall cliffs of Bandiagara to the winding streets and alleys of Timbuctu, to every Dogon.

Feast of the Assumption

<u>Cleveland, Murray Hill</u>   <u>August 15, 1999</u>   <u>The first little Y2K</u>

*The joyous annual celebration of the Feast of the Assumption of the Blessèd Virgin Mary into heaven, August 15, began with flowers, fireworks and feasting in Cleveland's "little Italy", Murray Hill. It was a Holy Day of Obligation requiring all Catholics, under pain of venial sin, to attend Mass. Moreover, the event fell on a Sunday, a once in seven years added blessing. At dawn the parish churches opened for early mass. The festival commemorated a divine miracle in which Mary, or Miriam, the **Theotokos** (Mother of God), joining an elite group which included only Elijah, Enoch, Moses, and her son Jesus, was spared death and was assumed directly into heaven, enwrapped in clouds of glory. The churches were packed with happy worshipers and at the largest, Holy Rosary Church, the Auxiliary Bishop, the Most Reverend Alexander Quinn, was present and personally assisted in the communion.*

At the same time, the first signs of Y2K panic were occurring just blocks away at Case Western Reserve University. The fateful GPS Week Number Rollover was upon them. The Global Positioning Satellite system had been set up to run 1024 weeks, modulo 1024, begun on January 6, 1980. Back then, nobody seemed to be concerned about what might happen in the far distant future, at the end of the 20th century. But it was now here. The final week—week 1023[1], began at midnight—00:00:01, August 15, and would end on August 22, 1999.

A few of the early computers were tied to the Global Positioning Satellites. Harking back to the '60's, they had been designed to record the year in only two digits to save a precious two bytes, "80", not four

---

[1]   Actually the 1024th week, but it all started with Week Zero, not Week One; thus 1023.

digits—"19-80", which to the computer was simply a rerun of their Day of Genesis—they would just roll over at midnight every Saturday, counting the weeks faithfully to 1024, and start over again.

The two zeroes in the date field, "00", did not mean the year 2000 but the year 1900, a fact that would prove of great significance on the stroke of the new year at Area 51, where the time experiments were conducted throught the use of high voltage expanding and collapsing electrical fields. There, the times and dates were tied to the atomic clocks, and tied in turn, by default, to the multi-state 750K transmission lines whose terminus was at Nellis Air Force Base, Area 51.

Back in Cleveland, the trouble was that nobody was very sure which computers still carried the fatal flaw or precisely where they sat within their respective networks, because those ancient, first generation computers were simple and uncomplicated, and had been working quietly and perfectly since they were installed back in the 1960's. The engineers only knew that they were out there—somewhere—and they had no means of detecting them except by sheer guesswork.

Panic would rise when systems failed, euphoria when they worked. Maybe the real Y2K wouldn't be so bad after all. Today, at least, worst case scenario, they wouldn't be going back all the way to 1900. Only a fifth of the way back, to 1980.

At Murray Hill, the masses ended and everybody walked out into a perfect day—and the celebration began. Music filled the air. Elderly Sicilians and Calabrese danced and pranced and sang and street musicians paraded up and down the steep hilly streets with accordions, mandolins, violins. Rainbow balloons strained at their tethers; some broke free and soared happily aloft.

Streets were blocked off for a real parade with a full marching band which would start at noon; picnics were held on steps, park benches and sidewalks. Street vendors selling gelati—spumoni, luscious sorbets and granita, and rich cannolas, and the 88 year old organ grinder, Amaro, complete with monkey and cup, now a celebrity, completed the picture. Annual fourth and fifth generation family reunions took place. *The bars and restaurants were packed. Wine and beer flowed freely; hundreds of students from the nearby colossus, Case Western Reserve University, and thousands of Clevelanders, including Italians, Poles, Slovenians, Hungarians, Irish and WASP's joined in the huge party. Everybody was Italian today. Over at the university, computer mavens and programmers, working past midnight, noted the entry into Week 1023—the final week before the rollover. How many computers lurked in the shadows with the dangerous two digit date field? Nobody knew. For safety's sake, a series of trial runs were made by setting those older computers whose location was known for August 22, just as they had attempted to set them for January 1, 2000 while testing for the main Y2K. They figured they could handle a reversion back to 1980 and correct it, with no serious consequences.*

All the tests passed with flying colors. With one exception. In Murray Hill hardly anybody noticed. At midnight, a major power outage struck and darkness enveloped Murray Hill and nearly a fourth of metropolitan Cleveland. One and only one vintage computer in the loop failed the test. Haplessly, a tech, after luckily discovering it, had neglected to disconnect it from the network during the test, and it reverted back to "80"—i.e., 1980, an invalid date, and shut down, taking the entire system down with it in cascade.

At nearby Case Western Reserve, work went on frantically through the night, anticipating the worst on the real ending of the G.P.S. cycle, August 22, then the 9-9-99 threat just around the corner, and by far greater extension, 01-01-00, January 1, 2000—or 1900—take your pick.

Murray Hill adapted, and the party went on. The soft velvet glow of candlelight flickered and gleamed through the slanting streets, still wet from the brief storm, while brilliant Roman candles whooshed into the moonless sky. There was magic in the night.

Revenge of the Nines

The sovereign State of California celebrated a birthday on this late summer day, 9-9-1999—the anniversary of its statehood—all of 149 years since 1850, prelude to the banner sesquicentennial celebration set for 9-9-2000. State and private industry computer programmers and operators throughout this wealthiest and most populous of states had survived the G.P.S. Week Number Rollover virtually unscathed. But they were more worried about September 9, because for any computer with a two digit date field, which would read out at 9-9-99, a different kind of challenge loomed: in the code of many of the early computers, all nines signified the end of the program, an automatic shutdown in which they would simply roll over to all zeros, requiring a resetting and a hands on re-programming.

Governor Gray Davis issued a warning of these dangers to all the public utilities, whose monopoly privileges were wholly dependent upon a single special proviso: that when emergencies arose, they were required by law to undertake extraordinary measures to resolve them.

California's largest utility, Golden State Gas and Electric, hadn't always risen enthusiastically to this perennial challenge. It existed amid perpetual controversy and acrimony. Their management, plagued by endless bickering, underwent constant changes, in which during one year, the CEO would be an accountant, in another year an attorney, and another year an engineer. The only constant in the equation was the unswerving loyalty of the Board of Directors to the stockholders, who preferred accountants. Cynicism abounded among their workers at all levels, from linemen to engineers, from lowly clerical workers to high executives.

Hundreds of lawsuits, civil and criminal, ranging from claims of simple overcharging to embezzlement, all the way to extortion and murder, hung over the company like the Sword of Damocles, while legions of rogue law firms kept the company's adversaries mired in endless delays and appeals, Erin Brockovich notwithstanding.

Exasperated Californians had another name for them, Golden State Graft and Extortion. The company had recently made a public apology to the millions of Californians they pretended to serve, and promised to do better. Nobody seemed to notice any difference. The Public Utility Commission would order them, from time to time, to return their constant overcharges to the public. Few ever thought it was enough.

The Board of Directors, pitted against the Public Utility Commission, the liberal press, the public, and their own employees, were sick to death of all this Y2K hype. Their stock had plummeted last summer and wasn't performing all that well even within the utility sector, and they were in an ugly mood. They voted to downsize even more than they had in the previous year. In a few months all this millennium bug nonsense would be over.

Over? Oh yes! **All** *over, pun intended, warned a group of concerned computer engineers, if the company failed to act. A single weak link could create havoc throughout the system, a handful could cause a chain reaction, a cascading shutdown with dire consequences. They weren't even talking about the real Y2K yet but the date 9-9-99. When they requested emergency funds to address the problem, they were heard politely, but nobody on the board took the 9-9-99 date seriously, and they didn't understand the engineers' technical jargon. The issue was immediately shelved. In private session, the Board had shouted it down.*

Most of the old computers were attached to switching stations and substations in the East Bay, especially Oakland; a handful still operated in the San Joaquin Valley. Oakland's Mayor Jerry Brown, during his two terms as Governor of California, had been, and continued to be, *an implacable foe of Golden State Graft and Extortion, and to the Board of Directors, he was the devil incarnate. They were not about to release critical funds to help **his** cause.*

On September 2, Oakland South, the newly built public hospital, officially opened and was assigned the most serious cases in the city and county. The hospital, a showpiece of enlightened public largess, featured a state-of-the-art intensive care unit, surgical theater, dialysis unit, cardiac and pulmonary wards including four iron lungs. It was the most modern public hospital in the county, and the patients, most of them collected from the other public hospitals around the city and county, had just been moved in. Many were seriously ill; most were black and poor. Students selected from the finest medical schools around central California would clerk and intern there.

A proud and visible accomplishment of the progressive new mayor, it was to be dedicated in a well publicized ribbon cutting ceremony on Thursday, September 9, 1999, the Golden State's birthday, by Mayor Jerry Brown, Governor Davis, and a group of other dignitaries.

The Nines struck the electric power grid seconds after midnight on September 9, taking out nearly the entire East Bay. A million people found themselves without power.

At Oakland South Hospital, in the bustle and confusion of setting it up, the emergency backup generators had not been properly hooked up and tested. Golden State's inspector hadn't bothered to show up to certify it.

By daylight, the death toll had risen to seven: three of the four patients in the iron lungs, two in the ICU, one in emergency surgery, and one in the dialysis unit. By day's end, the toll had risen to nine.

The Millennium Bug was on the march.

PART ONE

Time Currents

Time is the substance from which I am made. Time is a river which carries me along, but I am the river. Time is the tiger which devours me, but I am the tiger; it is a fire that consumes me, but I am the fire.

Jorge Luis Borges

Chapter 1

The Nuclear Briefcase

Vlashikha, near Moscow   11:10 PM   December 31, 1999

In an alcohol fog, Boris Yeltsin unsteadily made his way up the wide, plushly carpeted hallway to his fifteenth floor penthouse apartment—the official Presidential Suite in a newly remodeled government highrise in Vlasikha, a Moscow suburb, site of the headquarters of SRF, the Russian Strategic Rocket Forces. His aide, Lieutenant Yuri Idol, was nearly a head taller than Yeltsin, thin, meticulously groomed, bald at 28 with a sculptured short beard and mustache. He was the official nuclear briefcase bearer. Lt. Idol followed his boss into the spacious apartment, through the plush, Victorian furnished sitting room and into the main bedroom, setting "cheget", the black *átonmyi chemodenchik,* the briefcase, against the wall behind the bed. He then turned, stood at attention, and looked at Yeltsin expectantly.

"A happy New Year to you, Mr. President. And to your family."

"Thank you, Yuri. The same." They saluted. Yeltsin nodded, smiled warmly, shook his hand and dismissed him.

He loosened his tie, kicked off his shoes and flopped on the bed. *Happy New Year everyone; happy New Year, Mr. Clinton, Mr. Jiang Zi Min.* His temples were throbbing painfully. He sat up and poured three fingers of vodka from a crystal decanter into a water glass and polished it off with professional celerity. *Did I need this? Da! Everybody is drunk tonight. This is medicine, doctor's orders. No harm done.*

Wife Naina was away tonight in St. Petersburg with daughter Tatiana and grandson Boris. He'd have been there with them, only Security thought it would be a good idea if he stayed at the center of power until New Year's morning, what with all that hullabaloo about Y2K, here and in America, where it wouldn't start happening until morning. He didn't believe it, and almost defied them, but they insisted. *So who's in charge here? Am I under house arrest by these clowns? Oh, what the hell . . . Just tonight.*

He willed himself to sleep and began snoring loudly, down for the night. Happy New Year.

Nearly an hour went by. At the witching hour, the dawn of 2,000, church bells in Kremlin Square and all over Moscow began to peal. Boris began to wake up. The pealing multiplied discordantly, louder, jangling out of tune as more and more chimed in. He opened his eyes, then smiled. *Happy New Year, Mother Russia. Happy New Millennium.* Then he covered his ears with a pillow, rolled over and closed his eyes.

As he sank deeper into sleep and began to dream, something else interfered, something annoying. He stirred. *What is it? A swarm of mosquitos?* It ceased for a brief moment, then returned. An insistent high pitch emanated from the corner of his bedroom which lasted several seconds. In altered time it played in his dream, a long unbroken note: the angel Gabriel sounding the final trump under blood red skies.

4

He opened his eyes and briefly saw flashing red and blue glints on the ceiling, and then, a very loud series of staccato beeps which jolted him fully awake.

The briefcase!! Every muscle in his body tensed; his heart pounded as adrenalin coursed through him. Suddenly he was completely sober. He leapt out of his bed, stumbling over his boots, and fell flat on his face. It almost knocked the wind out of him. Then he heard loud footsteps outside his bedroom, followed by a crisp double knock.

"Mr. President! Boris! It's Aram. We have a serious emergency!" It was the voice of Aram Avedekian, his national security advisor.

"Just a moment, Aram. Yes, I understand. The briefcase is going mad." He pulled off his trousers and his rumpled shirt, then grabbed a fresh suit and clean shirt out of his closet and slid into the trousers. He walked across the sitting room and opened the door, fastening his trousers and belt. Avedekian, a short, stocky, nervous man with white hair and thick, graying eyebrows, was obviously overwrought. His left hand had a slight tremor, and his tie was loose "Come in, Aram; let me finish getting dressed. Get ready to call an emergency meeting if you haven't already done so."

Avedekian took a long breath and composed himself. "I shall do so the moment you give the word," said Avedekian as he entered the room. Yeltsin picked up the briefcase, opened it, and keyed in the 13-digit *Kavkaz* code. It didn't work. Twice more he entered the code before he finally got it right. Both men stared intently at the emerging picture. A map of eastern Russia showed on the screen with a flashing, moving yellow blip somewhere over eastern Siberia. Live telemetry data played on the bottom right of the screen. Yeltsin's eyes widened as he took it in. This kind of scenario had been altered, updated, rehearsed *ad nauseam* from the time he had taken office nearly ten years earlier. But this was real; it was only the second time the briefcase had gone off, the first in 1995—the Norwegian weather satellite that had been momentarily mistaken for an enemy ICBM.

He acted with calm and forbearance then; he would do so now.

Yeltsin turned to Avedekian and nodded. "Aram, convene the council!"

The telephone rang; Avedekian picked it up. It was General Markov, Chief of the General Staff. "Yes, Mikhail, yes. He is awake. We're just beginning to decode these messages . . . . Yes, I agree it is serious. The President has just this moment ordered me to convene a meeting of the Security Council . . . . Right away. Be certain everyone is notified . . . . Yes, we'll have a video conference downstairs in the briefing room. Five minutes . . . . Yes, Mikhail, it could be the real thing. This does not appear to be a phantom; it has been detected in Siberia. Less than five minutes ago. I talked to them myself. And by the way, their power is down. One of their major substations. Was it hit?"

"No," General Markov replied. "It may be this Y2K, this millennium bug business. Parts of their network are quite primitive, and aging badly; there has been no money to make these refinements. I'm expecting additional reports very soon. Did they pick the missile up on radar?"

"Not exactly. It may be equipped with stealth technology making it invisible to radar. Perhaps it is flying low, below the radar." Avedekian hung up the phone and turned to Yeltsin.

"That was General Markov, as I'm sure you know. His briefcase,[1] of course, went off at the same time. He is in Kurilovo[2], down in the war room with his staff, awaiting your orders. They are analyzing the data and assessing the threat independently. Defense Minister Sokolovsky is here in Moscow; his briefcase undoubtedly has gone off as well. I will call him now to be certain he will be at the meeting."

---

[1] Russia today employs *three* nuclear briefcases, all identical: for the President, the Chief of the General Staff, and the Defense Minister.
[2] *Kurilovo*, 100 miles south of Moscow, site of major underground defense installation complete with war room.

Yeltsin nodded. He was now fully dressed. He bent his head and squinted for a long moment at the single missile tracking on the screen; it was now well past Kamchatka and heading due west. He took a deep breath and breathed a silent prayer. *This mantle has been passed to me; I can save the world. Or destroy it.* He turned to Avedekian, speaking sharply. "Call *Kazbek*[1] right now; I want to talk to Markov privately before we start the meeting." Avedekian called on the secure line and handed the phone to Yeltsin.

"Mikhail! Yes, it's an emergency; you've seen it too. But as you can see, it's only a single blip, and I have serious doubts about whether it's even real. *But* I want you to monitor the entire network—cables, radio, satellites and relays—that controls the automatic response system, the so-called doomsday machine, and be very *very* sure it doesn't get activated in the unlikely event that it's a nuke. You know well that if it activates the dead hand, *we* will be the ones doomed as well. Alter the frequencies, jam them if necessary. If real, it could be an accidental launch or some madman trying to start World War III."

"I fully agree, Mr. President. I shall do so immediately. I hope all goes well."

Yeltsin did not know whether or not to trust Markov; this added another unpleasant variable to the mix.

They placed the open briefcase on a wheeled cart and rolled it over to the elevator. By the time they had descended to the ninth basement level, the war room, the blip had moved several more degrees, now turning slightly to the north. They entered the too brightly lit gymnasium-sized war room and viewed the huge screen on the north wall. As President Yeltsin entered the buzz momentarily quieted to a hush as he looked around at everybody, made a cursory bow and a quick wave.

Defense Minister Sokolovsky, a medium height, muscular man in his 60's, emerged through from the elevator, accompanied by two

---

[1]   *Kazbek* is the Russian military command and control.

aides, carrying his nuclear briefcase himself. Dismissing his aides, he quickly joined Yeltsin and Avedekian in an adjoining office, where they exchanged the same information. They emerged and sat down together, observing the exact details from the briefcase screen play on the gigantic screen before them. The room was filling up with military and civilian defense officials and their aides. Time and 40 years facing a global nuclear holocaust on hair trigger alert had taken its toll; faces had aged and hair had grayed. For some it was almost anti-climactic.

"The trajectory is already calculated," Sokolovsky observed. "Look here!" On the huge map of Russia on the wall, more than 100' across, they saw the light green arc, the projected time of impact flashing above it, and the most likely place of impact. It was north, several hundred kilometers north of Moscow, close to the sea.

Yeltsin felt trapped and his anger was growing. "Why did this have to happen on *my* watch," he asked himself out loud. His face reddened. He waved Avedekian into one of the cubicles in the cramped office.

"What do we *really* have here, Aram?!" Yeltsin growled in a low voice. "I know of nothing strategic. Are you absolutely certain it's not a weather satellite? This does *not* look like a nuclear attack. If it is a missile, it might be an accidental launch of some kind, and not all missiles are nuclear. And you haven't proven to me that it isn't just a computer phantom!" Staring intently at the screen, Sokolovsky was nodding in agreement.

"We must, of course, provisionally assume the worst," Avedikian nodded grimly. "And hope for the best, of course."

This irritated Yeltsin in the extreme. "Spoken like a true party hack! I hired you because I thought you were an independent thinker. You're a mess! Where is your mind? *Of course* it could be a phantom! Maybe a computer prank? Chechnyans, Libyans, Iranians, terrorists on the loose, teenage hackers, solitary madmen, most of whom would love to see Russia and America destroy each other! Look where it's heading! It makes no sense. Even if it's real and it hits there it can't do all that much damage. Speak to me, say something intelligent!"

Avedekian looked crestfallen. "Sir, technically it could be a phantom, but our system is programmed to eliminate false trackings."

"But nobody has seen it. *Was there a launch detection!?*"

Avedekian took a deep breath and shook his head slowly. He broke eye contact with Yeltsin, looking down. "*No* sir, but our satellite tracking is no longer perfect," he replied sheepishly. "We've had to make too many cuts in the budget." Minister Sokolovsky shook his head, rolling his eyes.

"No launch detection?!! This is getting more fantastic by the minute!"

"Except for that, everything's working perfectly."

Yeltsin was now exasperated. He felt like strangling Avedekian with his bare hands. "How fail-safe is it?" he snapped. "This may be an error embedded in your program that's just showing up now. I'm not going to start World War III on that kind of data. We'll even take one hit if we have to."

"But Mr. President, we cannot take the chance."

His face beet red, Yeltsin grabbed him by his necktie and shouted in his face.

"*You idiot!*"

Avedekian was terrified. "Are you going to murder me, Mr. President?" Sokolovsky, mildly amused, gently intervened. "Sit, my friends, sit down."

Yeltsin relaxed his grip and shoved Avedekian into a chair. He relaxed and began to laugh. "Not today, Aram. Not today, you thick-headed Armenian!"

Visibly relieved, Avedekian forced a smile. "You are under a great strain, Mr. President. Perhaps I should call your doctor."

Yeltsin breathed deeply and spoke to his advisor in calm and measured tones. "Aram, the entire world is at stake here. I have thought this through; now listen very carefully. Russia must now act with forbearance and responsibility. We have grown up, Aram; Russia has grown up. We must not act like children in a schoolyard or adolescents on a street corner. We must act as if this world were in our hands, because at this moment it *is* in our hands, and we must preserve, *we must save this world*. It is our only home." Sokolovsky, nodding gently, concurred. "Do you not agree, Robert?" he said, turning to Sokolovsky, who nodded in agreement. His cell phone rang;

"Excuse me, gentlemen; I must speak with my aide." He left the small office. "I will be right back."

Avedekian continued.

"But what if it *is* real, Mr. President?"

"Compared to all out war a single nuke would be like a small firecracker. Clinton would never order this without the most extreme provocation. If anybody from America set this off it would be some rogue general. They have their Zhirinovsky's, too."

"Well spoken, Mr. President." Avedekian said. "It is clear that you are in control of this crisis." He turned around and crossed himself. He turned again and looked at his boss carefully, speaking under his breath. "Boris, you look terrible. Your doctor is here. Have you taken your medicine?"

Yeltsin breathed deeply, calmed visibly, his voice lower, his tones measured. Normal color had begun to return to his face. "I will be fine, Aram. As to not taking the chance, Aram, that is my point exactly. We cannot take that chance. Neither of us wants to see mother Russia destroyed. This is clearly *not* how a first strike would be carried out. I'm convinced of that now. It would be suicide. What would they have to gain, except to give us warning so that we could completely annihilate them, while they were massacring us!? We're going to have to wait and see. If and when it comes time to act, we're well prepared, and we have plenty of time."

Avedekian seemed to relax momentarily. "That's very wise, Boris. But it could turn again."

Yeltsin punched in a code on the briefcase. "I am declaring our defense condition yellow," he breathed. The upper portion of the giant screen on the wall now took on a yellowish cast. "We will leave it there for the moment, Aram; I am not going to blunder into a global thermonuclear war! Only Kassidian and our Communist friends would opt for that; they're still fighting the cold war; they still believe there can be acceptable losses. If necessary, we will quietly go to orange, internally, without any overt moves. Our missiles need only be pointed in their direction; already dozens are aimed at strategic targets in America, and at NATO. I will call each of those operators personally and alert them to be on high readiness. If there are more, if it really is a first strike, it will take only minutes to target them with hundreds of SS-20's."

"Right as always, sir!"

"It must be this way—to prevent a series of errors that can't be reversed. The stakes are far too high; even a tiny error could burgeon into a disaster of immeasurable proportions, setting off the automatic response system, the doomsday machine. For now, God forbid, if such a thing is happening, it will be missile for missile."

"How so, Mr. President? How to respond to such madness?"

"With sanity, Aram. The only way. *For a Hartford, a Minsk*, to paraphrase an old adversary, McNamara. If we overreact, everyone will die. He called such a thing a horrible spasm. And he was right." Yeltsin was now calm, firmly in control. But he needed a drink.

Avedekian persisted. "Perhaps it's a kind of decoy, a prelude."

"A conspiracy? I hardly think so. That makes even less sense— it would take away the element of surprise. Clinton is not stupid, not by a long shot. *If* there's a conspiracy, it's being run by rogues, by extremists. Some of his generals think he is the devil. We've already had our own Dr. Strangelove—General Zhirinovsky—Dr.

Doomsday. Zhirinovsky helped to sell the doomsday concept to Brezhnev and Andropov; he virtually invented the doomsday machine. Kassidian is his fanatical disciple. I also know this kind of thinking goes among paranoids and red baiters in the United States military who think we're still Communists. If you want to think conspiracy, imagine people like that conspiring with their counterparts on both sides!"

"Colonel Kassidian is a loyal officer. We have to have somebody who can analyze the worst case scenarios."

Yeltsin shook his head. "Colonel Kassidian is a fanatic; he makes Zhirinovsky look like a pacifist." He had a sudden impulse to fire Avedekian on the spot. *Could he be colluding with Kassidian and his doomsday cohorts?*

Yeltsin took a deep breath. "We're still here, Aram," he continued. "Your grandchildren are still here; they are living the good life. Armenia would not be spared. Let our world be a safe one, pristine, free. Let all this become a memory, a bad dream! Let us do it for Armenia!"

Avedekian frowned; tears came briefly to his eyes. Yeltsin's words had touched him. "You are a great humanitarian, Mr. President."

Yeltsin put his hand on Avedekian's shoulder. "World War III isn't happening. On that screen there's only one possible missile, I say *possible* missile. *Not* the kind of scenario for a first strike. *We're not even that important any more,* I'm sorry to remind you. Now Aram, you must leave. I must talk privately to Sokolovsky." Avedekian nodded, quickly left the small office and walked out into the war room.

Yeltsin waved Defense Minister Sokolovsky over. He looked tired. His face was flushed and his bushy black eyebrows showed streaks of white. At Yeltsin's behest, they ducked into another office to talk privately, each carrying his nuclear briefcase. They shook hands. Yeltsin trusted Sokolovsky, more than he did Markov.

Sokolovsky's science aide, Lt. Vitaly Ivanov, knocked smartly on the door and entered. Sokolovsky opened the door. "Ah, Vitaly. Please come in. What do you have for us?"

Lt. Ivanov was a bit overwhelmed, but his demeanor was determined and dead serious. Yeltsin extended his hand, nodded and gave him a fleeting smile. "It's a great honor, Mr. President."

"Yes, yes," interjected Sokolovsky. "Show us what you have."

"We have traced the trajectory of this . . . uh . . . missile as far east as we could. I cannot guarantee it came from Alaska. Tracing it to the nearest sightings in Siberia, we must hypothesize that it could have originated near but west of the Bering Straits. Our guess is one of the islands of the Novaya Zemlya archipelago."

Yeltsin and Sokolovsky raised their eyebrows and lifted their heads in surprise. They paused and looked at each other.

"Do you have anything more specific?" Yeltsin spoke in a more agitated tone.

"Not yet, Mr. President."

"Then at this moment you cannot say with certainty that it didn't originate in the United States," said Sokolovsky sternly.

"No sir. We cannot rule it out. Over Kamchatka we saw it turn, so we cannot know if it turned earlier. We will continue to refine our data and inform you immediately."

"Thank you, Lieutenant," Sokolovsky and Yeltsin nodded. Lt. Ivanov saluted and left the room.

Yeltsin spoke low. "In a way I am not surprised, Robert. If this is a missile, it is either a mistake or a deliberate provocation by the likes of Kassidian or Korobushin, or some rogue party trying to start a war."

He gathered up his papers and stood up. "But now we have to satisfy the Council that all the proper measures are being taken. They are waiting."

"Are you ready, Boris?"

"Yes, Robert. But right now, I have another grave concern: of the doomsday machine being set off by a fluke. We cannot take the chance that the *fail deadly* broadcast will go out, just in case it is a missile and it goes off. We need to be truly fail-safe here, Robert, doubly, triply, redundancy upon redundancy. Please disable the radio broadcast to the secret bunker in Chekhov—find the frequency and jam the signal. Do whatever you can in every way you can. Do it immediately. And anything else you can think of. If we confirm that it came from us, we must minimize it and cast it as an accident and move swiftly to find the perpetrators. You know where to look first, Robert."

Minister Sokolovsky looked directly at Yeltsin with compassionate if tired eyes. He nodded assent, grasping Yeltsin's shoulder and squeezing gently. It was a highly personal moment for the two veterans, a closeness that had always dwelt between them but was rarely expressed. "Yes, Boris. In a way I, too, am not surprised, but we must act. I know who to trust."

Yeltsin, feeling revived, felt a momentary surge of optimism. If it appears likely that it came from Russia, the immediate risk of war was reduced. He activated the security computer that only he had control of, then returned to the podium. The Minister began typing in commands. Avedekian looked worried but said nothing.

It was now time to address the Council. The familiar face of General Mikhail Markov and others from the Kurilovo facility began to appear on the screen. Here in Vlashika, military brass and high level security personnel were still taking their seats. President Yeltsin drew in another long breath, brushed his hair back, and composed himself for the cameras. He stood in front of the central podium and addressed the council.

"Gentlemen, a happy New Year to you all. It is most unfortunate that we face a potentially serious crisis in the first minutes of 2000. We are looking at what *may* be a missile tracking, although I have serious doubts about this. Nevertheless, it cannot be ignored. This is what we know at this moment: no launch has been detected. And there have been no visible sightings. Also, there was a large power outage near Kamchatka, where the transmission originated—Y2K likely. So let us be calm. In the very *unlikely* case that it is an attack, we are fully prepared to respond in kind. At this point I do not believe it's a deliberate attack; it may be no more than a computer malfunction. In addition to which, nobody has actually seen any such missile, or aircraft—*all* the evidence, such as it is, is electronic. General Sokolovsky and I concur on this matter. We have declared yellow only as a precaution and do not wish to alarm the Americans, who in any case will instantly declare DEFCON 4 in return. We are investigating all other possibilities as to cause and origin, including all potential enemies and our friends as well." He paused and looked directly at the camera eye. "I will do what I must do to protect mother Russia, who in the past has paid a terrible price for her involvement in the world, for her very existence."

He lowered his voice, looking out over the audience. "I will now telephone the President of the United States. When I have finished, I will come back here. I will attempt to answer any questions you may have, and we will confer further."

Yeltsin stepped off the podium, turned to Avedekian and ordered him to get the translator on the line After a few seconds, Avedekian handed him the phone. He withdrew from the cameras and walked into his office and punched a button to connect to his translator.

"Podolsky!! Wake up, you drunken fool!"

The translator spoke smoothly; he had been awakened with everybody else when the red alert went off. "Da! I am here, Mr. President. I am here!"

"Podolsky, are you sober? Get ready!"

"I am ready. As always, Mr. President. My mind is crystal clear." He was not entirely sober but he never slurred his speech.

"All right, Pavel. We are calling the President of the United States. There could be an emergency, and you know the dance. Engage your mind and don't make a fool of yourself and me. I am coding in your number now, so wait for the signal, get on your phone and be prepared to translate. And be prepared to be surprised! I presume you are in position. In approximately one minute I am going to call President Clinton."

Boris Yeltsin picked up the red telephone receiver in the briefcase, punched a button and waited. The translator's phone connected.

While he waited, Yeltsin briefly glanced at the monitor from Kurilovo. His heart stopped. There, in the lower left of the screen was a short muscular man standing stock still, steel grey hair, jaw set, pale blue eyes fixed solemnly on the screen. It was Colonel Kassidian.

Chapter 2

The Football

<u>The White House</u>   <u>5:10 PM</u>   <u>December 31, 1999</u>

A few minutes after 5 PM Washington time, President Bill Clinton took the elevator from the Oval Office upstairs to his private dining room for an early dinner. Hillary and Chelsea were waiting for him, already seated. The burly Secret Service man carried the American nuclear briefcase, "the Football," titanium, ovoid, nearly a foot thick, placed it behind the President against the north wall, and left the room.

The long mahogany table was set, and wine—a crisp Merlot at cellar temperature—was served with a flourish, a gentle bow and a smile to the first family by Lemuel, a White House veteran who had served four presidents.

President Clinton was inwardly very content; the dust had settled after the Monica debacle and the failed impeachment; his presidency was finally back on track. The nation was prospering as never before; the world was at peace, and he knew he'd had a lot to do with it. The 1900's would be history in a few hours; all the numbers would change.

17

Emerging from his reverie, he smiled warmly at the tall, impeccably attired elderly black man who was serving them. "Thanks, Lem, I don't know what *any* president would do without you." Lemuel then served the first family a salad with crisp new greens, tangerine sections and walnuts along with a silver cruet on the side filled with a delectable semi-sweet raspberry dressing. He then quietly disappeared.

"Look out the west window, Chelsea," said the President, returning to his pleasant thoughts. He pointed to the setting sun, emerging below a cloud near the horizon, suddenly brightening and flashing out brilliant rays. "Look at those gorgeous pinks, the fire orange, the brilliant red streaks on the clouds. Now look Chelsea, look Hillary. The whole sky is beginning to turn. What a sublime ending of the 1900's; what a perfect beginning! I think I can say, *all's right with the world.*"

"You forgot *God's in His heaven!*" chided Chelsea gently. "But yes, it's a sunset I will never forget," she breathed. Hillary smiled softly in assent; the hardness, the glitter in her eye was gone. She was quite beautiful tonight, and she looked more relaxed than she had in years.

In unison, the first family raised their glasses in an early toast to the millennium.

Suddenly, a loud wail began to emanate from the briefcase. Momentarily transfixed, the President put down his glass, picked up the 40 pound "football" and set it on the table in front of him. Adrenalin coursed through his veins.

Before he could enter the code and open it, Sandy Berger, his National Security Advisor, accompanied by his chief deputy, Warren Wiley, strode into the room. John Nevsky, Clinton's Russian translator, was with them. Their faces were grim. The Russian military had suddenly gone on yellow alert and there was detectable movement of aircraft, ships and submarines, though not on a large scale. Could this be the prelude to an attack against NATO?

The President keyed in the codes and opened the briefcase. The screen quickly appeared and they all saw the blip moving across eastern Russia. As Clinton reached for the red telephone to call Yeltsin, it rang. Boris Yeltsin and his interpreter were already on the line.

"Hallo, Mr. Praa-si-dent," Yeltsin spoke, in his thick Russian accent. "Happy New Year. I am sorry to intrude."

"*Dobriy vecher!!* Happy New Year to you, Mr. President," Clinton replied. He summoned Nevsky, who had his headphones on and was already connected. Podolsky, Yeltsin's translator immediately came on, and all four were connected. They punched in the codes and the conversation resumed through the translators.

"Good afternoon Mr. President," Pavel Podolsky translated, in clipped tones, in British English with scarcely a hint of an accent. He was sharp tonight. "I will come straight to the point. We have detected what appears to be a missile on our radar, coming in from the east. We are tracking it now. From its trajectory we've traced its apparent origin to Alaska or some point east. It cannot be an aircraft because it is moving too fast."

"I'm looking at the blip on my screen," replied Clinton. "One second." Berger signaled him, walked over and whispered in Clinton's ear. Clinton nodded and resumed. "It's definitely not from North America. I have given no such order, Boris; we are allies and we are friends. Over great obstacles abroad and at home, we have taken great forward strides together. No missile has been launched: for one thing, our satellites would have immediately detected any launch event originating here, or anywhere else for that matter. We did detect some activity near the Novaya Zemlya islands, but it was ambiguous—there was other noise at the same moment—a lot of it—and that may have obscured it. I was not informed until just now."

"We have detected no launch either, and we are checking for a possible computer malfunction. But as a precaution we have put our forces on yellow alert. I'm sure you understand."

Clinton's mind was turning furiously; he was assessing the immense gravity of the risks at hand. *I must do whatever I can to save the world.* After a brief pause, he replied to Yeltsin.

"Fully, Mr. President. For similar reasons, I am declaring DEFCON 4. Our military, like yours, gets very nervous about such matters, and that should satisfy them. Now: what about Y2K, the millennium bug? You're already past midnight. Have there been any power outages.?"

"Possibly. A few minutes ago information came in from a city near Siberia about a power loss in a large area."

"NSA will investigate this thoroughly. A good day to you, Mr. President. We will remain in close contact and I will share any findings with you the minute I know. Is Avedekian with you?"

"Yes."

"Mr. Berger is here and would like to speak to him."

Chapter 3

Y2K Olé

It was the last flight of the night, the year, the century, the millennium at Sky Harbor. Escalators and moving ramps creaked to a halt. The Y2K scare, despite a huge ad campaign of disclaimers by the airlines and the government, had caused the cancellation of thousands of flights, many at Sky Harbor.

An announcer's voice echoed through the darkening corridors in the nearly deserted airport as final boarding was called for America West's Flight 2849. Eighteen passengers filed past Maria Teresa Padilla, the pretty young Mexican-American employee at the ramp, who glanced casually at their boarding passes, smiled and wished each of them a happy New Year. As a colorfully dressed group of mariachis from Sonora, Mexico passed, instruments in hand, she switched to border Spanish. She smiled at Gabriel Alcaraz, a handsome, energetic, swarthy young man, lead trumpeter.

"Feliz ano nuevo! Vas a hacer musica en el avion?"

"Si si! Gracias! Somos Los Mariachis Dos Mil! We are thee Mariachis of 2,000. Por supuesto! Vamos a Reno a tocar toda la noche. Tocar y jugar!"

As they stepped from the bottom of the ramp onto the plane, the passengers could feel the sting of the fine, cold droplets of rain striking their faces as gusty winds suddenly picked up. It was a cold night in Phoenix. Two stewardesses, Monica and Vanessa, welcomed them cheerfully aboard the new A320 Airbus. The cockpit door was open and the captain and co-pilot, Anastas "Ani" Deukmejian and Seiji "Bubba" Kazaoke, readying themselves for the flight, nodded smilingly at the boarding passengers.

"Sit anywhere you like; we're nearly empty," said Vanessa. "Happy New Year!"

At 11:25 the plane was towed away from the gate. After an interminable wait, a de-icing truck appeared, doused the wings, and at 11:49, the plane lifted off the wet runway and headed north for Reno and Seattle. As the lights of the Valley of the Sun disappeared under the clouds, the inevitable cart appeared and Vanessa began serving drinks, including champagne on this special night. The mariachis began unpacking their instruments.

Seated on the right near the front of the main cabin, Dr. Nano Brown, 46, a senior Boeing engineer, well dressed, medium height, with chiseled features, penetrating grey eyes and a curly mop of sandy colored hair, smiled to himself and opened up his new Toshiba notebook. Ideas were flowing; he began pecking away. Two rows back, Ian Marley, a tall, slender young Jamaican with smooth coffee colored skin and large bony hands, a devout Rastaferian, set his bongo drum in the seat beside him and had a powerful urge to light up.

Seated in facing rows in the front of the cabin were the Romney's, a Mormon family of four, all progressively myopic with china blue eyes behind their coke bottle glasses At this moment they were trying to console their five year old, Brigham, who was whimpering and snuffling. Monica smiled at him and patted

22

his head; he jerked away from her, sticking out his tongue. His mother, Katherine, a thin, careworn woman in her mid-forties, with thin, blond wispy hair, wearing an ill fitting front buttoned dress with a large blue bow, gently rebuked him, picked him up and put him in the lap of his sister Jane, a gawky sixteen year old with psoriasis and severe acne, dressed in red gingham, the red and white check oddly matching the hues of her red blotchy skin. All were freckled. Their father, Joseph, a Mormon Bishop, was a portly man with a large, fleshy face and thinning hair swept up from the side in a low part and plastered to his head. He wore a black suit with a clip-on sky blue tie.

Most of the passengers were in a reveling mood as the Airbus rose through the thick clouds.

Drinks were served by Vanessa and Monica and a New Year's party began; champagne was served. In the cabin the small movie screen hung down every fourth row, began to flicker. A few passengers opted to buy the movie; Monica shook her head, smiling, and handed out a half dozen headsets free of charge.

On the left side to the rear sat the mariachi band of five, swarthy, short and muscular, with huge sombreros, guitarron, guitars, violins and trumpets, accompanied by Marta, the mother of two of them, a diminutive, aging flamenco dancer in heavy pancake makeup. All were dressed in colorful splendor. Directly across from them on the right sat a very large man, Reverend Lazaro Luna, a Mexican-American Foursquare preacher from Wink, Texas. In the next row were the newlyweds, beautiful and supple, greeneyed Wanda and strikingly handsome Warren Whipple, young, upwardly mobile Microsoft engineer-technicians, already fastened in a passionate embrace. Two rows toward the front sat Jesse Maxwell, a slim, tall, good looking 15 year old traveling alone.

The flight movie lit up the small screens, and as thunder and lightning and music surged through the headphones, the gaunt figure of Doc Brown was seen dangling from the clock tower in Hill Valley, awaiting the lightning strike. *Back to the Future III.*

The shining silver bird soared above luminous white clouds, under a crowd of stars.

A bell rang in the cabin. The captain's voice came on.

"Less than a minute to midnight. We're entering the 21st century."

"Not for another year, dingbat!" Nano Brown muttered to himself. Monica's voice purred through the speakers, her voice cultured but recognizably Southern.

"Ten…nine…eight….three…two…one…Happy New Year!"

Champagne was noisily uncorked and poured into crystal goblets borrowed from the galley in the empty First Class section. Seated on the left side four rows from the front of the cabin were Dolly Klein, a tiny, attractive Jewish grandmother with big hair, and Kitty Schrödinger, an elderly dwarf. They began singing Auld Lang Syne. All of passengers chimed in. Wanda and Warren Whipple broke their embrace and toasted themselves and the New Year, then resumed. Nano Brown took off his glasses and slugged down his beer, then sipped his champagne, enjoying the light, fruity bouquet and the tingle on his tongue. *Not bad, not bad.*

The mariachis picked up their instruments. Exhilarating music surged through the cabin. Brigham Romney stopped screaming and smiled. Ian, the young Jamaican, took out his small bongo drum and started a Reggae beat. Marta pranced up the narrow aisle flashing her skirts. Kitty Schrödinger and Dolly Klein were singing and laughing, struggling to get into the aisle to dance. Dolly had her eye on Ian Marley, forty years her junior, across the aisle one row back. He pretended not to notice. As the mariachis passed him in the aisle, Brigham, the five year old, held his hands over his ears and screamed as his mother and sister tried to participate and settle him down at the same time.

The captain announced a minor weather problem with snow and winds in the higher elevations of northern Arizona, and promised to do his best to avoid the rough spots. Nobody's spirits were dampened; many were on their second drink.

The plane suddenly hit an air pocket; Marta fell sprawling on her back, revealing fishnet stockings and torn red underwear. Her face saddened and one could see the age lines and the dark circles under her eyes become more pronounced. She tottered and reeled through the turbulence back to the lavatory. Kitty and Dolly were thrown roughly back in their seats. The plane descended. Kitty looked severely distressed. Dolly moved across the aisle to sit next to and care for Kitty, then loudly called for a stewardess to help. After a fairly steep descent to a lower altitude, the plane swung sharply to the east. They found smooth air and continued to fly low.

The cabin quieted down and a few of the passengers began watching the movie. In less than an hour the brilliant neon lights of Las Vegas flashed in and out of the cloud cover, reflecting briefly in the cabin windows.

The bell rang and the Captain's voice came on. "We're going to celebrate another New Year's right here! We're in the Pacific time zone now, so we've gone *back in time. Back to 1999!* We're going to climb to 30,000'. It should be as smooth as glass up there." The altimeter spun clockwise.

Through the headphones in the cabin, Huey Lewis and the News were singing "Back-in-Time." The volume and the palpable beat increased substantially as the captain's voice faded.

Jesse Maxwell, precocious great great grandson of the pioneering Scottish physicist, James Clerk Maxwell, suffered from multiple sclerosis, and was headed to Seattle to participate in a promising new treatment for this stubbornly resistant ailment. During the three years since it had been diagnosed, Jesse's condition would range widely from crippling debility, in which he could scarcely walk, to nearly complete remission. Tonight his symptoms were minimal and his coordination was good.

Jesse was awed by Vanessa's alluring beauty, her perfect breasts, her sensual mouth, her soft eyes. He glanced down at his Pokemon program, folded up his laptop and put it away. As she passed by he pulled at her sleeve.

"Can I have a Pepsi?" he asked her tentatively. His voice was changing and modulating—back and forth—between a man's and a woman's voice. "And one for my POcKEt MONster!" She smiled at him. Their eyes met.

"Wow, she's like a movie star!" he whispered to himself. "I'm in love!" He pushed a button on the Game Boy and immediately Arboc, the Pokemon cobrA, spread his shawl and flashed his forked tongue as his eyes widened.

The mariachis lurched into the aisle, lifted their horns to play, and begin their theme song, Las Mananitas. The two trumpets, playing in thirds, were in such perfect tune with each other that the chords rent the air.

More drinks were served. The passengers grew louder and rowdier. Once again the plane hit heavy turbulence. Reverend Lazaro Luna, heading towards the lavatory, tumbled headlong into the aisle, his huge red bible falling on top of him. He grinned weakly and several passengers bellowed with laughter as he struggled to his feet. He pursed his lips and gritted his teeth, saying nothing.

"Have another drink, Riverend!"

The plane was being buffeted by exceptionally high winds aloft at 30,000' and was blown eastward several miles off its course. The bell rang again, seconds elapsed, and the pilot's voice came on.

"Looks like we've encountered some more rough air, so we're going to fly just a bit lower. Sorry about that. We should be out of it in a few minutes. Just keep those seat belts fastened—for now." The altimeter needle spun counter-clockwise as the plane descended, enveloped by the thick cloud cover.

More cheers and singing. Monica and the cart zig-zagged up the aisle. Another round of drinks.

The air now became smoother as the plane continued to descend, still veering eastward.

"This is your captain. Looks like were out of the turbulence. I've turned off the seat belt sign and you're free to move about the cabin. By the way, it's just about five minutes before midnight. Get ready for another celebration! Monica will start the countdown."

The passengers cheered and started singing again. Jesse looked out of his window seat. Briefly he could see the ground through the clouds; only a few widely scattered lights remained visible over the vast Nevada desert. He wondered who was living down there. Vaporous clouds began rushing by again, and soon they were engulfed once more. Again he gazed longingly at Vanessa as she passed. She noticed and smiled knowingly at him.

In the cockpit a stern message burst over the radio: "You have entered a restricted military area. Identify yourself!"

"This is America West flight 2849 out of Sky Harbor, destination Reno."

"Climb immediately to 21,000 and maintain a heading of two-niner-five. You're barely at 15,000. Over and out." The pilot obediently began a gradual climbing turn. In seconds the plane was again in turbulent air.

Ani looked at his watch and flipped the audio switch. "We're going through some more rough air; fasten your seatbelts for now. We should be out of this in a few minutes. By the way. It's getting close to midnight in Nevada! Happy New Year; we're flying back into 2,000!"

Bubba, the co-pilot, switched to the weather channel, listening to the constant droning voices and static. Unusually high westerly winds aloft. He checked his VOR position and ground speed.

"Better maintain three-zero-zero, Ani; for sure we're getting blown off course again. We've got a 170 mile crosswind!"

The radio crackled again; this time the controller's voice was sterner.

"This is a warning. You are still over restricted air space at Nellis Air Force Base. Head two-eight-zero immediately and do not turn north until you are out of military air space!"

"Roger. Over and out." The captain looked at his watch again and announced to the passengers: "This is your captain. Two minutes to midnight—a *new* New Year. Synchronize your watches; I will start the countdown."

Ani and Bubba smiled at each other as the radio droned and crackled. Monica and Vanessa were now in the cockpit. Monica stood next to Bubba, stroking his thick black hair, then kissed him hard and long, while Vanessa chugged a water glass of champagne. She then tipped up the near empty bottle and drained it dry.

The air smoothed out again. The passengers began cheering and singing and the mariachis tuned up as Vanessa reentered the cabin and popped a fresh bottle of champagne for the passengers, pouring another liberal drink for herself.

The plane hit another air pocket, and the pilot descended to 20,000'. Vanessa, already tipsy, lost her balance and nearly hit the floor, spilling her drink all over the Reverend Luna and his bible. She apologized and patted him with a napkin. Staring vacantly ahead, his face taut, the Reverend turned to the brightly illustrated Apocalypse and began frantically flipping the rice paper pages, tearing some of them. Two seats behind, Jesse Maxwell was looking furtively at Vanessa.

A little dizzy, she sat down next to Jesse, who took a quick breath, shutting off his Game Boy. The bell rang and the fasten seat belt light came on. She noticed a swelling bulge in Jesse's pants. She put an arm around him, gently kissed his cheek, and patted the bulge affectionately

"Naughty boy. What's your name? How old are you?" she whispered to him, caressing the bulge lovingly. Swaying slightly, she looked down at Jesse's Game Boy. "Is *this* your pocket monster?" she slurred, squeezing the bulge.

Jesse grinned, taking another quick breath. *This is the luckiest day of my life.*

"My name's Jesse. I'm fif... uh... seventeen." He was flustered but delighted. "You're really beautiful, you know?" He caught his breath, blushing deep red. "I've got to go to the bathroom."

"You're becoming a *man!*" Vanessa whispered, gently prodding and rubbing the bulge. Jesse turned to her with a bewildered smile on his face. "I can help!" she whispered softly and lovingly in his ear. "It's *time.* Go on back."

Jesse got up and walked self-consciously back to the lavatory, his new navy blue, gold buttoned blazer draped carefully over his arm to hide the bulge. Vanessa flitted to the rear, smiling at the passengers as she passed them. She knocked on the lavatory door, whispering loudly.

"Open up, Jesse."

The latch clicked. With another glass of champagne in her hand, Vanessa eased her way into the cramped space and locked the door.

"Have a sip of champagne, Jesse; it's the new millennium." Jesse complied. She ran her fingers through his thick auburn hair and softly kissed his lips. His pants were open. "This was *meant* to happen! You're going to be a hunk, a heartthrob," she breathed, as she crouched down.

Monica began the countdown to the next New Year. "Ten... nine..." Gabriel picked up his trumpet and blew a long perfect high C, which pierced the air. "Eight... Seven... six... five..." A 'Y' flashed on all the movie screens; it was the flux capacitor in the DeLorean, filling with plasma. The long C continued, intensifying, echoing. A symphony orchestra playing the *Urlicht* from Mahler's Resurrection Symphony seemed to pick up the precise trumpet note, long and plaintive, intensifying to fortissimo.

"Four... three... two..."

A grunt and a muffled cry emanated from the lavatory.

Chapter 4

Explosion!

<u>Above Groom Lake, Nevada   Midnight   January 1 2000/1900</u>

At that instant there was a brilliant green flash, a dazzling, palpable surge of light, throwing everything out of focus, leaving eidetic doppelganger photon trails. The plane lurched violently. All the gauges in the cockpit fluctuated crazily. Eerie shadows bent around the cabin in black and green as the plane was engulfed. Fiery coruscations of white, orange and yellow now appeared and disappeared in the cabin and the cockpit, suddenly becoming grainy, then fading. Crazy zig-zag patterns danced on the television screens. A moment of utter blackness for all, of brief unconsciousness. Flesh crawled and extremities tingled.

"Wow!" Jesse exhaled. "I never knew it would be like this!"

Screams from the cabin.

"It's a bomb!"

"We've been hit by lightning!"

"It's a missile attack, just like TWA 800!"

"Jesus, we're all going to die!"

"It's a *mishegas!*"

"Carramba!"

"Praise the Lord!"

"What the hell happened?!"

"Don't worry, be happy!"

"Arghhhhhh!"

The TV images snapped into consonance, and Doc Brown's Flux Capacitor filled all the screens in the aircraft, seeds of fluid golden light, time liquefied and flowing, pulsating through the narrow end of the Y, which brightened to a blinding white light. Cabin lights flickered. Then the screens went dead. Ian Marley lit up a joint during the confusion, inhaled deeply, and smiled.

The pilots breathed a temporary sigh of relief. Lights came on in the cabin; the TV screens came on again, but the movie had stopped. The passengers suddenly realized they were flying again. Only seconds had elapsed. Everyone exhaled a sigh of relief.

Vanessa swallowed hard, planted a long wet kiss on Jesse's mouth, then cautiously opened the lavatory door and eased out. Her makeup showed streaks and smears and her hair was awry. She quickly ducked into the other lavatory and straightened herself up.

The bell rang and the Captain spoke. "Calm down, folks. We're OK now! It's over! Whatever that was, it's gone."

Pandemonium slowly subsided as it became evident that there was no smoke, no fire; the plane was flying. The stewardesses restored order.

"We're all right. We're fine!"

"It's the New Year!"

Faint cheers from the cabin.

Jesse pulled himself together; he looked in the mirror, looked away and looked again. He felt different and suddenly realized that all his MS symptoms had completely disappeared. He was exhilarated. The peach fuzz on his face had turned darker. He rubbed his chin and felt a roughness—stubble. He shook his head in bewilderment. "She *said* I was becoming a man!"

The bell rang; it was Ani, the captain.

"Settle down, folks. That was quite a scare but everything is just fine. Looks like we've encountered a weird weather phenomenon— maybe some kind of ball lightning, maybe St. Elmo's fire. Relax. It was a heckuva scare but we're completely out of it! Everything's working per-fect-ly."

A few minutes elapsed. "It's New Year's!" shouted Nano Brown. "How 'bout a drink!" The passengers looked around; Monica pushed the cart up the aisle, passing out juice, coffee, drinks.

Jesse emerged disheveled from the lavatory, tucking in his shirt, and returned to his seat. His penis, rigid as an iron poker, throbbed almost painfully. He rubbed the stubble on his face again—still there. He'd forgotten to zip up his fly. Nobody noticed.

The Romney's held their Book of Mormon and prayed. Their father Joseph, a Mormon Bishop, led the prayers authoritatively. Others were stretched out. Kitty Schrödinger, the dwarf, was bent over in her seat with her hands over her head; Dolly was caring for her. They both headed for the restrooms and Kitty was suddenly sick, throwing up at lap level all over the Reverend Luna and his bible as she passed. Wiping himself off with his sleeve, purple with rage, veins standing out on his temples, teeth clenched, he clutched his bible and fumbled with his Roman collar. He was mute. He pulled the white plastic insert loose from his collar and threw it and the bible on the floor. He exhaled, his lips moving silently, eyes bugging out.

The mariachis and the flamenco dancer had now changed in appearance, their colors softened. They stood in the aisle, picked up their instruments and began to play Guadalajara. But the sounds were also muted. Bewildered, they stopped, stood straight at attention, bowed quickly, and sat down. Ian Marley's bongo drums sounded shrill, a penetrating, fading vibrato tailing off to silence.

Marta lay her head in her son Gabriel's lap, and he whispered consolingly to her.

Monica waved off a handful of dollar bills from a passenger. "Drinks are on us!" she announced as she poured. "Happy New Year!!"

Dolly called out to her urgently. Kitty Schrödinger, the elderly dwarf, appeared both dead *and* alive. She was now slumped in her seat, eyes rolled up and mouth agape. Monica checked her vital signs; she had the ghost of a pulse. They brought her water and partially revived her but she was obviously a very sick lady.

In the cockpit, both pilots were frantically turning knobs and pressing buttons trying to get *any* response on the radio, the VOR, the GPS, or the emergency frequencies. Zero response. The radios had all gone silent except for an occasional crackle.

"Dammit—they're all dead. Try to get that military controller. What happened to our VOR—nothing! This is ridiculous!" The co-pilot began surfing all the channels.

"Nothing but atmospheric static." Bubba checked the signal. "No signal! Where the hell are the satellites? Nothing!"

"Whaddya mean, nothing on satellite? That's impossible."

"Well, impossible or not, I can't get it. Wanna try, Ani?" The captain keyed in all the satellite frequencies. Nothing.

"It's gotta be a malfunction, Bubba! It shows it's working in here so the reception's been interfered with. The lightning must have struck so close it created a surge through all our radio equipment."

"OK Ani, I'll keep trying. I might be able to make an emergency repair, though I probably forgot most of what they taught us—in one day. What about the transponder?"

"Green like everything else. It thinks it's working fine."

"Where are we?" They began checking all the electronic equipment on the aircraft. Methodically, the co-pilot checked all the gauges, then rechecked them. Ani nudged him.

"The cloud cover is gone! Look! It's crystal clear out there!"

The plane glistened under an iridescent, moonless sky.

Bubba looked outside, then at the altimeter. "21,000 feet. He noticed the ground speed indicator. "The winds have let up. Look at our ground speed!"

He gazed out the window. There were no lights below He looked up; just stars, brilliant stars. They were still checking all the instruments. For a brief instant a voice came on, then clipped off. They surfed all the radio frequencies but couldn't get it back.

"Did you hear that?"

"What?"

"The radio. Wait—I think it's coming back! I thought I heard a voice Listen."

"I didn't hear a thing," the pilot replied. Power . . . radios . . . transponder . . . altimeter . . . oil pressure . . . fuel . . . manifold . . . temp . . . vacuum . . . lights. Then he checked the aircraft— elevators, rudder, ailerons, landing gear. Every indicator shone brightly forth in readiness. The Airbus was in perfect operating order.

"Shall we send a Mayday?" asked Bubba.

"No, no. We don't seem to be in any kind of trouble at this point. I'm sure we'll fly out of this, whatever it is. Maybe we can still make Reno on time. That sick woman may be coming around."

"Well, keep trying to get them on the radio. This is really strange. I'll try all frequencies. Try the military base again!"

"This is surreal! It's weird beyond belief. Something must be jamming us. But how could they jam the VOR's? Maybe we're in some kind of VORtex. And what's wrong with the satellites?"

"Where are we?"

"We're just a little north of Groom Lake, at the far north end of Nellis Air Force Base; that must have been where we were hailed. Area . . . uh . . . 51—I think that's it—uh . . . weird science—you know, alien spaceships, little gray dudes with almond eyes."

"Dead reckoning is the answer for now." The co-pilot pulled down his maps and began to calculate the proper heading for Reno. "Maintain three-oh-five and we'll be heading straight for Reno."

Silence. Their concerns mounted as they rechecked every instrument and re-read every gauge.

Another crackle on the radio—from the control tower frequency at Groom Lake. Bubba pointed downward.

"Look down there, Ani. No lights—none. The power must be down all over."

Ani looked hard. "Yeah, you're right. Haven't seen any sign of life since this thing happened. If it's that way in Reno, how can we land in the dark? Too risky."

"Why don't we hone in on that signal we just heard. At least they're functional. It's a military base; they'd have a backup if the power was down.

Ani nodded energetically.

The radio crackled again.

Ani spoke up. "There it is again, Bubba! You were right. Guess we better get back in range. It's the only thing resembling a signal out there. We'll have to wing it."

"Wing it! Right! Well, you're right. We've gotta do it. That controller's gonna climb all over our asses, though."

"Yeah, but we've got a medical emergency, get it? He can't argue with that. FAA regs! OK, let's do it, Bubba."

At 12:07, a radio voice faded in and out. They were now 65 miles northwest of the Area 51 complex. The pilot banked the Airbus into a 180 degree turn and honed in on the elusive radio signal. He got the controller on the headset.

"This is Captain Deukmejian, America West 2849, destination Reno and Seattle. We have an emergency. You're the only thing alive on the radio. I can't raise anybody in Reno or anywhere else; I can't even pick up a VOR. *One of our passengers is critically ill.* Something very weird happened to us, but we seem to be OK now; I think we may have been struck by lightning."

"Roger," the controller responded. "We had something very strange happen here too—some kind of green explosion. All land lines are down and all our external power, too. We can't get anything on the radio or on satellite. Just a moment."

A wiry, grim faced Marine Corps Lieutenant Colonel, with hollow steel grey eyes, stiff reddish hair tinged with gray, and a bony face, flanked by two large armed guards, burst into the cab of the tower. He grabbed the microphone, out of breath.

"This is military security, Lieutenant Colonel Cassidy. Identify yourself immediately!"

"Ani Deukmejian, Captain, America West, flight 2849. Originating Sky Harbor in Phoenix, destination Reno, Nevada and Seattle, Washington."

"What are you doing flying over a restricted area?"

"We were in very high prevailing winds and also trying to get out of severe turbulence. We got blown farther east than we realized. Request permission to land; we have an emergency."

Cassidy's face was contorted with anger; veins were standing out on his face. "Permission denied! We are in a *national emergency.* Turn northwest and get out of our airspace right now! If you continue on your present course we're going to light you up!"

Ani and Bubba looked at each other, paused, and nodded. Ani spoke. "But sir, this is a class one emergency! We're following FAA regs to the letter. Right at midnight we were hit by this tremendous flash of green light; sparks and weird lights flashed through the plane and then it was over. The cloud cover went away and so did the high winds. Then all our radios went dead along with the GPS and the VOR signals . . . ."

"Get to the point!" Cassidy shouted.

"You're the only live signal we could get, so we flew back within range. *We're in trouble.* We've got a elderly woman on board who may have had a heart attack. There's no doctor on board."

The controller took a deep breath. "They're probably legitimate, Colonel."

Cassidy raised his voice. "Transmit the coordinates!"

"How much leeway are they allowed? They don't know our airspace."

"None! Remind them that no deviation will be tolerated! Keep them in the widest possible pattern, pattern F. If they deviate in the slightest degree they will be blown out of the sky."

The controller shrugged and spoke to the Airbus again.

"All right. You are ordered to remain in a wide pattern until you are cleared to land. I am transmitting the coordinates. Be prepared to remain in the pattern for some time. You must *not* deviate from the pattern! Our base is under the highest alert."

"Roger," said Captain Deukmejian. "Our GPS is disabled, and we can't get anything on satellite. You're all we've got. Anyway, there's plenty of fuel."

Lieutenant Colonel Miles Cassidy, Chief of Security, was beside himself. He had just attempted to call NORAD[1] on the hot line and got nothing. All the land lines were dead. Fearing that NORAD had been destroyed in a sneak attack, he swung into action. He assembled his security team, all Marines, immediately ordered Class One military alert status, only allowable under DEFCON One and read out the rules of engagement; everybody was to be considered a potential enemy, no one was to be believed, and in any situation even remotely suspect, the orders were to shoot to kill.

---

[1]   NORAD: North American Air Defense Command

Cassidy turned to his guards and the controller. "As you know, we've been at DEFCON 4 since mid-afternoon; something serious is going on. This so-called commercial flight could be a stealth force, a vanguard. I can't get through to Nellis, I can't even get NORAD on the dedicated line. We may be at war and NORAD may already be gone!

Cassidy picked up another phone and tried NORAD again. The line was dead. His deputy, Major Bud Wingard, who had been standing in the doorway listening, entered the cab of the tower.

"Shouldn't you call the General?" Major Wingard asked pointedly. "I'll call him at his quarters if you like. He's coming down with the flu and he didn't go to the New Year's party; I was there. I'm sure he went to bed."

"Not yet! Not yet!" snapped Cassidy. "I need telemetry on that so-called Airbus, anything. I've got it in a pattern now. I can't confirm a thing. The Cray is working, so see if you can confirm the flight and the crew. And get the passenger manifest. They can stay in the pattern until hell freezes over as far as I'm concerned. I'm declaring a red alert, and if they make any suspicious moves, I'll light 'em up! They're already well targeted."

"With all due respect, you've got to clear all that with the General! I'll call him right now."

Cassidy's face was flushed with anger. "No! Wait. I'll call him myself." He picked up the phone. keyed in a phony extension, and pretended the General was on the line. "Good evening, General . . . . There's been a huge explosion . . . . We've got a serious emergency here; all links to the outside world appear to have been cut off. Right now there's a possible enemy aircraft descending on us." He paused, pretending to listen. "We're already at DEFCON 4. Then that green burst, then no communications. Not even satellites. We may be at war and we don't have any way of knowing whether the President has declared DEFCON 1." Another pause. "Fine, General; whatever it takes."

Major Wingard, who disliked and mistrusted Cassidy. saw through the ruse but did not let on. He stepped out, quietly telephoned Col. Pick, the second in command on the base, and told him what he knew. Both immediately agreed that the General should be awakened immediately.

Cassidy signaled his Marine SWAT team, then turned to the computer screen just as the passenger manifest on the America West flight appeared. Flight 2849, check. Pilot Deukmejian, co-pilot Kazaoke. *Damned foreigners, a Russian and a Jap.* Then the passenger manifest. Maxwell, Brown, Whipple, Klein, Luna, Marley, Romney. It looked genuine enough. He shook his head in disgust, and then nodded to the controller.

"Flight 2849. You are cleared to land on runway 9-27; enter your pattern and land from due East. We'll light up the runway. We'll have a doctor there."

"Roger. Thank you. We are now heading for your . . . uh . . . base."

Colonel Cassidy's voice boomed through the microphone.

"When you land, *you will await our security team.* Nobody is to deplane until we you are cleared!"

"Roger. Over and out."

As the Airbus prepared to land at Area 51, the passengers began to stir. "Why have we turned around?" some of them murmured.

The bell rang and Ani came on. "This is your captain. You all experienced the flashing lights and the disturbance. FAA regulations—we're going to land at a base right near here and have everything checked out. They've got advanced technology there and a hospital—everything. We're *very* lucky, I mean very, very lucky. It means we won't get to Reno or Seattle on time, but, you know, America West's first concern is the safety of its passengers. There'll be a doctor there for the sick lady. Promise we'll get you all out of there as soon as we can!"

There was a stir in the cabin, grumbling, along with interest and anticipation among some, including Wanda and Warren, who briefly broke their embrace, came up for air, and looked around. The Boeing engineer, Nano Brown, was now very curious and animated; he began pecking furiously on his laptop. Reverend Luna was catatonic.

Jesse was sprawled in his seat marveling at the new millennium, his miraculous recovery, and his luck. A non-smoker, he had an urge for a cigarette. Ian Marley reached back and gave him a crooked one. He lit it up and coughed violently; he could not inhale. Kitty Schrödinger's condition had not changed—she remained as if dead *and* alive.

Dolly Klein, still attractive at 65, struck up a conversation with Nano Brown, 46, and was now flirting with him. Brigham Romney's crying settled down to a whimper. Monica offered a drink, then coffee to the Romney's. Being Mormons, they indignantly refused.

"Mormons don't pollute their bodies with drugs—including alcohol and caffeine!" Monica was told in no uncertain terms. She apologized and then handed two 7-ups to Katherine, the mother.

"Why two, Kay?" asked Joseph, the father. Kay kept one and gave the other to Jane. Monica offered peanuts to Brigham. He threw them at her and started screaming again.

Soon the runway lights came into view. Bubba switched on the Airbus's brilliant landing lights; they negotiated the low, rounded hills as the controller guided them in to the runway, and they landed. As they pulled to a stop, they were surrounded.

Chapter 5

The Bubble

Area 51's main research facility was a huge 21 level, 1,400' underground bunker built into the side of a mountain and downward, surrounded by protective steel plates three feet thick, and poised, like NORAD, on mammoth steel springs, making it virtually invulnerable to atomic attack.

In the spacious lounge on Level Two, the base string quartet had just finished Schubert's *Death and the Maiden* quartet to an audience of nearly 100. It included Dr. Sandor Rakoczy and Dr. Alfonso diGiovanni, violins, the beautiful and sensual Dr. Ludmila Ivanova, viola, and Conch the Nommo, the four-fingered space alien survivor from the Roswell incident playing cello, decked out in a specially tailored tuxedo. They were playing in absolutely perfect tune; the performance was magical. When the piece ended, the champagne was poured—a toast to the New Year.

As they refilled their glasses at the stroke of midnight, the all-pervading green burst engulfed the bunker. The champagne held the green glow in the darkness. A few seconds later, the ground began to shake, and suddenly a bone jarring earth tremor hit with a huge bang. The entire bunker shook violently on its springs, which emanated a rising, ominously pervading low tone, which slowly tailed off.

Everybody was thrown off their feet, some off their chairs. Crystal goblets shattered on the floor. Pandemonium.

No aftershocks followed. There was a moment of eerie stillness as the springs vibrated to a stop.

The alien and his human companion, the ancient Dogon, Puplampu, quietly walked to the stairwell unnoticed and disappeared. A small, dark man accompanied them.

All the power was down. In a split second the emergency generators kicked in, life support first. A fraction of a second later the lights came on in the lounge; power was restored everywhere. Suddenly everybody was awake and alive; there was frantic activity. Most moved towards the elevators, some for the stairwell; a few stood their ground. The scientists and technicians instinctively headed for their labs.

At the exact moment of the flash, time on the astro clocks registered 1-1-1900 instead of 1-1-2000. The atomic clocks hiccuped. The technicians worked feverishly to correct the error. No detectable error. All the land lines were dead. No radio signals, no satellite signals. Nothing.

A loud alarm bell clanged mercilessly in Brigadier General Thomas Mills' quarters, Area 51's emergency alert system. The General had a cold, had skipped the celebration and gone to bed early. He bolted awake and grabbed the phone. It was his second in command, Colonel Walter "Wally" Pick.

"General, this is Col. Pick. Sorry to awaken you. We have a major emergency. Basewide—and possibly beyond. All communications are down including satellites, VOR's, GPS, all outside lines. We can't even contact Nellis or Edwards. Everything from the outside is dead."

The General was suddenly wide awake. "Have you contacted security—Lt. Col. Cassidy?"

"They contacted me. In fact. Col. Cassidy thinks World War III is upon us, and he wants to declare the highest security alert. Says he tried to contact NORAD and the lines were dead. Plus a commercial airliner has just called with a medical emergency and the same complaint—no satellites, no radio—except at our base. He thinks it might be a vanguard—an invading force. They're landing now or are about to land."

"Keep me fully apprised, Wally. We'll get to the bottom of this as quick as we can. I'll call a base wide meeting of all the engineering, maintenance, electronic and science people immediately. You handle Security and Col. Cassidy. And watch him closely. Keep Major Wingard apprised; he's Security's second in command. And trustworthy."

"I'll do it, General. I'll keep an eye on Cassidy; he may already have overstepped his bounds."

"Let me know what's going on with the airliner. I'll alert Dr. Ivanova and the medical team."

After placing the entire base on alert, the General called an emergency meeting of all department heads to be assembled and meet in the Science Division on Level 18 as soon as possible.

The elevators were quickly packed to capacity. At the retractable control tower, no traffic had been due until 6:45 AM, until the America West Airbus radioed in its emergency; then the tower rose miraculously out of one of the low hills to its full height of 100', looking like a huge phallic monolith suddenly infused. All the lifts in the bunker were working; others started pouring out into the cold moonless night and milling around.

It was now nearly 12:30 AM. The Airbus had landed minutes earlier. Cassidy dispatched his heavily armed SWAT team to secure it as a potential enemy aircraft. "I'm declaring Class One status, effective immediately. Go! Remember, things are not what they seem." They all knew the drill; they had rehearsed it time and time again. The crux of Class One: trust no one, shoot first and ask questions later.

He would take no chances.

As the Airbus sat silently on the runway, two grim security officers arrived at the same time as the chief base physician, Dr. Ludmila Ivanova, accompanied by two medics. All five boarded the plane. The NCO in charge, Marine Sgt. Marvin Daumer, ordered the baggage compartment emptied immediately and searched. The contents were unceremoniously dumped on the ground. Two of the Marines, 6'3", 270 pound identical twins, entered the passenger section, checking everywhere with detectors. They were met by a spirited flamenco strum from the guitarron and a blast of the two trumpets. They drew their guns. The mariachis stopped in terror and sat down; Marta sobbed audibly. The Whipples, horrified, sat up straight, holding hands tightly. Dr. Nano Brown quietly switched on his pocket recorder and sat expressionless, trying to look unconcerned. Jesse switched off his Game Boy, fidgeting in his seat. He quietly zipped up his fly.

Joseph Romney opened up his Book of Mormon to Alma 32, clasping Katherine's hand firmly, pointed to a passage and softly read, "I behold that ye are lowly in heart; and if so, blessed are ye." Brigham Romney, on his mother's lap, cried loudly and impetuously; he was ordered to shut up. Jane Romney sat stiffly, her lips pursed, legs crossed, left leg swinging.

Kitty Schrödinger was stretched out prone on the seat while Dolly Klein, kneeling in front of her, held her head and gently stroked her face. Reverend Luna continued to sit motionless, staring sightlessly, his fists clenched. Ian Marley's stomach was rumbling; he began to perspire. He started to get up to go to the rest room and was rudely shoved back into his seat.

Dr. Ludmila, stethoscope dangling from her neck, was directed to Kitty Schrödinger; she listened to her heart and lungs. A short stretcher was brought aboard. Dolly Klein insisted on accompanying her and they refused. She became furious and strident, hassling the medics and the security men, calling them Nazis and then cursing them in Yiddish. "Ah schvartz chalerya af'n zee! Farshtoonkeneh mumsers!"

"Wonder whut in the hail she meant by that," drawled one of the security men.

"It means Happy New Year, *schmegeggie!*"[1] she smirked. She was ordered to sit down and shut up. "Shtarkers!"[2] she muttered to herself. Her anger was feeding on itself; she was hopping mad.

The stewardesses, Monica and Vanessa, were frisked *very* thoroughly, along with the lovely Wanda Whipple; observing this, Dr. Ludmila laughed loudly and scornfully. The pilots and stewardesses were taken directly to Col. Pick's office at headquarters. Kitty was placed in the waiting ambulance and Dr Ludmila accompanied her to the base hospital on Level Four of the main bunker. Another physician, a Punjabi blue turbaned Sikh, Dr. Narayan Singh, examined her, nodded to Dr. Ludmila, and took over.

Each passenger was checked out by the security officers and frisked. Ian Marley, momentarily flatulent, was ordered to drop his pants, and a small bag of pot was found between his cheeks. He could not hold back; he expelled a powerful jet of moist, pungent gas which blew the tiny plastic bag into the next row. Undaunted, the twin security men, Sgts. Marvin and Melvin

---

[1] *Schmegeggie* is a colorful Modern Hebrew cognate to the Yiddish *schmendrick*, which means a fool, buffoon, oaf, or an apathetic or incompetent person.

[2] A *shtarker,* literally a strongman, is basically a bully, a loud, intrusive, insensitive or harsh person. From MHG, *stark* harsh, strong, also desolate or bleak.

Daumer, retrieved the bag; each sniffed it thoroughly, each nodded knowingly, in unison, to his counterpart, and then confiscated it. Marley was handcuffed, grabbed by his dredlocks, and marched roughly off the plane.

Suddenly Reverend Luna came alive. Eyes bulging, he leapt up from his seat, and with almost superhuman strength, wrestled one of the security officers, Marvin, to the floor and began bludgeoning him with his huge red bible. They drew their guns. Marvin's twin, Melvin, fired. Reverend Luna tried to use his bible as a shield, but the bullet ripped through it and entered his chest. He collapsed in agony.

With great strain the medical corpsmen and security men placed his 290 pound frame on a stretcher and tried to remove it from the plane. As they exited with it, they slipped in his blood, and the body tumbled helter skelter off the stretcher and on to the ground. The passengers sat in stunned silence.

They continued to check out and frisk the passengers. The Romney's were cleared and taken to one of the Mormon residences, where they were welcomed. The mariachis were allowed to deplane but their instruments were confiscated, as were Nano Brown's, Jesse Maxwell's and the Whipples' laptops, and Jesse's Pokemon Game Boy.

Dolly Klein, loudly defiant, was taken into one of the security offices and harshly interrogated; she first requested a lawyer, then a Rabbi. She castigated them mercilessly in a stream of ferocious guttural Yiddishisms, whose meaning reached them despite the fact that they did not know the words. They gagged her with grey duct tape.

Air Force Major Laura Schenk, MSW, who had come to interview the passengers, quietly alerted Colonel Pick of the shooting on the plane, the condition of the other passengers and the abuse of some of them. Col Pick reacted strongly. Laura and Lt. Col. Cassidy were natural enemies; they despised each other.

Having little or no pretext to hold Dolly, the twin Marines, Sergeants Melvin and Marvin Daumer, whose unofficial nicknames were Dumb and Dumber, escorted her to the hospital room where Kitty lay in a deathlike coma. Sgt. Melvin Daumer then called Lt. Col. Cassidy.

"This is Mel. I'm sorry, colonel. Marv was attacked by one of the passengers and I had to shoot him—the passenger, that is."

"What was his name? Did he survive?" Cassidy asked.

"His name is Luna, Rev. Lazaro Luna, a preacher. He's probably not gonna make it."

"Mexican?" Cassidy asked. "Well, too bad. If he dies, I'll help you out with the paperwork. There'll be a lot of it and a review. I'll back you up. This may teach them the meaning of Class One security on our base!"

"Thanks, Colonel. Marv and I feel really bad about it."

"Don't!" Cassidy replied coldly. "Lessons will be learned and good may come of it. Meanwhile, we're assembling our Class One security team—Capt. Panic, Lt. Moore, Sgt. Russo, and you and your brother. We're going to make a couple of surprise visits! Remember, we remain on Class One rules of engagement!"

Major Wingard called Col. Pick, asking him to meet him at Security Station 3. Pick told him about the violence in the Airbus, then called Base Hq. and ordered a bus. He stopped at the red police call box where Wingard was waiting. They drove to Headquarters. Entering General Mills' office, they saluted.

The General saluted perfunctorily and nodded. "Sit."

"Sir, minutes after the power went down, an America West Airbus out of Phoenix came into our airspace, flying over us," said Wingard. "They radioed in with a severe medical emergency. Lt. Col Cassidy waved them off and told them to keep going, even threatened to light them up, but the pilot started quoting FAA regs for medical emergencies in flight, so he allowed them to land. Col. Cassidy was very agitated, practically out of his mind. He told everybody we were probably under attack, that World War III had likely already begun. and that the Russians had already taken out NORAD, so he was going to declare Class One Security right then and there."

"That's *my* prerogative," asserted the General. "But so far so good. You say he tried to call NORAD?"

"Yes. He claims the line was dead . . ."

"Then I understand his action. It's his job to take the strictest precautions under a potential emergency, especially one with as many unknowns as this one appears to be so far. How do *you* feel about esclating to Class 1 on the base, Major? You're second in command at Security."

"There should at least be a modicum of evidence—internal or external. If it is a knee jerk reaction to any unknown, people may die. The airliner would be the first potential threat, but now we know it is not a threat. And . . . ."

The General interrupted. "My thoughts exactly, Major. I'd better call Cassidy right now. If there is any indication whatsoever, I will authorize him to declare Class One rules on the spot."

Major Wingard was shaking his head, and held up his hand. "But wait, Sir, there's more. Declaring Class 1 is your decision and yours alone, but Cassidy may have jumped the gun; he may already have done so."

The General's eyes narrowed. "What gives you that idea?"

"When the commercial airliner called the tower, I volunteered to call you right then and there. But Col Cassidy grabbed the phone out of my hand and said he'd talk to you himself. That's when he *pretended* to call you."

"What, *pretended*?!"

"That's what I've been trying to tell you, General. I knew he was confabulating. And as soon as the phony call ended, he formally declared Class One, emphasizing the nation was probably at DEFCON 1, and Security would now operate under Level One rules of engagement. Deadly force."

The General's eyes widened, his jaw set and his face reddened. "What?! Do you have confirmation of this?! This is an outrage! Somebody could get hurt—or killed."

Col. Pick's cell phone beeped. Major Laura Schenk, the base social worker, was on the line. As he listened, his jaw dropped and his face grew pale, "My god, Laura, good God. This is awful. Is he still alive?"

"What is it?" demanded the General.

"They shot someone on the plane. May have killed him." He spoke quickly into the phone. "I'll get right back to you, Laura. I'm with the General.

"Get an ambulance there, quick!" He turned to Major Wingard. "Looks like somebody *has* been killed!"

"Col. Pick's phone beeped again. It was Dr. Ludmila. "The sick passenger is in ICU, and the Daumer twins and two others are already in the plane and they're roughing up the passengers. They're out of control. I passed another ambulance going the other way. Something else may have happened on that plane. I'm going to call the General"

"I'm with the General, doctor. Bad news. Sergeant Mel Daumer shot one of the passengers." He heard the ambulance siren over the phone. "They're arriving right now." He hung up; it beeped again. It was Major Schenk.

"I'm at the hospital emergency room. Reverend Luna is unconscious, and Dr. Singh and his staff are prepping him for emergency surgery. Apparently the bullet lodged in his spine. They're not optimistic about his chances. I'm going back to the plane to interview the passengers. Incidentally, they're just passengers. Not an invading army!"

"Enough!" interrupted the General, turning to Major Wingard. "I'm downgrading the security alert from Class One where it never should have been.

Inform all the parties, Major. I will deal with Col. Cassidy myself." He turned to Col. Pick. "What about the rest of the passengers, the crew?"

"Scared out their minds, but OK."

"Get a bus over there," ordered the General. "Bring 'em to the reception center. I'll meet them there in about 20 minutes"

"Roger, General. Meanwhile, give me a few minutes to get over to Security. I'll signal you; then call. Right now I'm going to the plane to check out the passengers. I think Major Schenk will be there."

Col. Pick and Major Wingard drove quickly back to the Airbus. Pick ordered a bus to drive to the runway and await his orders. He whispered quietly to Wingard, who immediately confronted the Marines at the site.

"I have just come from the General's office. You are ordered to stand down. Return to Security headquarters immediately. That's a direct order."

Sgt. Marvin Daumer spoke up. "But Major sir, we're operating under Class One Security; we cannot stand down."

"The General has just countermanded any such order and declared Class 3, which is normal for our base. I've just given you a direct order, Sergeant, which I will not repeat. Move it!"

The twin sergeants and the other two Marines complied and drove away in their vehicles. Major Schenk stood near the plane with the remaining passengers. The were standing outside the plane in the 30° air, shivering in cold and fear. She consoled and reassured them as best she could. Major Wingard and Col. Pick walked over to her, shook her hand, then greeted each one of the passengers briefly with a reassuring handshake, informing them that Major Schenk was recording all of the conversations for the Base Commander. She also asked them to remember every detail. At that moment an old blue Air Force bus with small windows, rounded corners and a long hood pulled up in front of the plane. All the passengers got on.

Col. Pick and Major Wingard then drove quickly to the long, white, one-story Security Headquarters building, which resembled two large, white double-wide trailers hooked together, with a small annex on the west side which served as a brig when necessary. There were no occupants today.

They mounted the eight stairs to the front door and strode in authoritatively. As they walked in, the red emergency phone rang. Cassidy made a grab for it but Major Wingard was too quick for him. It was the General. who repeated the official downgrade order, automatically reducing the severity of the rules of engagement. Wingard listened and nodded furiously, glancing over at Lt. Col Cassidy, who was glaring back.

"What in the hell is going on, Major?" Cassidy demanded.

"The General has confirmed the order to stand down the Class One alert effective immediately. I've already informed the Daumer twins. We're now back to Class 3," Wingard countered, still looking at Cassidy, knowing he had faked the call to the General. He cupped his hand over the phone. "General; Colonel Cassidy already briefed you a half hour ago . . . ."

"*What do you mean he briefed me?! Colonel Pick woke me up only minutes ago! Put Lt. Col. Cassidy on the line!*" Cassidy was furious as Major Wingard, with a fleeting smile, handed him the phone.

"What's wrong, Colonel?" *If looks could kill,* Wingard smiled to himself as Cassidy grabbed the phone out of his hand. He could hear the General's voice shout "Explain yourself." He listened silently, tightlipped, gray with fury.

Wingard couldn't resist. "Something wrong, Colonel?"

"We've been ordered to stand down! *That includes you,* Major!" Cassidy sneered. "So stand down!"

Laura Schenk had just entered the building and heard everything. She wanted to laugh aloud; she tightened her lips but couldn't suppress a smile as she gazed triumphantly at Col Cassidy, who glared silently back at her. She turned away with a flourish, nose in air, left the building and returned to the Airbus passengers. Cassidy whirled around, stalked into his office and slammed the door. They heard a yelp; it was his dog.

The big blue bus arrived at the base reception area with the Airbus passengers. The pilots, both active Air Force Reservists, were warmly welcomed by the General's adjutant, Major Ike Sizemore, who accompanied them to base headquarters along with the stewardesses, Vanessa and Monica.

Nano Brown, the Whipples, Monica and Vanessa, and Jesse Maxwell were the first to be escorted into the reception center, a long room with black couches against the wall and rows of upholstered chairs with foldup seats like theatre seats, all black. On the long wall on the north were mottled marble like counters with large windows that reached to the ceiling. As they entered, the lights went on behind the windows, and an Air Force enlisted woman, a staff sergeant wearing a name tag, "Gaudet," slid the window open at one of the stalls. It was nearly 2 AM; the center was now open for business.

"Good morning. Happy New Year to all of you and welcome! I'm Staff Sergeant Gaudet. Sorry your flight was interrupted. You may come up here one at a time. I need to register each one of you as a visitor.

Immediately the bank of pay phones on the west wall was mobbed; change was demanded. Soon, however, everyone realized that the lines were dead.

The Base Commander, Brigadier General Thomas Mills entered and quietly addressed the group in his Tennessee drawl. "Welcome to Nellis Air Force Base, folks. Please sit down. First, I want to inform you that your diminutive friend Miz Kitty Schrödinger is in good hands. She's holdin' steady. The Reverend—well—he's still a'hangin' in there. We're all prayin' that he'll be all right, and we're doin' everything we can." There was a collective sigh of relief. The General continued. "Second, I want to apologize to y'all for what happened on that airplane. I'm responsible for everything that goes on here, and you can be sure that those security men that got out of hand will be held fully accountable for what they did. I can tell you their commander thought the base was under attack by a foreign power, but I can also tell you that there was no justification for their violent behavior. Major Schenk will see to it that your needs are tended to and try to make you as comfortable as possible, and she'll have some more questions for you. I'm also sorry you can't get in touch with your families just now, but something very strange has knocked out our power and our communications. We'll get to the bottom of as soon as we can, and meanwhile we want you to know that you're our guests. Any questions?"

Jesse Maxwell raised his hand

The General smiled. "What's you name, son?"

"Jesse, sir. Jesse Maxwell. Is this really Area 51?"

"Indeed it is, son. You're here and you're a welcome guest, you and your fellow passengers."

"Is everything top secret here, like aliens and spaceships?"

"Careful, son. If I could tell you it wouldn't be a secret, would it? I wouldn't want to arrest you!" Jesse grinned; the passengers laughed. Tension in the room subsided.

"I'd love to meet some of your scientists," Jesse added. "I love science. And my great great great grandfather was a famous scientist, James Clerk Maxwell, the one who discovered electromagnetism."

"Impressive, Jesse!" the General nodded. "We studied him in my *alma mater*, Georgia Tech. Electromagnetism. And one of the fathers of modern physics to boot. We'll talk further."

Nobody else volulnteered, but the passengers were breathing easier. They were safe.

"Present your I.D.'s to Sergeant Gaudet," General Mills told the group; "She'll print out your guest ID's and give each of you a name tag. And let Major Schenk know if there's anything you need. She will be talking to each of you about what happened on the plane." He left the gathering.

The passengers lined up and presented their ID's to the reception clerk, Security's computer, attached to a Cray YNP, immediately accessed its immense database, spit out a detailed report in seconds, and printed out an identification badge for each passenger with a three line mysterious bar code. The Cray held information on virtually everyone—anyone alive or dead who had a Social Security number, a criminal record, military service, an FBI or CIA file, newspaper writeup, or involvement in any militarily or politically sensitive matter.

When the reports came up on Dr. Nano Brown, and on Wanda and Warren Whipple, they were impressed. Science division was called, and the scientist who took the call, Dr. Willie Gates, a metallurgist and first assistant to Dr. Alfonso diGiovanni, already knew Brown by reputation, and despite all the tumult and chaos in the bunker, hurried to the reception area to welcome him. When he discovered, to boot, that the Whipples were top echelon software designers and engineers at Microsoft, he felt that he had discovered a gold mine. Security issued special badges to Brown and the Whipples. The Whipples were pried apart, and the three accompanied Willie Gates down to Level 12.

Ian Marley was released with a stern lecture, and he and the Mariachis, including their mother, Marta, were issued badges and housed in the BOQ. The various laptop computers, and the Mariachis' instruments were returned to their owners. Ian Marley begged them to return his "tobacco." This they refused.

Kitty Schrödinger's condition had worsened. On a respirator, she lay in a coma, holding at the precise point between life and death, under the care of Dr. Singh. Dolly Klein remained steadfastly by her side.

Jesse Maxwell was placed in the care of Vanessa and Monica. His voice had changed completely, and he now knew that the demon of multiple sclerosis had completely departed from his body. The three were issued badges and escorted to an empty trailer. Monica quickly joined her boyfriend Bubba at another residence.

Jesse and Vanessa were now alone in the trailer, where for the rest of the night, Jesse's initiation into manhood was deliriously, deliciously, exhaustively, blissfully fulfilled and completed.

At 4 AM security finished up, and the reception area closed. Reverend Luna was now in the ICU. Dr. Singh and his nurse, shaking their heads, stabilized him as well as they could, but held out but scant hope that he would recover.

Chapter 6

Borrowed Time

*I could be bounded in a nutshell and count myself
a king of infinite space.*

Hamlet

The Physics Labs, Level 18,   1 AM   January 1, 1900

Deep in the Area 51 compound, over the past year, a series of hyper-secret, advanced Philadelphia type experiments were being conducted. The research was in its very earliest stages, sending inanimate objects accompanied by plants and laboratory creatures—mice and insects—backwards and forward in time for seconds or minutes.

The device, the DIBC—short for *dilating isotropic biophase converter*—was operated by the selective activation of *scalar* tachyon fields—stable, invariant, even under the most extreme transformations. It was nicknamed *Dybbuk*, a ghost that occupies a living body. The fields were generated *cymatically*. Visible effects were achieved through Professor Sandor Rakoczy's brilliant breakthrough, the creation and utilization of virtual tesseract and simplex crystals. The trick was to generate a powerful, spherical electrical field, and then collapse it through the crystals, creating a polar time axis upon which the entire sphere, including any object or creature placed within, would move forward or backwards through time as if they were on a straight rail, the time dimension seeming to adopt certain spatial qualities. Upon activation, temporal shock waves were created, surge clouds which behaved like cocoons surrounding and engulfing the subjects.

Sending them minutes forward would allow them to watch the object or creature materialize before their eyes. Surprisingly, powerful energy readings for a measurable period of time were registered up to a minute before their re-materialization, readings that showed unique harmonics and visible chromatic harbingers of the actual gross matter just prior to manifestation. *Transporter effects in the time stream!*, scientists and techies would humorously observe; *Star Trek science!*

The scientists had made huge breakthroughs and had been ambitiously testing the tachyon pulses on their subjects, increasing the size of the collapsing sphere so they could send them into the past or the future for up to a half-hour. Where? For now, until further breakthroughs were in the offing, in precisely the same space—the straight rail-like axis.

Sending them backwards in time created what must have been live paradoxes such as mice and insects reproducing in the past, but the continuum miraculously appeared to absorb those in stride. How was this possible? Did they return on the same time vector, implying that other vectors existed? Did the existence of other vectors serve as a proof of parallel existence, parallel universes? Did the reproductive act just not "take" in those conditions—in the "past"—i.e., was it less real? And finally, is the past what our dubious commonsense thinking thinks it is—eternally and utterly fixed and inalterable? Is it a dynamic set of collectively concurrent opinions held in living minds, tailing off as the earlier ones expire and continuously renewed as the current, prevailing aggregate flows into the new minds? *Or does it really exist independent of those minds, still permanently fixed and inalterable?*

They thought not. It was clear that the existence of time vectors *and* parallel universes was implied, *proven*, some thought.

The questions were endless—but exciting. This was uncharted territory—real science in the best sense of the word. And philosophy—live ontological and epistemological questions. Only experimental research would offer the possibility of gleaning truth—usable facts—out of these questions.

They soon learned that whatever was sent back, even for minutes or seconds, would create violent fluctuations, palpable vibrations and an ear-piercing howling sound. Hapless insects would be fused with any material, such as a cigarette butt, a napkin, a staple, a coin, even dust, competing for the same space as the subject dematerialized in the present moment and materialized in the past. They quickly learned to keep the affected space clear. They sealed off and sterilized the room and filtered the air, making it virtually a laboratory clean room. Airlocks were on the drawing board.

The time machine was tied directly to the star clocks. Precisely at the witching hour, Y2K had struck Area 51, which, with its major electrical sub-station, was situated at the westernmost terminus of the multi-state power network which included northern Arizona, all of Utah, and portions of Nevada, Idaho, Wyoming and Colorado. Two of the old computers on the PST side of the network, buried deep within the complex, hybrid multi-state switching system, reverted to "00", which meant 1900 instead of 2000, only a few milliseconds apart. It created first an enormous power surge through the 750KV transmission lines, followed instantly by a cascading shutdown, ending at Area 51, the terminus, which created the huge collapsing energy field with a five mile radius that engulfed the center of the base.

It was the collapsing field that overwhelmed the date-sensitive electronic switches in the Dybbuk and maximally activated the tachyon pulses. The affected area now formed a spherical bubble covering the same five mile radius. The bubble also engulfed the America West Airbus which was flying directly overhead, its altitude below 20,000'.

Commanding General Thomas Mills ordered Area 51's three chief scientists, Drs. Sandor Rakoczy, Alfonso diGiovanni and Robert Rose, and the base physician, Dr. Ludmila Ivanova, all of them civilians, to call a meeting immediately at the emergency conference room on Level 18. The scientists and techs began assembling there.

Rakoczy, 47, was chief scientist and inventor of the time machine ; he and the much younger Dr. Ivanova were an item. Second in rank in the science division was diGiovanni, a chemical engineer and metallurgist, who headed up the Roswell Division. One of the jobs of his team was to continue to reverse engineer the alien spacecraft that had crashed at Roswell 52 years previously, and to maintain a mutually fruitful relationship with the live alien, Nommo and his Dogon shaman, Puplampu, as well as the ancient speckled dolphin, Lantos, and see that all their needs were met. As a metallurgist, diGiovanni had just succeeded in duplicating the incredibly pliable organic metal/plastic alloy that was the skin of the ship, which also bore an uncanny chemical/biological resemblance to the skin of the alien. Dr. Ivanova, a biologist and physician, was the Base's chief medical officer, and was Nommo's doctor. Through the good fortune of having the world's only known live alien as a patient, she had become by default the world's leading exobiologist. Dr. Robert Rose, astrophysicist, formerly chief astronomer at Lick Observatory, ran Area 51's base observatory with its 108" telescope and state of the art technology

At 12:40, Rakoczy and his associates quickly gathered in the large, oblong conference room on Level 18. The room was a mess. Glasses and napkins and coffee cups were still on the long, walnut table; the 12 plush brown leather chairs were awry. *Somebody didn't clean up! The General will be here any minute.* They picked up and straightened up quickly. He was unable to get either diGiovanni or Rose on the phone, and was ready to dispatch one of his techies to find them.

Gerhard and Mikhail, Rakoczy's best techies sat down; other scientists and techs from the various labs showed up. More chairs were brought in. At the end of the long conference table was a squat podium and a wall of whiteboards. The meeting was called informally.

Everybody was trying to make sense of what had happened. Their instruments told them that the tachyon generators had maximally activated the virtual simplex crystals well ahead of a scheduled series of tests to expand their range. The astronomical clocks—"star clocks"—were calibrated to earth's precise position on the ecliptic—the solar orbit track—primarily through the Global Positioning Satellites, and reconciled secondarily through direct reference to the positions of nearby stars with large proper motion[1] such as Alpha Centauri A, Procyon, and Sirius A. Their fix on the stars was lost, and the clocks, too, appeared to have completely lost their orientation, defaulting to the time registered through the electric power network, which showed 12:00:01 AM, 1/1/ "00"—i.e. 1900.

Rakoczy had to began to suspect that they had either altered space-time or that there had been a planetary polarity shift causing global magnetic chaos. His mind raced. *What set off the tachyon*

---

[1] *Proper motion* is the rate that a star moves in relation to other stars—from the vantage point of earth, of course.

bursts?! What caused that single big tremor with no aftershocks? One: external power could have been knocked out causing a massive power surge and collapsing field, setting it off—Y2K?! Two: a planetary polarity shift causing huge differentials in electrical potential and creating maximal phase shifts, setting it off. Three: it's the peak of the solar cycle; today it's the strongest it's been in 40 years; the solar storm could have killed the satellites, to be exceeded only by tomorrow—and the next day—and the next. Four, less likely, a magnetar in the immediate stellar neighborhood, overwhelming everything remotely electrical or electronic including the satellites. Five: any combination of the above, hastening the long overdue planetary polarity shift. Six: none of the above; something unknown, unheard of and potentially deadly. Theoretically, we've gone back in time. Theoretically. But suppose it's true! If you bend Nature's laws, you have invoked Maxwell's Demon and she will bend them back! If that's true, we're in some kind of bubble, and it's eventually going to burst. Tortoise and hare: if the FTL[1] tachyons have streaked way ahead, the tardyons—the slower-than-light particles—will arrive late—and when they finally catch up, they'll engulf it! God knows what might happen then!

He thought harder and sat up suddenly, speaking out loud. "My God. If we've moved in time we're in a limbo between the tachyons and the tardyons—a time vacuum that nature must hasten to fill. If that's true—then we're all carrying a huge negative potential! That explains the glowing champagne."[2] He rushed into the laboratory and found the experimental animals intact. They were agitated but alive. Their eyes were glowing green. *Yes! Yes! They're charged! I've got to call diGiovanni and Rose. This is crucial!*

He dialed diGiovanni's office, then his residence. No answer. Message machine. He left a message: "Get your ass down to the

---

[1] FTL: faster than light.
[2] The negative charge was actually at one further remove—an *imaginary* charge . . .

lab stat. Major emergency!" He dialed Robert Rose's number. Same message. Then Dr. Ludmila's number. Same message minus "your ass."

He brought up experimental tachyon data on the powerful Cray C916 and began making calculations at a furious rate. He laughed at the date on the astro clock—January 1, 1900. Then he stopped short; the thought struck him like a thunderbolt. It couldn't be! Not the whole base! He rocked back and forth wrestling with the thought and then began calculating furiously. *Ah: it may be a powerful nearby event causing a distortion in the lens of space. But not likely—just a pet theory.*

He noticed a small discrepancy, but didn't have an astronomy program to verify what could have caused it. *Rose—Robbie Rose. He's got the program; he can calculate that in a heartbeat!* He dialed again and again got the message machine. He called Rose's residence—same thing. He slammed down the phone. *To hell with it; I'll calculate it myself! Solar year: 365 days, 5 hours, 48 minutes, 46 seconds. Simple calculation; I can get it to within less than a minute. Twenty four leap years, one leap second added per year since 1972; wait—I don't need those.* His fingers flew; numbers leaped on the screen of his laptop. *We're all back in 1900?!* He laughed again.

The idea began to sink in again. *Solid earth; everything is working! What about the tremor and the quake?! Of course! It adds up. If we're really 100 years back in time, the earth must have shifted that much naturally before they even began excavating for the base!*

Strong evidence, but he still didn't believe it. Suddenly it seemed absurd, impossible. *New issues. Most of the base seemed to have been physically transported to 1900, but did this leave a five mile deep semi-spherical hole in the ground, and did it replace its counterpart in 1900? Did a huge sphere of dirt and rock 10 miles in diameter get sent back in time? Absurd! The obvious answer: no. The more obvious answer: rephrase the question!*

*Could it insinuate itself in between discrete quantum moments in time-space? One absurdity after another. Final speculation: a supervening reality. Meaning? Dominance over the events it was overriding. Inference: dominance of the human and other wills over actual events. Provisional inference: a valid reality, and possibly a dominant one, can be created and driven by collective will. STOP!! ENOUGH ALREADY!! **I'm chasing the mice around in my skull.***

He shook his head hard and slapped his forehead with a glancing blow. He walked into the restroom across the hall and splashed cold water on his face. It felt good. He let the water run colder and splashed it on his face and neck. Now he felt that he was coming to his senses.

Still, it seems we have all materialized back in 1900!

He strode quickly into the conference room. *I can't just up and tell them that! We'll let them figure it out—if they can. There has to be some other explanation.*

The others assembling there still had not understood what had caused the upheaval but were beginning to suspect a massive, cascading power surge causing the main power transmission lines to go down. Some were speculating along similar lines as Rakoczy.

While the star clocks, quite independently of the Cray and the other super-computers, also registered 1900, six minutes early, all of their PC's and laptops faithfully registered 2000, synchronized perfectly with their watches. *That* had to be a major coincidence, that the collapsing field whose magnitude set the time interval was somehow synchronous with the date registered in the external power system.

None had yet heard about the violence on the Airbus.

Rakoczy called them to order, briefed them on the General's imminent emergency meeting, and lectured them on the dangers of the security team taking rash action, and the imprudence of jumping to any premature conclusions.

"They know nothing. Keep it that way. Keep your mouths shut. Maintain a *very* low profile. I'm going to tell them it's a major solar storm—they can confirm that—it might even be true! Also: watch out for Cassidy. He's a mushroom: feed him shit and keep him in the dark. By the way, they don't call him Mad Dog for nothing."

"Cassidy's such a gnarly little bastard! You'd think that'd make him a little humble," added Rakoczy's 28 year old technician, Gerhard, 6' 1" tall with a triangular face, blond hair and eyebrows, a spare build and very long arms.

"*Zhopa!*" translated Mikhail, Rakoczy's chief technician, a stocky young man of 26 with a round face and dimpled cheeks. "A flaming esshole! But if you are so *og*-ly, you know, you have earned right to *be* esshole. Because you are already *lllooo*king like one! We have proverb." He paused for a moment and grinned, showing the gap between his front teeth, resembling a young Ernest Borgnine. "Also, in Russian, you know, word for *esshole* is same word for *black hole. Cassidy* is black hole."

They agreed among themselves to inform no one else as to what they suspected had happened, except possibly the General, whom they were more inclined to trust, *if* he was capable of grasping the whole picture.

A phone rang. Rakoczy answered. It was Lt. Col. Cassidy.

"This is Security. Remain where you are and keep everybody there. Nobody is to leave Level 18 until you are cleared. We have new threats and I am treating the matter as Class 1, with Class 1 rules of engagement."

Rakoczy was irritated. "Sorry, Colonel, but you've been overruled. I believe that is up to the General. He will be here shortly."

"Follow this procedure or there will be consequences!" shouted Cassidy, who slammed down the phone. "Goddam civilians!" he muttered to himself. "This is a top secret military base!"

Base Commander General Tom Mills arrived. The military people saluted, some of whom had rarely seen him up close. He was shorter that they anticipated but had an athletic build for a man in his 50's, not an ounce of fat. His face defined him, straight nose, prominent jaw and high cheekbones, but above all his eyes—deep blue and deep set. His gaze was direct and penetrating. A tolerant man, he nevertheless radiated authority.

Two of his aides entered the conference room with him. He summoned Rakoczy.

"Get diGiovanni and his staff up here into the conference room; we're going to have a meeting right now. Get your people together; we'll start as soon as they're here." He took Rakoczy aside and pressed him hard about what might have actually happened.

The General spoke in a cultured dialect of his native Tennessee. "What in the wide, wide world of sports has happened here, Sandy?! Are we in any real danger?"

"No immediate danger, it would appear, General. Of course, we can't be sure," replied Rakoczy.

"Call me Tom."

"No immediate danger, Tom. We don't have a consensus yet. DiGiovanni may have a theory. There are too many variables. We know that the tremor happened *after* the flash—that's crucial. We also know that today the sun is more turbulent than it's been since before the electronic age began—and it's getting more so by the day, nearing the peak of the 11 year cycle. That could have explained why the satellites went dead, and it could have affected communications worldwide."

"What about all this folderol about Y2K. Could it have really caused this?"

"Theoretically, yes, General, it could, and it very well might have. We got sick of all the hype because the media were blowing it up and building a whole industry around it. But, it could have taken out the power grid, caused a surge, and set everything off. Remember that GPS Rollover event in Cleveland in August? The 9-9-99 fiasco in Oakland—nearly a million without power?

"Yes, but those were just flukes, weren't they, Sandy?"

"Not according to the engineers at Case Western, my former colleagues. They know more about Y2K than anybody—and they experienced an early version of it with the GPS rollover last August when nearly half of Cleveland was blacked out—and that was only supposed to have been a test! It was a stupid accident—with consequences. They've *really* been sweating the millennium bug. Their suspicions may have become fact, right here, right now, tonight! And God knows where else, Tom."

"You know the Russians went on yellow alert this afternoon— hours ago?" observed the General. "Just after midnight their time. And we went to DEFCON 4, in fact we're still at DEFCON 4 unless it's got worse in the meantime. We also know there was a Y2K event in western Siberia, a huge power outage. And a blip on Russian radar that might have been mistaken for a missile."

"General, I caught Wolf Blitzer's report on CNN earlier this evening," Rakoczy observed. "He said Clinton made light of it, that he wasn't worried at all. Anyway, it seems Yeltsin called Clinton, though the White House hasn't released any further information. And I don't think Yeltsin was calling just to wish him a happy New Year. And Wolf thought Clinton did look a little worried. I hate to say it, General, but it *could* set off World War III for obvious reasons—if any missile system including our own is still on hair trigger alert, which I pray is not the case. A malfunction could easily trigger a launch sequence—*if* they were on high enough alert. Don't forget that the offensive systems are hardwired on both sides, and *they* would function with deadly efficiency even if nothing else did. Plus, it's rumored that the Russians' doomsday machine is still operational." He paused, looking the General in the eyes. "Anyway, why am I telling you all this, General, Tom; you're the military man." The General nodded. suppressing a smile.

"Yes, but I'm glad you understand it as well as you do. There was that fluke in 1995 when Yeltsin's atomic briefcase got activated. That was a close one! Turned out to be a Norwegian weather satellite; the Norwegians informed the Russians, but somebody dropped the ball and the information didn't get passed along to the right people. It was nip and tuck for about 15 minutes. And he's got a *serious* drinkin' problem!"

"I remember it well, Tom."

"Anyhow, I was referring to your fancy array of detection devices. I've already had a look at the seismic data; nothing at all since that first bang. I'm surprised there weren't any aftershocks."

"Me too. But as far as being attacked by the Russians or anybody else, don't forget that *everything* is dead on the outside. We've still got a wide range of emergency frequencies, even though the satellites are down. We've tested them and they're operational. No attack could have been so totally comprehensive that there wouldn't be signal one anywhere at all. The Russians couldn't have done that with every ICBM in their arsenal—when they *had* a full arsenal. Above all, *we'd* have been a prime target, right here at Nellis where we sit. No, I think whatever it is, it's not hostile. I certainly hope not! Something entirely different is going on here."

The General nodded and raised his eyebrows. "What about those time experiments you've have been working on. I understand you've made real progress. What would've caused the flash? And the quake, if it was a quake."

Rakoczy nodded and smiled. "I can't do that, Tom, but I can tell you what I think is most likely."

"You think it was Y2K?"

"That's a strong possibility. A gigantic power surge: don't forget, Nellis is the terminus for the entire interstate power grid—750K transmission lines—three quarters of a million volts. It so happens that the tachyon generators were maximally activated. They had been tied to the GPS clocks, but the electricity system, the interstate power grid is a default, a fail-safe if the GPS quits. The system registers its own time and date when any kind of glitch occurs, and if it registers '00' it means 1900, not 2000! So, the near instantaneous shutdown and startup, must have caused it. The two were only microseconds apart, likely caused by the Y2K business, and overwhelmed the crystals with a gigantic expanding and collapsing energy field, driven by nearly a million volts."

"But wouldn't a huge surge like that fry the crystals?"

"You'd certainly think so! Our experiments up to now have been very modest; most of the spherical temporal fields we created were only centimeters in diameter—verging only seconds or minutes ahead into the past or future. The crystal arrays and the circuitry were beefed up to protect them from surges, but we just didn't know how well!" He grew serious. "You know, Tom, we're in completely uncharted waters now. We need to pool every brain cell in the compound! We know that the collapsing energy field engulfed us, that the time current flowed backwards to a certain point and then reversed again. The currents seem to be flowing at a normal rate forward again—that is—a rate that at least seems normal to our organisms."

"You actually think we've traveled in time?"

I'm not sure that 'travel' is the right word, but yes, that's what it looks like. My calculations confirm it, but I've been wrong before, all too often. *If* our organisms, as you call 'em, are intact, it doesn't seem likely they've been sent through a time warp. But, whatever it is, it's very likely unstable. Something's going on and we have to get a handle on it."

The General furrowed his eyebrows. "Intriguing thought! Which way did your so-called chronon flow go, backward or forward?"

"Ha! Chronons indeed! Anyway, backwards. Back in time. I know because it was the simplexes that were activated, not the tesseracts. Why, I still haven't figured out."

"But *my* own time keeps moving forward, and that's all I've got to go on."

Rakoczy continued. "Shared subjective time; subject prior to object. I've thought of that, too—that we can face in any temporal direction and *our* sense of duration, Bergsonian *durée*, is still valid. Doc Brown really *could* talk about spending his retirement years in his favorite time period, the Old West."

"That's a mind blower! Scary!" blurted Rakoczy's chief tech, Gerhard,

"Sounds like sacred geometry," Mikhail quipped.

"Profane geometry," responded Gerhard. "God is not there, and the devil is in the details!"

"What do you mean?" Mikhail asked.

"Just the fact." Gerhard replied, "that in any given period of time all the astronomical bodies in the universe have shifted, including of course our own spaceship earth—our private ecliptic. If we went ahead or back in time, following those worldlines, then we're in a different sector of absolute space—we'd be residing at a different address on the Great Grid.!"

Rakoczy nodded vigorously. "Stay on that track, Gerhard! You're on to something."

Everybody took a breather, got up, walked around and drank some water or stale coffee.

"So how do we restore the status quo?" the General asked.

"The first step is to find out where and when we are. And, yes, a time shift is a real possibility," Rakoczy replied.

"Could it be a group illusion, a group hallucination?" asked Gerhard.

"Could be," Mikhail commented, "but with time travel, could be same phenomenon. All is in our minds. No less danger, maybe more!"

Rakoczy raised his hands. "Yes, and a group hallucination, as you call would make it *more* real in a way, not less! Isolated reality in a group mind. But gentlemen, **here's the onion**: create the algorithm that could track earth's corkscrew ecliptic through space to the exact spatial coordinates it passed through in 1900, since that's what our instruments are appearing to tell us. That's where you were going, Gerhard."

"Sounds impossible," said Gerhard. "Can't trace the variables. Orbits within orbits. We don't know enough."

"You're right. We can't! A supercomputer couldn't do it. And yet, here we are."

"So how did this happen? It makes coincidence sound like a force of Nature!" said the General

Rakoczy nodded vigorously. "Shakespeare thought the same thing, General. So did Milton. The answer is clear: we cannot *create* such an algorithm."

"But we must have left a wake behind us—a particle trail," replied the General. "Stardust! Or maybe in altering space itself— isn't the aether coming back into vogue among your kind?"

"Precisely! We can't create it but maybe we can detect it. Good thinking, General. I like the stardust metaphor. I'm thinking: maybe there's even a visible trail—like the luminous trail of algae stirred up in a ship's wake."

"Good image yourself! Were you a Navy man, Sandor?"

"Actually not, General. I had a high lottery number—243. Three to the fifth power! Perfect for a physicist!"

"In your first experiments, sending things a few seconds or a minute into the future or the past, what was the actual magnitude of the collapsing field?" asked the General.

"Very small, the largest about 17 millimeters in diameter—that would send them back or forward one hour," Rakoczy replied. "We *were* being very cautious—preparing to extend it—very gradually. Looks like Y2K may have done it for us—in spades!"

"That was the space to enclose the objects. How did your crystals actually get them backwards or forward in time?"

"Very simply. We increase the time interval by proportionately dilating the diameter of the collapsing field activating the crystals, creating a special kind of ripple effect—like a stone dropped in a pond, except that the rear bank was moving away. The ripples—meaning the waves—hit the fixed shoreline—always the present, the point of origin—and created regular interference patterns in the present. But it kept flowing backwards, unimpeded for the radius of the field *plus* the *actual distance* our entire system has traveled in spacetime—the field was stretched about 1,000 miles as earth moved through space on the ecliptic."

"So far so good. But doesn't the whole solar system move through interstellar space?"

"It does; in fact, it's part of an ascending series—actually kind of like a corkscrew. The universal center of mass is the last and greatest in the series. *Anyway*, we increase the radius *and* the interval by increasing the voltage. We actually had fun calibrating the clocks in the past or future by setting the date—almost like punching in the date on the DeLorean in *Back to the Future*. We never dreamed that it would work. We never expected this! We're still calibrating the radius, but it's over 24,000 feet—nearly five miles."

Chapter 7

Y2K and the time machine

Nommo's pool, Level 21   2:30 AM   January 1, 1900

Dr. Ludmila and the Dogon, Puplampu, sat at the corner of the 100' long, 35' deep water home of the alien, Nommo and his dolphin companion, Lantos. Her feet were in the water, on the first step of the pool stairs. Nommo rose out of the pool and placed his right hand on Ludmila's left shoulder, one of several ways he made physical contact with her—top of head, forehead or shoulder.

She had gone there to do a routine physical check on the three, but it was obvious Nommo had something to communicate to her. Images and a meta-language flowed through his four-fingered hand-fin into her mind for five full minutes. She understood his wider meaning—that time had changed and that it would be OK—but the bulk of the message would unfold for her, like a download following an upload.

"It's the alien! He's doing it all! So says Dr. Ludmila." Rakoczy told the General. "And he talks to her in musical tones and intervals!" He paused and laughed to himself. He was mentally

72

tired and he was getting punchy. "Sorry General! All seriousness aside, I've got to take a break. I'm tired and a little dizzy. I need a few minutes.And I could use a drink!"

The General nodded. "By the way, Sandy, what about diGiovanni? And Rose?"

"I'll call them" Rakoczy reassured him. "Or I'll send one of my men to find them." As he left the room, he turned to Gerhard and spoke softly. "You know, I could use a stiff drink . . . . Excuse me." He walked out in the hall.

Gerhard followed him and produced a chromium flask. He handed it to Rakoczy. "Here, Sandy. Drink. It's Ratzeputz, nearly 120 proof It will clear your mind."

Rakoczy frowned, gritting his teeth "Ratzen putzen!? That's Yiddish. I hope that's not what it sounds like!"

Gerhard laughed. "It's an old traditional German hard liquor— been around since the 1800's. Even has medicinal properties. It serves its purpose! Drink; you'll find out. You'll enjoy it!"

Rakoczy smiled gratefully, opened the flask and took a sip. "My god, you're right, Gerhard. It's good!"

"Drink up!"

Rakoczy took a long pull and noisily slammed down half the flask without taking a breath. His eyes rolled up into his head. He exhaled audibly. "It's great! Thanks, Gerhard. I feel better already!" He took several deep breaths and another short pull on the flask. He handed it back, smiling broadly. "Great, Gerhard! And it has a great finish! I can still taste the ginger."

Gerhard opened it and took a short pull, smiling and exhaling noisily; "It does that to you," he smiled. "I've got more; quite a little stash!"

They walked back into the conference room.

"Feel better?" the General asked.

"Much, much better," Rakoczy exhaled.

"Now—*the alien*, you say is causing this? Are you pulling my lariat? You can understand if I'm just a bit skeptical of your theory!" laughed the General.

"I'm semi-serious," said Rakoczy. "But Dr. Ludmila really believes this; she talks about it every night. And for a mystery of this magnitude nothing is off limits; nothing is too improbable. When she arrives ask her yourself. We'll examine her thoroughly. *I have to find out for myself!*"

"But let's suppose you're being serious, Sandy. I've never known you to be a practical joker. Now, if your calculations really tell us we've gone back in time, how do we confirm it?"

Rakoczy smiled and nodded. "Very carefully!" he quipped. "General, skepticism is a step in the right direction! And no, I'm not joking. But I'm seriously considering it, crazy as it may seem. Every theory seems insane, impossible. Being here is insane. If we have all of them we have to choose the least improbable, at least provisionally."

"Fair enough," agreed the General. "Let's hear it again."

"When the power shut down and almost instantly came back on, 750,000 volts, the radius of the collapsing field was *humongous* as you know. Simple formula, voltage, current, resistance. In four dimensions, not so simple. Are you with me?"

"I'm with you!" the General said with some pride. "Masters at Georgia Tech, double E, thesis on small arms wireless energy. Just two years ago."

"Whew!" exclaimed Gerhard. "Scary stuff, Star Trek stuff—set for stun or set to kill!"

"Right you are, Gerhard. And disable any electronics within range. But back to the matter at hand."

Rakoczy continued. "We've unearthed a very stange fact in our modest experiments with the 4-D matrix. I've explained it and I'll explain it again. When we set and activate the collapsing field, *the greater the radius, the longer the time axis*—in direct proportion, in other words, *bigger payload, further back or forward in time.* Current density is a variable we control. But not this time!"

Gerhard was intrigued. "I'm trying to visualize the time axis stretching back on the prime ecliptic. It's like a long cylinder with a semi-sphere on each end."

"Differential geometry. And integral geometry. Just add one more dimension! Then apply to our virtual simplexes and virtual tesseracts."

"Do we know the spacetime coordinates?" Gerhard asked. "Our address?"

"Wish we did! But I think we can return to our earlier state by the same means we got here, wherever or whenever 'here' is—path of the least resistance. Problem is we still don't understand how electricity behaves in a four dimensional matrix, especially at this magnitude. We were in the early stages, as you know, sending things backward and forward in time."

Rakoczy looked up; every eye was on him; every mind in the room was riveted, hyperfocused on his words.

"Take a breath," said the General, "take a break!"

Rakoczy stood up, then walked over to the water fountain. Tension in the room subsided. But he was tired again. "Anyway," he continued privately to the General, "It's not a joke. And Dr. Ludmila says it came from the alien, Conch—based on harmonics—on sound sequences he put in her head in a kind of Vulcan mind-meld. She played them on her viola and our instruments recorded some extremely precise harmonic sequences, a melody!"

The General was incredulous. "She translated the music?!"

"Yes! It's quite beautiful. And she thinks it'll all be just fine. I'd love to agree with her, except . . . ."

"Except what, Sandy?"

"Well, maybe I'd better show you." They turned and walked towards the laboratory. At that moment, the elevator doors opened and Dr. Alfonso diGiovanni appeared.

"Where the hell have you been?" Rakoczy demanded.

"Sorry! I guess my communicator was turned off." They walked into the lab. Rakoczy dimmed the lights, and all the lab rats had a green glow in their eyes. DiGiovanni and the General were astonished.

"What does this mean, Sandy?!"

Rakoczy looked them in the eye. "Your guess is as good as mine!" he said ironically. "My flabber has been gasted, too!" He turned to diGiovanni and spoke seriously. "Al, we need your input. We're trying to brief the General on what might have happened. He needs to craft a response to this bizarre event. I don't think any of this is laid out in his, uh, manual. You're an unconventional thinker. Time to plug it in!"

DiGiovanni shook his head slowly. "I need time to think. Why are their eyes lit up? Ours don't seem to be. Sandy, let's put it all together and collect all the variables, even the most improbable. Neglect nothing; in a mystery like this the truth can turn on the tiniest, insignificant fact."

"Yes, the truth may be hiding in plain sight. So what was your very first impression, Al?"

"I don't think it's my alien, if that's what you mean, though I can't completely rule him out," diGiovanni said.

The General pondered for a moment, then became very animated, raising both his arms, his eyes widening. "But *gentlemen.* Maybe it's just *us* that are isolated, and not the whole damned planet! That'd be a little easier to believe." He paused and added. "And to isolate." They all nodded. Respect for the General rose. He can think on his feet. They also found his homespun humor diverting, what little it of they could comprehend. He talked country, but he knew how to use the English language. Sort of like his fellow Tennessean, Vice-President Gore.

Suddenly Lt. Col. Cassidy strode into the room, flanked by Marvin Daumer and two other Marines. They saluted summarily.

"He's got his twin apes with him," whispered Rakoczy to the general. "That gives me *tsores!*[1] Wait—only one. Where's the other one?" he asked himself.

Upon seeing Cassidy, the General's hackles rose literally.

"Excuse me General, but I wasn't informed of this meeting," said Cassidy loudly with a hint of menace in his voice. "We've got an emergency of the first order on our hands, and there is a lot to protect here. Our national security, for example. Our world."

Ignoring his diatribe, the General asked Cassidy: "Where is the other Sergeant Daumer?" He looked at Marvin. "Where is your brother?"

"In his quarters," Cassidy and Marv Daumer replied simultaneously.

"That's the correct procedure, Colonel. We will keep him under house arrest pending court martial until and unless another determination is made."

Cassidy nodded, frowning. The General continued. "But interfering with this meeting is *not* correct procedure! I have just released you to limited duty and you've already lied to me and overstepped your bounds. This was convened as a scientific meeting, clearly not your area of expertise. I am obligated to organize our response to this emergency, and your job is to follow my orders."

"Sir, I am only trying to protect this base, you, and the United States of America. Something is going on that we don't yet understand and it's my duty to protect, even to use extraordinary measures."

---

[1] *Tsores*, always plural, means severe annoyance, aggravation, or just plain misery.

"Well put but dead wrong" replied the General. "I have made the decision. Your unauthorized declaration of Class 1 has been cancelled!"

Cassidy glared silently, jaw set. "Now, listen up and listen good," asserted the General. "Until I restore you to your *full* duties, you will await my orders and carry them out as I issue them. There appear to be no injuries here except those who got knocked down or fell out of their chairs—and the man Sgt. Daumer shot!"

He stopped for a moment, and began speaking in a low voice, in measured tones. Those who knew the General well knew that when he became this quiet, to watch out. He marched Cassidy outside the room where the others could not hear.

"An innocent man is dying, a man of God, due to your overreaction. We will address that situation when this is all over. *You* may continue to perform limited duties temporarily pending an official review of your acts at the earliest possible time, because right now we need all the help we can get. Meanwhile, do not go beyond your purview or you will find yourself locked up and facing military justice!"

Cassidy responded with thinly veiled defiance. "Sergeant Daumer acted in self-defense; the man attacked him."

"Yes, with a Bible, I understand. Maybe he was trying to beat some religion into him. No excuse for shootin' the man. Strike two."

"There may be enemies among us; General. I still believe I was justified in declaring Class One security, and I felt I had to act quickly." Cassidy had an unconscious habit of baring his teeth when he spoke. The General was incredulous.

"Son, you don't know whether you've been shot, fucked, powderburned or snakebit! I'll be the judge of that! You acted on your own without my approval. You overreacted. The Christian minister your subordinate has probably killed could hardly be classified as an enemy. We will act strictly by the book. So let's get on with it. You will confine your activities to damage assessment and information retrieval and *that's a direct order!*"

Cassidy was exasperated. "Let the record reflect that I personally disagree with the General and believe this situation should be treated as Class One security." The General did not answer. *Mills is a patsy, thought Cassidy, a sheep in wolf's clothing. Air Force!*

He and his contingent saluted and got back on the elevators.

Chapter 8

The Gate of Horn

Area 51, Nevada   January 1, 1900   3 AM

Rakoczy was now very tired. He needed to unwind, to restore himself. He walked back into his office to think, sat down and put on his headphones. He then put Bartok's obscure second viola concerto on his CD, a rare and welcome gift from Ludmila. *Bartok! Unrivaled master of dark tonalities, magnificent Hungarian who loved and taught my father.* He turned the volume down, leaned back in his plush chair with his head at an odd angle, and closed his eyes, savoring the ascending atonalities like fine wine as they moved his mind palpably, chromatically, through strange but familiar corridors, the subtle discords like insignias from unknown sources. It seemed to play in a part of his brain that processed both sight and sound; colors played in a strange synchronous accompaniment.

He dozed off and found himself in a backlit mist, stepping into an ancient chariot, dissolving into a rainbow cloud as it accelerated into oblivion, the vehicle of a vivid time dream, *awakening in the stream that transported him to 1900.*

He is in India on a pilgrimage with Oppenheimer, and they sit in a yogic posture before a shrine in Orissa of an immense green six armed god along with many chanting Siddhis and Swamis, some in *dhotis*. As he gazes in fascination, he falls into trance *within the dream.*

First his entire sensorium leaps out to a perfect spherical form. He is on the inside of a sphere, an eye whose concave inner surface is infinitely sensitive and reactive. The multi-limbed god takes on a dolphin-like configuration. It is the speckled dolphin, Lantos, who duplicates herself, and she and her male counterpart oppose themselves in a yin-yang. The entire figure begins to whirl slowly in a counterclockwise direction

A brilliant point appears in the exact center of the sphere. Two more points emerge and the three begin to spin. He intuits these as the Sun, Sirius, and a Pleiadian star. A point appears in the center, the four points expand to an equilateral tetrahedron—a perfect four sided pyramid. The points of light liquefy and merge, then, as if it were being inflated, the tetrahedron burgeons in two stages into a tiny sphere, and begins a gradually accelerating spin in a dervish dance.

Another eye appears to open within his forehead, triangulating with the other two, and the scene leaps out in *tri*-scopic vision. He is now seeing vividly in four full dimensions.

Within the strangely coherent, increasingly glowing blur, first the yin-yang begins merging, re-forming and devouring itself at its busy boundaries, then becoming triadal within the sphere, pervading it throughout with its three divisions radiating in laser-precise blue, green and red, phasing to their anti-colors, yellow. magenta and cyan. Like quarks and anti-quarks, they show forth as natural *tri-polar contraries* instead of bipolar opposites, three centers remaining at points dividing the sphere perfectly into 3 reciprocating equivalencies which emerge exactly at the point where the yin-yang is now yin-yang-yung, transmuted from two to three, swirling at the divisions into the new forms and growing. Threeness! This becomes unstable and begins to change again. An anti-pattern of golden-white dots appears and these grow into brilliant semi-spirals, all counter-clockwise, as the entire field and ground shift to stabilize as a hypersphere with a new *fourth* axis—the temporal axis—upon which it travels backward or forward through the continuum—*ana-kata*—forward in time or backward in timespace.

Each major change is now accompanied by a symphony of color changes, drums, and doppelganger pitch bends, continuous tones of sound and color playing out their entire range in a reciprocating glissando spiral. Yeats's interpenetrating gyres! At the final mutation, a new depth-glow is superadded, blooming within in a uroboric swirl and merging Rakoczy's burgeoning consciousness into utterly new perception, the 5-D ultrasphere, shedding hyperspheres like soap bubbles.

He holds the image of the ultrasphere for a long moment, then it collapses in stages, space dimensions and time dimensions, all the way back to a single, luminous, dancing point, which slowly fades.

Rakoczy's brain awoke. Or so he thought. He struggled through successive awakenings through various dreamscapes, each more convincing, more real. When the brain seemed to come fully awake, the body was paralyzed. He discovered that could not move. *Locked-in* syndrome. He tried to force sensation into his toes and fingers. No luck. Something told him he must not try to re-enter the dream.

He could breathe slower or faster and move his eyes. The prospect of falling back into sleep terrified him. He didn't dare—something told him he might not wake up if he did—or worse.

He could not cry out. Finally with a superhuman effort of will, he appeared to gain control of the body, and energy seemed to flow into the spinal cord.

Through a window sunlight shone directly on his face. But there was no sunlight and no window; he was hundreds of feet underground and it was night. Where was the light coming from? He calmly observed the scene through his eyelids, watching a moving sea of precisely distinguishable particles, now symbols, flowing from left to right, blood red, vermilion. It was punctuated, not by dots, or chaotic shapes, but by Arabic numbers and actual letters—Latin letters, Greek letters, Cyrillic letters, mathematical symbols—letters and numbers he somehow knew. And they carried meaning, all of them. *How could this be?*

Finally he gained full control of his body and violently pulled back his arms and his legs. His heart was pounding but he was immensely relieved.

His neck was stiff—his head had been tilted at an odd angle. The Bartok had ended. *Now: the dream. What a dream!* He remembered every detail. With Oppenheimer! He *had* met Oppenheimer briefly—but only once.

A threeness dream! Threes in quarks, threes in the procession of the Unmanifest, now threes in vision, threes in a yin-yang, yin-yang-yung! Three strands in reality, satthwic, rajasic, thamasic.

I move backward through childhood and return to my mother's womb—and go to seed!

The dream does have electrical reality, no question about that, so what particle or particles could it be composed of—the light that I am seeing? The ghost of a photon? Virtual virtuality? And what's it interacting with? Been here before, déja vu. Didn't I just say that? The dream has a rhythm, but the music is between the cadences—in the spaces. Again, in the spaces, the boundaries. Ah, Bartok! Are you responsible for this? It's like a filmy aura, delicate. You can tear it. But it leaves a trail, elusive strands. The trail fades, before, maybe behind your eyes.

And it has a glow, like cold fire. Are they special photons? Do they carry a mass or a charge, frequency, momentum, spin, phase, density, intensity, chirality, dimensionality? It behaves like ordinary space; there are axes. Potential energy? Pre-potential? That could explain it. And what unmatched power can organize them into such coherence, set them dancing, grant them ongoing life—instantly? And my consciousness at the exact center of it all. It's my show. Oh brother Higgs, where art thou?

Not completely. A vision, a sense of Conch the Nommo deep down.

Rakoczy's mind probed further. That dream; could he re-enter it now? That frightened him. Then Nellie came into his mind.

My dear Swedish poet friend, Nellie, whose images came directly out of her dreams, a direct link to her unconscious. When we met we each felt a rotating energy in our torsos. Magnetic, electric. I wonder if an encounter like that inspired Maxwell!

We had the best sex together, ever! When I reached her cervix she ignited, ascended like a Roman Candle; I planted myself there, almost entering. The cervix was like a light bulb socket; the rapture, surged into me like a high voltage current. It's been 20 years, but just that once in my life, not before or since, even with Ludmila.

The dream images moved her soul. Strange girl, brilliant, beautiful in her own way, beyond me in her own way. We might have married. I did love her then, even now. But she didn't love herself.

She said to spread your fingers and catch fire, catch the dream between the webs. But her webs are brittle and they tore like a delicately lacquered fan. She has no idea how much she opened up my mind—and my heart. She called them moonstone cadences. The rhythm of the dream.

He pulled up a screen on his laptop, and with flying fingers, brought up her poem.

> *Moonstone cadences*
> *Pass over folded fans*
> *Lacquered together*
> *Never to fold apart.*
> *Taciturn dreamer,*
> *Where do moonstones find space to live within cadences?*
> *What gives one the power to open something lacquered*
> *Without tearing hidden folds? What is the thing*
> *Which upon passing over reveals the dream bringer?*
> *Only the wishbringer knows the hows and whys*
> *We may only marvel or cry*
> *Or be taciturn dreamers.*

He typed in some of the highlights of the dream, and saved it. Then he put it aside, leaning back in his plush chair with his hands behind his head, concentrating hard on the extraordinary events scarcely three hours old.

He sat up suddenly. *Have we really gone back in time? Surely it can't last. If you bend Nature's laws, you are in her debt. Maxwell's demon! She will collect. She will bend them back. It has to revert!*

A powerful but tranquil emotion, suffused with light, washed over him, a palpable presence. A key audibly turned the tumblers in a lock. The door! He stood up and opened the door to find Nommo and the smiling, very young Puplampu standing there. As he began to speak, they faded into transparency and disappeared.

Rakoczy shook his head, pinched himself and touched the solid wall. He was awake but definitely in an altered state. As he sat back down the thoughts reverberated. *I can't ignore this any more. I must know.*

He closed his eyes and was quickly, almost physically drawn into a trancelike state.

Nommo and Puplampu seemed to appear before him once again. Their images were inert—they did not move—yet they radiated some kind of energy that he could glean information from. He began to introspect. *Puplampu is the first key to this mystery. Yestserday he was old; today he's young. Is this a true 1900 version? I've never taken a really good look at him. He's seven feet tall and only slightly stooped, slender and muscular, and not badly wrinkled. His long sinews stand out and firmly define the long muscles and his mahogany skin shines. Now he's talking to me and now he's smiling. I'm allowing myself to open up to him, or to his image. It is actually very consoling, very.*

His smile cannot be described except to say that it conveys great comfort and forgiveness, even a kind of absolution. Now he is smiling inside my mind, and suddenly it's more than an image—he's there, he is inhabiting it and giving it life. Despite his deep humility and mildness, and his disarming laughter, there is wisdom and power, as if a god were operating through him, a god that could hurl thunderbolts or shift his shape—or kill you with a look. And he's been with the alien more than 50 years. with the captive alien, Conch

He forced himself awake. Stop! I'm being swept away by this dream or whatever. Enough! Enough! He took several deep breaths, then called Ludmila's number. No answer. Then he was drawn back into his trance; his thoughts were flying as if on automatic pilot. *Ludmila was right all along; he is a collective being. They don't need names. She thinks that the Nommo are as far beyond our species as we are the amoeba.*

His cell phone vibrated in his pocket. It was Ludmila. "Get back down here, Sandor. Something's happening. The General is worried and DiGiovanni is in a panic. The crystals in the Dybbuk are glowing and pulsating. *Hurry!*"

Chapter 9

The Higgs boson: God particle or *deus ex machina?*

Area 51, Nevada   January 1, 1900   3:30 AM

Rakoczy rushed to Level 18 and ran into the clean room that housed the Dybbuk. The glow in the crystals was fading but they were still pulsating; whatever had caused it was waning, or so it appeared. He watched it grow weaker over the next minute, and the next. DiGiovanni and General Mills were standing with him, They both breathed a sigh of relief.

The cell phone vibrated again.

"I was just with Nommo . . . Something's wrong and he's trying to deal with it."

"Deal with it?"

"He's back in the water but he's still transmitting to me. It seems technical; maybe I'm not getting it. He's using musical intervals that are strange to me, yet something comes through. Maybe I can decipher it, maybe you can decipher it. What is a quantum tetrahedron?"

"It's a collection of four quantum triangles. Why is that important?"

"I don't know. It's very technical—I didn't even know he could do this. It could be lost in translation. All I know is that it relates to the time machine, and that there is some danger. You have to fix it . . . . *Wait . . . . It's religious . . . . High Mass.*"

Rakoczy frowned. Obviously a threat existed and it wasn't coming from the Church. *High mass . . . . Wait, how high?!*

"Leptoquarks!" she blurted out. "Wait, there's more . . . . One TeV."

Unheard of! Unbelievable! he thought. He didn't speak out loud because he didn't want to alarm the General. But he understood. *Only a couple of years ago at Fermilab. The Tevatron was creating them in pairs at 210-215 GeV, billion electron volts. The particles they were decaying into were very high energy—destructive to any sensitive electronics, even fairly crude electronics. And this is nearly five times stronger.*

"What else?" he asked, almost afraid to hear the answer. "How could that happen here?"

"Wait . . . . They happened . . . . wait . . . . around 1933. The time stream transmitted them along with all of us! . . . . Wait, there is more . . . See dee tee? Wait, those are letters. C D T. Central Daylight Time. Impossible! Casual?—no *causal.*'

"Dynamic triangulation? Causal dynamic triangulation?"

"Yes, yes. That's it."

"That has to do with our simplexes—4-simplexes—the pentatopes. My God, how could he know that?! It's an advanced theory, very new stuff. Moving variations in space itself!—Or moving violations! What else?"

"Message is finished. I'm coming up. Focus on leptoquarks now."

Rakoczy shut down the electrical interface to the Dybbuk. The crystals ceased to glow; the time machine was now inert. Ludmila came through the door into the time lab.

"It's done," he said simply. "These smarmy, snarky little beasts hitched a 33 year ride back to 1900 but they didn't pop out with the rest of us. They waited nearly three hours. How, I haven't the remotest! But they almost fried the Dybbuk!"

Ludmila smothered his speech with her soft, full lips. It was a long kiss edged with passion. "I am proud of you, Sandor." He joined the General and the others; she stopped in the ladies restroom to freshen up. Kissing him had aroused her;, and as she looked in the mirror and brushed her hair back, her nipples came erect. She touched herself; she was aroused; she was wet. Ovulation was just starting. *Those eggs!* she thought with anticipation. *They are ruling my life again.*

Rakoczy walked into the conference room. They all moved close to him; he was nearly mobbed. He stopped near the squat podium and took a long breath, then another. Time seemed to stop. An audible group sigh filled the room; they needed him to tell them what was going on.

"What the hell is it, Sandy?" demanded diGiovanni

"What do you have?" asked the General.

Rakoczy smiled. "Leptoquarks."

A quizzical look crossed the faces of some in the room; others fully understood. All were relieved by his demeanor. Ludmila opened the door from the hallway, stopped and listened.

"Leptoquarks," he repeated. "Most powerful I've ever heard of. They're unstable, they decay and emit destructive particles. But they're supposed to bind positrons to quarks. Our time circuits have no tolerance for anti-matter. And one TeV! That's one scorching, sizzling projectile hurtling through spacetime – like an exploding shell. It's a monster quark. We're dealing with the strong force unleashed. Could have destroyed the time machine. We lucked out"

"That's a relief," nodded Gerhard. "Is our luck holding?"

Rakoczy grinned. "Seems to be. Anyway I disconnected the Dybbuk—pulled the plug. There's no danger—for now. But those little beasts seemed be the key to what just happened, and they've brought the laws of physics with them. They appear to live in pure, unmitigated Hilbert space—to symmetrical Fock space."

His love, the unabashedly sensual Dr. Ludmila sauntered through the open door, draped her arm around Rakoczy's neck and kissed him softly on the lips. "I think you mean *Dilbert* space, darlink. And *fock* space! Oh la la!"

"Filbert space," Rakoczy quipped. "You know, where Jocko put the nuts."

Dr. Ludmila turned to diGiovanni. "There is my good friend Al," she said in her sultry voice, lightly kissing his lips. "Smile, Al! You and I can understand all this. At least *we* have connection— biology and chemistry. Makes biochemistry! Wormhole connection, Al. I have wormhole, you have worm! And fock space!"

"I've got some theories of my own," said diGiovanni to Rakoczy, managing a brief smile and pretending to ignore Dr. Ludmila. "I suggest we put them all together as quickly as possible. I believe you are right. I've just been boning my—*oops*—I mean boning *up* on my Maxwell. Yes, it looks like we're on borrowed time, a pun my word. I think it's a zero sum game. Now tell me more about your leptoquarks."

Dr. Ludmila smiled, pursing her lips, raising one eyebrow.

Rakoczy replied thoughtfully. "Zero sum. Hmmm. Yes. Well. The leptoquarks may be a mediator between matter and anti-matter—a third term maybe living on the boundary. Professor Higgs's peripheral nervous system. Wheeler's quantum foam with sub-microscopic wormholes near the scale of the Planck radius. The leptos may be crucial in creating a super-symmetry"

"Blah blah blah!" mocked Ludmila. "You're chasing those mice again!"

He looked at di Giovanni intensely, who was shaking his head.

"You mean implicate order, unbroken, underlying unity. God particles? Higgs bosons? Nobody's ever seen one. Extraordinary theories require extraordinary confirmation, extraordinary solutions. The standard model may be sub-standard. Leon Lederman is full of baloney. His God particle is a *deus ex machina!*"

"Good one!" laughed Gerhard. "But he earned himself a Nobel Prize. And he's a sport. Actually, I'm inclined to believe him."

DiGiovanni smirked, shaking his head.

"Listen to me, Al. Consider first: the Higgs field is a ubiquitous *physical* entity that is hypothesized to give, to grant the mass to quote-unquote *observed* physical particles, as opposed to unobserved physical particles. What does that tell you! On this note look carefully: the *unobserved* physical particles—the so-called virtual particles—are the basis of *charge*, which is readily observable and quantifiable. So don't duck the question: realize that the bulk of observable, or at least calculable reality is based upon mythical beasts no one has ever seen."

"*Stop it!*" interjected Ludmila. "Now your mice are multiplying! They're scurrying everywhere!"

DiGiovanni spoke up. "Higgs granting mass to all? Very generous for a thrrrifty Scotsman! Maybe he can turn virtual into true! Sounds busy!"

Dr. Ludmila broke in passionately. "Give me a break! All you Uranian characters! Leptoquarks shleptoquarks! Higgs, figs! Do you think you're at the bottom of the well? There is no bottom, just worlds within worlds within worlds. I feel it!" She placed her hands under her ample bosoms, pushing them up. "Here. Here is where I feel it. Here and in the gut. You are too much Virgo, Sandy, easy for you to take things apart, hard to put back together. Even your name has sand, tiny grains. Put all sand together and look at rock! Where did sand come from, hey? From rock. Where did rock come from? From mountain. Where mountains? Third rock from sun! You study too much physics and not enough biology! And you, Al, even worse! Stubborn Taurus! Ignoring evidence is not science. I thought you were looking for truth, not hiding from it!"

"I think you mean geology," diGiovanni quipped. "And, by the way quit, filling my wife's head with all that astrology mumbo jumbo. She's using it against me!"

"Smartass Al! Biology! I am biologist. I am Pisces and so is Marina! So was Einstein. Science of life! Astrology is cosmic biology. Marina knows more than you because she sees big picture." Di Giovanni shook his head. This isn't the time and place for this conversation.

Dr. Ludmila continued. "Nommo is my patient; he lets me probe him. When I do I have images, I have sense of great harmony, everything is one. Better than sex—at least—most of time. Everything is living, even your . . . leptoquarks. Life is beautiful, Al. You look just like Roberto Benigni, why don't you act like him?! Be Italian. Be passionate. You are too much American!"

"How about reproductive biology!" di Giovanni gibed, finally looking Dr. Ludmila straight in the eye. "He-she's a hermaphrodite, your friend Nommo. Consider the possibilities!" He turned to Rakoczy. "Settle her down, Sandy. She's *your* concubine."

"Thank you, Al," Ludmila retorted. "And he is *my* concu*bone*, thanks very much! But I am changing subject. Something you don't know about Dybbuk; something I know from Nommo. Dybbuk is living organism. With sense of humor even. Our Nommo controls that machine, the machine is alive, too, and the machine thinks Nommo is its mother. Nommo will get us back. He talks to me and I know how to listen!"

"We are on borrowed time, Ludmila," Rakoczy observed. "We may soon be out of time."

"Who is the lender?" she quipped. "Whoever it is, we are paying interest."

"The lender is James Clerk Maxwell," diGiovanni retorted. "The mad Scotsman! Only it's his evil twin. He's a loan shark, and he's the enforcer! Maxwell's Demon!"

Chapter 10

Planetarium

At 3:30 AM, lanky, athletic, dark haired Dr. Robert Rose, astrophysicist and base astronomer, walked out of one of the external residences. At a small private New Year's party there, he had had a lot to drink, and enjoyed a brief affair with the hostess, Melody. Immediately afterward he had stretched out on the bed and fallen asleep. When he awoke everybody was gone. *Where the hell did they go? Where did she go?*

He strode towards the bunker, deeply inhaling the brisk night air and clearing his head. He looked up and to his great surprise saw a moonless sky teeming with brilliant stars horizon to horizon, brighter than he could ever remember. *Thought it was going to be cloudy tonight!*

As he approached the bunker, security men met and briefed him on the strange events that had begun at midnight. Incredulous, he hurried inside, shaking his head.

He entered the small observatory on the third level and pressed a button to position the 108" telescope for viewing, programming the coordinates. *Damn—it's after three. All the clouds are gone and it's crystal clear. Wanted to catch the first moonrise of 2000, with no other planets above the horizon. It rose at 2:35; I'll still catch the first rays.*

He checked his messages; found the cryptic messages from Sandor Rakoczy, then singlemindedly turned to his telescope and programmed it, refusing to speculate on the weird events of tonight the guards had told him about. The boundless universe was his opiate, his refuge, his home.

Camouflaged solid earth moved aside on a high adjacent hill and a large rounded turret arose, rotated rapidly and winked open. Data unfolded on Rose's screen. He lit his pipe and watched. *No moon! That's impossible!* Quickly he checked his indicators and his watch. Everything was working. *Something strange going on. Never mind; Venus is going to rise at 3:55; that'll be a sight to see!* He shook his head and put on a pot of coffee. *Guess I had a little too much to drink. Clear my head and try again.*

At 3:49 he trained his telescope on the eastern horizon; sure enough, a planet was rising, but it was several degrees off the calculated location of Venus, and a tad early. He shifted the telescope to the rising light of the planet and watched it wax bright on the screen as it broke the horizon several minutes early. He watched the disk slowly emerge, saw the horizontal bands and suddenly realized he was looking at Jupiter! He watched in open-mouthed, stunned fascination for many minutes as the Great Red Spot to the south, looking like a bleary eye, slowly rotated into full view. The disk of the volcanic moon Io snapped into focus. *Impossible!! This is crazy!! Jupiter set in the west only two hours ago! Wait. This can't be live. Some joker has set it to play back another viewing.* He looked at the date readout on the astronomical clock. January 1, 1900. He laughed aloud in spite of himself. *I wonder who pulled this stunt! Had me going for a minute!*

At another level he suspected that the telescope was working perfectly; his expression changed to perplexity and his heart raced.

He then programmed the telescope to pinpoint dim Barnard's Star, a red dwarf that was the closest to earth with the exception of the Alpha Centauri system. It took him minutes to find it. It was nearly 17 arc minutes off—over a quarter of a degree, which meant that it could be nearly half a light year farther out! That would take 100 years, all right. Then he looked directly through the eyepiece. His heart stopped. There was no disparity. He rechecked it three times. No disparity.

He buried his head in his hands and breathed deeply, rocking back and forth for minutes. His heart was pounding. Then he checked it again.

In shock, he picked up the phone to call his friend Rakoczy.

"Sandy, you will not believe this. Get up here right away and don't bring anybody else!"

Relieved to hear from Rose, Rakoczy wore a poker face for the others. "OK. I'm on my way," he spoke softly into the phone. "Been trying to get a hold of you for three hours. We have a major emergency. I've been with diGiovanni; I'd like to bring him too."

"O.K., but nobody else!"

"What about Dr. Ludmila?"

"O.K., O.K., bring her but *nobody* else!! Don't bring the goddam alien! Or his witch doctor. Or the General!"

Rakoczy and Dr. Ludmila, hand in hand, casually walked over to the elevator. Di Giovanni was already on it. Rakoczy nervously lit a cigarette and blew smoke at the Positively No Smoking sign.

"Now what!? What the fuck is going on, Sandy, with you crazy mad scientists? The whole place has gone coocoo!" She smiled demurely, deftly plucked Rakoczy's cigarette out of his mouth and took a long drag on it, delicately exhaling the smoke. They all rode to Level 1, got in their cart and drove to the observatory building. Rose was standing there as the door opened.

"Hello, Robbie," said Dr. Ludmila, lightly kissing his lips. "I heard you came here from Lick Observatory. I would lllove to work there!" Rose did not smile. His heart was still pounding.

"You will not believe this!" he spoke rapidly. "Let me show you something you will not believe! It is unbelievable!"

They took the elevator up to the viewing room, which housed a small planetarium. Rose set the program for 4:15 AM, January 1, 1900, and punched it in. The deep velvet blue hemisphere above lit up with stars like the brilliant night sky. There was Jupiter just above the eastern horizon. There was no moon. He then took them in and showed them the live view from the telescope. Then through the eyepiece. All were identical.

A few minutes later, as the three walked stiff-legged back to the elevator, Rose shouted at them. "Didn't you know what you were fucking with with your stupid time machine?! You put us all at risk. We may be stuck here forever!"

They entered the elevator. Dr. Ludmila was even more aroused and breathing heavily; her lips parted. She leaned heavily with her ample bosoms on Rakoczy. They were all transfixed, but excitement was stirring in them.

"Let us go home, Sandy. Now. I want you to teach me about Fock space!"

Chapter 11

The Wild West

A phone jangled, insistent, loud and unwelcome. Area 51's top rated F-16 pilot, 26 year old Air Force First Lieutenant Bobby Wilson, was jarred awake. He grabbed the phone. It was Colonel Pick.

"Good morning, Bobby. This is Colonel Pick. Report to the flight line immediately. We're already prepping the F-16B. There'll be a car at your door in five minutes. Lt. Joseph will be your co-pilot."

"On my way, Colonel."

Bobby's lover, helicopter pilot Captain Mary Mulligan was half awake. They had partied all night and smoked a small but sufficient quantity of top secret Area 51 premium red dirt homegrown. He was still high. He poured a water glass full of yesterday's cold coffee and slugged it down. It wasn't enough. He turned the shower on cold, braced himself and danced, shivered and yelled for a half minute, then stepped out. That worked. *Or so he thought.*

Mary was awake now and concerned. "Bobby It's early. What's up? It's Saturday morning!"

"*I'm* up," he replied. "Up in the F-16B. Colonel Pick just called, I have to go in—flying with Lt. Bates Joseph. Something's wrong; something's going on."

"Good luck!" said Mary, sardonically. "He's a religious nut. Anyway, he'll try to save your soul?"

"No such luck! I'm a nonbeliever. Lord, help thou mine unbelief! Bates is a damned good pilot, though.

"So what's the emergency, Bobby?"

"Colonel Pick didn't tell me and I didn't ask. I'll find out when I get there," he sang.

Col. Pick then called the home of 28 year old Lt. Bates Joseph, another rated pilot, and a 1995 Air Force Academy graduate. His wife, Ellen, answered.

"Good morning. This is Colonel Pick. Please let me speak to Lieutenant Joseph."

"Bates is over at the Chapel. We're Seventh Day Adventists, you know," she told him proudly; "We worship on Saturday. He's preparing our 10 o'clock service. You're invited, of course, Colonel Pick!"

"Thank you, Mrs. Joseph. 'Fraid we've got a bit of an emergency, and I'm going to have to call him to duty. *Excuse me for a moment.*" He put her on hold and called his Adjutant, Major Ike Sizemore, who was already at headquarters. "Go over to the chapel and pick up Lt. Joseph right away. Take him straight to the flight line. We're sending him and Bobby Wilson on a little reconaissance mission ASAP." He clicked back to Mrs. Joseph. "Sorry."

"Oh! Well, that's all right, Colonel. We can postpone our services—there are only four Adventists on the base! I'll tell them."

"Fine. We'll get him back as soon as we can!"

"Is he flying alone? I always worry about that."

"No, another pilot, Bobby Wilson will be flying with him."

"Oh yes. Bobby. We've met him." She hesitated. "Colonel, I don't mean to pry, but I really need to know: is Bobby Wilson a Christian?"

Col. Pick hesitated. "Well . . . . I think so. Actually, I don't know." He paused. *Why do you want to know if he's a Christian?*"

"Colonel, this may sound very strange to you, but we're a very religious family. We're firm believers in the Rapture."

"Fine. I respect your beliefs. What's that got to do with Bobby?

"Colonel, if Bobby is a Christian, and he and Bates are taken up in the Rapture—well."

"Well what? Isn't that a glorious thing for a Christian?"

"Of course, of course it is, Colonel." She was almost warbling with joy. "But . . . ."

"But *what*, Mrs. Joseph?" he asked tolerantly but impatiently.

"Colonel, they're going to be up in a plane together . . . . If . . . . uh . . . . You know . . . . If . . . ." She hesitated to spell it out. After a long pause, she said. *Colonel, do the math.*"

At 7:10 AM, at first light, the F-16B was scrambled, with instructions to fly to the south end of Nellis Air Force Base in Las Vegas, which had remained strangely silent throughout the night, even though Area 51 was unofficially a part of Nellis. Seconds after takeoff the plane penetrated a strangely translucent green aura. It did not register on his instruments and he was through it before he knew it.

"Make a note of that, Bates," Bobby told Lt. Joseph. In fact I'm turning the cameras on right now. Make detailed notes of everything—and note the time—to the second if possible."

He then flew southwest toward the main base of Nellis, seeing nothing. Certain that he had not read his instruments correctly, he swung back to Area 51, flew back through the bubble, checked his instruments, and tried again. No VOR, no satellite signal—no GPS. He had to fly by the seat of his pants.

This is nuts. Bobby muttered to himself.

Lt. Joseph pulled his map down. "Where're we going?" he asked.

"In a long, narrow oval," Bobby replied. "We're establishing a perimeter around the base, about 300 miles wide and 600 miles long. Say south of Kingman—the Hualapai Reservation to Carson City and Reno."

Lt. Joseph plotted a course as accurately as he could. Bobby agreed to it and activated the cameras. They were flying low. He noted the familiar landmarks: dry riverbeds, low mountain peaks in the Nellis Range. The main base, Nellis Air Force Base, only minutes away, just wasn't there. He swung to the southwest. Where the glittering Las Vegas strip was supposed to have been, they saw nothing but a few houses and barns, dirt streets, mules, and a few trails leading out into the desert. He swung southeast towards Kingman, Arizona, crossing the Colorado River, which was nearly a half mile wide. *What happened to Lake Mead?! Hoover Dam? Where the hell are we!?*

He banked the jet left to the southeast over Mono Lake, mist rising, frost glistening, pristine and enchanting in the dawn hours. *There's Yosemite Valley, Half Dome, Merced River, Mariposa—no question about that.* He breathed a momentary sigh of relief and slowed the craft to 300 knots, flying low.

Lt. Joseph nodded. "It's all here, Bobby." A few gravel roads and trails were visible; no pavement. Every geographical landmark was in place; he now knew exactly where he was on the map. They crossed the Colorado River. "Bobby, you missed Hoover Dam. I don't know what happened. You should be over Henderson right now. *And what happened to the GPS?* Zero in on a VOR—the max distance is 115 miles."

Bobby Wilson nodded, punched a button, shook his head, and then swung the F-16 northwest in a climbing turn. "Sorry,

Bates. I'm not detecting any. I'll worry about that later. We have a complete photographic record. I'm heading for Carson City and Reno." He banked right, rose to 10,000', hit the afterburner and raced northwest at Mach 1.2. The streaking thunder of the sonic boom reverberated over the desert.

Obadiah Hardesty, a grizzled gold prospector, an original '49er, half asleep in his hermit shack in the desert near Chloride, Arizona Territory, woke up at midnight. He saw the sky glow green for an instant. It was cold. He huddled tightly in his blankets and his red woolen *gatkehs*[1] and went back to sleep. He awoke a little after seven in an alcohol fog, took a pull on his whiskey bottle. Hair of the dog. He climbed into his bib overalls, pulled his boots on, and donned a soiled parka. He was disturbed about last night and wondered if it was a dream. He grabbed his pick and walked outside. Then he watched the F-16 go over, heard the roar, saw the fiery exhaust. The sonic boom knocked him down. Non-plussed, he checked his bottle—nearly half full. He was still drunk and his face was deeply flushed. He took another long pull on the bottle, then decided to amble over to his claim. He sat down on the ground, stopped to think again and began to weep. He poured the remaining whiskey on the ground.

White Cloud, chief of a dwindling band of Pomo Indians, heard a hissing sound which grew louder by the second. He looked up and saw a huge silver bird streaking overhead with fire shooting out its rear, then the bone jarring shock of the sonic boom knocked him to his knees. Returning to his band, mumbling in a strange tongue that sounded suspiciously like Yiddish, he invoked a sacred

---

[1]   *Gatkehs* (or gotkeys, if you prefer) underwear, a funnier way of saying underwear than "underwear." Also remember that in Yiddish, all underwear is long underwear.

pow-wow. He and two other Pomos walked over to the community fire and began sending smoke signals.

Panic began to rise. Lt. Joseph was fearful but highly animated, breathing heavily. "Do you know what, Bobby? These are signs we're seeing—they're signs of the Last Days. Bobby, I know you're a Christian, but do you really believe?"

Bobby was preoccupied and still a little high. "Sure, Bates," he replied distractedly. "We're Methodists."

"But are you a strong believer?"

"*Why are you asking me this?*" he snapped.

"It's the Rapture," said Bates Joseph with great emphasis. "I think it's happening!"

"Jesus, man, we're a little busy here. *Can this wait? Until after we've landed?*"

Lt. Joseph looked at Bobby quizzically, then sadly. In a near whisper he said, "OK. It'll be OK." His eyes were rolled up in his head and he was praying.

Just what I need, Bobby muttered to himself. He pinched himself to see if he was in a frighteningly realistic dream. *Did I party too much last night, he mused; maybe it was that little bit of smoke. Guess I shouldn't have.* He slowed down below 300 knots, then swerved downward to the right to avoid a flock of birds and nearly brushed the ground. He pulled up, felt the violent G-forces, and was now certain he wasn't dreaming. In the adrenalin rush his heart pounded. *Got to find civilization,* he thought urgently.

He descended to 400' and slowed to 200 knots. He swung over Reno and flew low and slow over Carson City, the capital, at 300'. He looked down, saw a knot of people. They were looking up. Then they saw what appeared to be a movie set in an old Western: horse drawn carriages, Indians, a shiny open carriage with huge spoked wheels that looked like an early antique car, women in parasols, chickens, kids, dogs, people gawking at him and pointing. "Look man!" he shouted to his co-pilot. "Look!"

Lt. Joseph snapped out of his reverie and saw the turn of the century scene below. He bobbled his head but said nothing, and started silently praying again.

"You all right, Bates?" There was no response.

Confused and concerned, Bobby radioed back to base. He was ordered to return immediately. As he neared the base, he passed a chopper flying in the opposite direction. It looked like Mary's Huey, but he couldn't tell. He flew through the bubble again, and told the radio operator that he had a very strange tale to tell about Western movie sets. He now began to convince himself that he must have missed Nellis, the Strip and all of Las Vegas.

Security was there to debrief him and Lt. Joseph. *Hope they don't piss test me,* Bobby thought anxiously.

Chapter 12

Echoes

Today time took its time. Precessing inexorably round the globe, starting in mid-Pacific at the International Date Line, 1900 swept Westerly an hour every 15 degrees, as the 18's clicked audibly into 19's in each time zone, coming full circle in the 24 hours. It was the first day of the 1900's, an orderly triumph of positional notation over civilization. A printer's bonanza. It was a day of fresh hope as the new century—the twentieth—was born in number though not in numerical truth; that birth lay just a year ahead. There would be a year to savor the transition, a year in which Physics would be reborn.

In the Höttingen District of Zurich, Switzerland, Albert Einstein, a smartly dressed young man of 20 sporting a bushy new mustache, a full head of black curls and a chic fedora, strolled out into a sunny, crisp New Year's morning and strode buoyantly towards the trolley stop. It was a warm day for January, breezy, almost a harbinger of spring. Most unusual!

Regina Holstein, a comely, buxom Swiss miss, emerged from the apartment house with a black briefcase in her hand, ran after him and finally caught up with him, out of breath.

"You forgot your briefcase again, Bertie darling," she exhaled. She put her arms around his neck, smiled and kissed him sensually on the lips. They ambled to the trolley stop hand in hand and she waited with him until the brightly painted car arrived. It clanked and hummed to a stop and she kissed him again, slipping her tongue into his mouth.

"Come home soon, Bertie; I'll be waiting for you!"

He boarded the trolley, firmly grasping the steel bar with one hand, and muscled himself into the car in a single motion. It was almost empty on this New Year's morning. A group of young nurses clad in white with Red Cross pins and freshly starched caps sat near the front, energetically chattering away in Switzerland's quaint German dialect, Schweitzerdeutsch. It was a holiday, but the university labs knew no holiday; neither did the hospitals.

A stale alcohol smell greeted him from the seats behind him; he chose to ignore it—New Year's Eve revelers with burgeoning hangovers dragging themselves to work.

As the huge trolley lumbered down the long hill on the wide cobblestone thoroughfare, his body and mind fell into the rhythm of the familiar clatter and rumble. He felt his body sway under the Newtonian dance, dominated by the physical forces controlling its mass and motion. But not his mind, strangely detachable from his body on this day. He could count the stones, detect their size and grouping by the short, low, occasionally shrill musical bursts, and place them into neat interacting sets, dancing geometric shapes enhanced by competing interference patterns, timing them, uniting them, conducting with his baton. Short semi-melodic passages were punctuated by the loud clang of the trolley bell, sometimes once, sometimes twice, as the lumbering iron beast periodically squeaked and groaned to a stop. If he had been blind he could have constructed a palpable moving sound picture, new sight, a substitute for sight. Music of interference patterns. Mozart must have known that; Bach surely felt it, saw it, knew it. He mouthed the words silently: I will draw the patterns with the intervals moving in an out of consonance, assign the key and play the relative frequencies on my fretless instrument! I will send it to Mahler.

Now the human voices, words only occasionally discernible, ebbed and flowed into a surreal Doppler chorus, and as the trolley sped up the cobblestone chorus grew shrill in an accelerating glissando, reaching a zenith, then curving back.

The shriek and groaning of steel wheels against rails, two too-loud clangs and a hard jolt jerking his body forward and backward, snapped him out of his reverie. Time to get off.

Off the steep trolley landing he stepped, onto the slippery cobblestones. Down the hill he looked long and hard. Swimming into his view, shores of the Zürichsee glistened at the bottom, 100 meters below, waves played palpably on the shore. His peripheral vision merged into an intense wide angle view, everything in a single dance, a peculiar order. Fleeting shafts of sunlight punctuated the moving landscape with strobe-like rhythmic glints off the waves.

Up rose a stiff gust, nearly blowing his hat off. The spell broken, he sniffed, inhaled and composed himself. Hand on hat, he briskly strode eastward toward the grey, austere building that held the physics labs.

He mounted two flights of stairs and walked into his shared office, sat in his chair and put his feet up on the desk. The phone jingled. It was his office-mate Heinrich, an older fellow student; his wife was about to deliver, so he wouldn't be coming in today. To be sure!

Endeavoring to regain his focus, he removed some papers from his briefcase. Some of Poincaré's latest work. He already knew many of the equations by heart; more were forthcoming. He could write them on the slate within his brain, but today they were strange hieroglyphs; within them lurked a mystery. They pulsed, they danced.

Suddenly something lit up, glowed bright green in his brain; an image of streams of brilliant light flowing into one. He lapsed briefly into unconsciousness, then snapped awake, disturbed at losing control of his mind even for an instant. He looked up at the clock on the mantelpiece; its bell sounded, three sets of three. It was exactly 9 A.M.

Threeness! Three majestic chords in E_b major, three flats, *portamento,* echoing the number 3, three triumphant major chords ending the opening movement of Beethoven's Eroica, the third, breaking forever free from Papa Haydn, free to burn his own shining track into the earth. The music played in his mind, dictated the time, saturating spaces of time, times of space, infinitely expandable, compressible, in inverse proportion. He fastened his mind to the rhythm, partially dissociating to observer within observer who took snapshots in the rhythm—elastic trajectories at zenith and nadir conversely crisscrossing, expanding and compressing. His perspective foreshortened to a disappearing point and instantaneously dilated to infinity in a timeless still-point moment, now reversing, time resuming. Ever discernible times of space, spaces of time, space peculiarly curved, the curve ever palpable. He could feel its arc; he traveled on the light beam, upon its arc.

He was momentarily disoriented. A sudden insight like a bursting sunrise appeared on the inner horizon of his concentric consciousness, rising, quickly illuminating the entire sphere. He strove to rivet his focus on it, drawing it into the light as it dawned on him, reviewing, replaying. He tightly focused the ray of his mind's eye upon the outer layer of the sphere, outer reaches of its tether, a concave mirror, in novel ways reflecting, amplifying, revealing all that emanated from within in a language of flashes, glints and shafts; new in-sights. Alive and active; it was a newly functioning part of him. He listened with inner gaze.

Deeply embedded in those hieroglyphs lurked a mystery; suddenly he saw patterns in them, patterns of jade light; parts of the equations seemed to rise off the page and glow; they played; the flat printed page two-dimensional grew a third axis and then shimmered on a fourth, a moving axis, alternating, merging and remerging from the infinite to the infinitesimal, maxima and minima. Minkowski, my dearest teacher, are you with me?

Re-replaying the journey, he focused anew on the hieroglyphs, concentrating harder than he had ever done. The secret was in the curves and in the interference patterns. Time *and* space? *Time-space?!!* An epiphany. Could it be? He concentrated long and hard on the thought, scribbling furiously, hiding his papers under other papers whenever someone entered the room. There it was, waiting for him all the time. *Zero sum*, a dance, a *coincidentia oppositorum*. Why couldn't Poincaré see it? He *must* have seen it; could he ignore it?

His heart pounded, his shallow breathing punctuated by powerful cadences that shook his frame. What time is it? Indeed!

Several students and assistants had entered the electrical lab in the next room. He hadn't noticed until now. Minkowski was in Bern for the holiday; he wouldn't return until next Thursday.

Einstein's fellow students passed like moving shadows back and forth before the open office door; caricatures of themselves; their voices a dull cacophony; sounds blurred, the occasional pop and sizzle of the electrical devices. Nobody greeted him; he was alone in a small crowd. His center of consciousness hovered at the edge, the breach in his mirrored sensorium, the inside of the reflective sphere where time-space had intruded. Simple question. He looked out his office window at the huge clock on the grey monolith of a bank building; the minute hands moved visibly; he could feel the crawl of the hour hands.

He gave a start. It was a quarter of eleven. Where had two hours gone? Putting both hands down on his desk he bent forward until his forehead touched the cool desk. It's all right, he thought; this is all new; this is a breakthrough. He sat up as awareness grew of the depth and intensity of this insight. Bubbles of light pulsed upward into his back brain as elation grew—a broad smile emanating from the depths; his whole being smiled.

Suddenly he realized he was hungry. Grabbing his notes, he quickly descended the narrow stone stairway, inhaled the bracing air, and then briskly walked nine blocks to the Pantheon, a well known Greek restaurant in downtown Zurich. He was early; only a few tables were occupied.

Sophia, the owner's daughter, a slim, sultry lass who liked his trim good looks and his penetrating eyes, gave him the menu and lingered, trying to catch his eye. Too preoccupied to flirt with her today, he ordered his usual lunch—a bowl of hot soup and a lamb *souvlaki*. Barely acknowledging Sophia as she decorously set his food in front of him, he ate quickly, slurping the soup, pushed the plate aside, and resumed his intent concentration.

Scarcely aware of the passage of two entire hours, he remained in the mahogany booth, filling an entire notebook with arcane mathematical symbols. The owner, George Theophanopoulos, became annoyed; he was monopolizing the booth for too long. He stood before the booth, arms akimbo, but before he could utter a word, Einstein glared at him angrily with luminous green eyes. Theophanopoulous retreated in terror muttering Greek imprecations, performing an elaborate Orthodox sign of the cross.

When he returned, in a virtual trance, he had the lab office to himself. He worked most of the afternoon, and at about 4:45, heard a clamor in the next room where several men were crowding around the wire, chattering excitedly. Something big had happened.

At his spacious new rented building in Colorado Springs, next to the Alta Vista Hotel where he was staying, 43 year old Nikola Tesla was eating his lunch as he and his trusted assistant, Prescott Walker, worked tirelessly between bites on his most ambitious invention—harnessing terrestrial stationary waves, which would allow power to be transmitted huge distances without wires. He had just lit up an entire town 26 miles away—without wires. With his help, albeit unacknowledged by Marconi, who took full credit, the first transatlantic radio transmissions had been made less than a year earlier. He was excited that these huge breakthroughs came just as the 20th century dawned upon the world.

This apparatus was literally attuned to the earth's own unique range of frequencies, and the crude pen graph had recorded a severe anomaly—off the chart—in the middle of the night. It logged in at 6 minutes before one. He now remembered he had briefly awakened by odd rhythmic pulsating noises on his radio receiver, and was pulled back by an irresistible force into a vivid dream, virtually a lucid dream, in which he was visited by an extraterrestrial being—clearly an amphibian. Without speaking, the being had placed its hands on Tesla's temples, who fell into a deep, blissful trance within the dream.

At 1 PM his teletype began chattering away. He allowed the message to finish and casually walked over to it, picked it up and read it, did a double take and read it again. His eyes grew wide and his jaw dropped. He sat down, took several long breaths, and then sank into deep thought for several minutes.

He knew what he had to do. He telephoned Union Pacific. While his assistant packed and loaded his carriage, Tesla began sending out teletype messages all over. They packed an elaborate amount of special equipment, then headed for Denver. His assistant, Walker, drove. At the Union Pacific Station, he purchased tickets to Reno, Nevada. With only minutes to spare, they loaded their equipment and boarded the train at 7:00 that evening for the 39 hour trip to Reno.

Paris, France   January 1, 1900   N o o n

At his suburban Parisian villa, 73 year old Jules Verne picked up the telephone. It was his younger friend Henri Poincaré, the mathematician, who excitedly related a bizarre event that had just occurred in the western United States. Verne listened intently. They had both had vivid dreams. Poincaré invited him over for lunch.

An ultra modern "fly"—fast one horse carriage with ball bearings, guttapercha tires and sleek aerodynamic design pulled through the high, ornate wrought iron gate into the courtyard of Verne's lavish home, and the well groomed Poincaré quickly emerged. He was met by the elderly Frenchman in the garden. They embraced.

"Riri![1] Bienvenue. Entrez!"

"Ah, Jules! Ce jour c'est toi qui es devenu un prophète!"

A sumptuous four course lunch with a delightful, light and fruity cabernet was served by Poincaré's chef and his assistant in a walnut paneled dining room as Verne, his wife Honorine and Poincaré engaged in spirited, serious conversation with much gesticulation.

"C'est Tesla!" Poincaré said excitedly. "Il a découverte l'usage des vagues terrestriel; tu savais ça déjà. Mais aujour d'hui, il y a quelque chose même plus intéressant."

"Quoi, Riri? Quoi plus?"

---

[1]   *Riri* is a French nickname for Henry, their version of Hank.

111

"Quelques voyageurs du futur! Soyant arrivé a l'ouest des Etats Unis en bateaux volants. Bateaux volants, je te dis! Incréiblement avancés, volant en velocités énormes! Plus que cent ans au futur!"

"Humains?" queried Verne ironically.

"Oui, oui. Américains. Je n'ai pas surété. Mais oui, humains, bien sur!"

"Impossible," said Verne, shaking his head. "Une violation des lois de la Nature!"

"Mais, mon cher Jules, c'était le sujet de tes livres! C'est toi qui doîtes savoir, avant de tous autres. Allons nous a l'office télégraphique en Paris. Allons! Il y en a plus de nouvelles! Tesla est la avex eux. Maintenant. En Amérique!" Skeptical, Jules Verne was stirred, despite himself.

Electrified, they climbed into Poincaré's sleek carriage and headed for the telegraph office at the center of the city.

Chapter 13

Carson City, Nevada

Bobby Wilson landed his F-16 at Area 51, and was met and debriefed by Colonel Pick and General Mills. He explained what he had seen, or rather what he had not seen. The Colonel asked if he had picked up any kind of communication. He had not, but he had recognized Carson City, even though it looked like a big movie set. He mentioned the green screen he had flown through. Col. Pick immediately commissioned an Air Force chopper to fly there.

Upon learning this, the General quickly walked into the bunker and took the elevator to Level 18. He strode into Rakoczy's lab.

"What did you find out, General, that is, Tom?"

"Well, for one thing, the F-16 pilot flew in and out of some kind of green bubble about five miles out. He said he saw it before and as he was approaching the base he could see it again—like a transparent dome of some kind. Also, much of our security perimeter is non-existent, since the Global Positioning Satellites, which are crucial in maintaining it, still appear to be non-existent."

"Just as I suspected," nodded Rakoczy briskly. "We need to get out there and get some instrumentation on it." He called in Gerhard and Mikhail, his two best *tinkerniquers*. "Get your full array of wave detection equipment together right away." He ordered. "Load it on the Land Rover and our truck. There's some kind of standing bubble wave surrounding the base about five miles out and we have to go out there and check it out. It may be the key to this whole thing. Bring radio equipment too and we'll see if we can pick up anything outside of that perimeter."

The techs began gathering up the equipment.

Rakoczy turned to the General. "Want to come along, Tom?"

"No, Sandy, I'll leave that to you. I've got a lot on my plate; we've got that Airbus and all those people to deal with, and, frankly, I'm getting a little concerned about Colonel Cassidy. Got to keep an eye on him. Plus a million other things. Get back to me as soon as you know something."

Good-natured, good looking, redheaded Air Force Captain Mary Mulligan was awakened and summoned to duty shortly after Bobby left. When Bobby returned to their flat, she was gone. She had already taken off in her Huey chopper, flown through the bubble, and immediately reported the total electronic blackout. Familiar with the area, she flew northwest to Carson City at top speed. She was astounded as she arrived over the center of the city; huge crowds of people were yelling and gesticulating. Indeed it is a Western movie set, she thought, smiling, marveling at the size of the production. She found an open lot about a mile off and landed the chopper. She pulled off her helmet, strawberry blond curls falling about her head, and began reporting her findings to the base on her radio. She watched with amazement and growing alarm as crowds of people started moving towards her craft. Some of them were running the other way in panic. Most were in Western garb, their six-shooters hanging heavily from their waists.

"Bobby's right," she radioed Security at the base. "They're making a Western. Oughta be a good one—it's quite a production!"

At the front of the crowd stood Mayor Clinton Yarborough, a tall, well dressed gentleman of 50, slender, in a black coat and string tie, Lincolnesque, with a well trimmed but ample mustache. He was flanked by two other men in coats and string ties.

"Howdy!" one of them yelled as he saw, to his further amazement, a woman in a military uniform staring back at them, and recognized military insignia and an American flag on the helicopter. The flag looked somehow different.

"Keep your distance!" Mulligan shouted back in through a speaker. "This is Captain Mulligan, U.S. Air Force, and this is a military aircraft on official business. What's going on? Are you people making a movie?"

The three men stopped and waved the crowd back. A woman giving orders! The county sheriff and several deputies on horseback rode up nearby and the sheriff tried to take charge. They, too, had seen it hover and then land.

"What in tarnation *is* that thang?" drawled the Sheriff. They moved cautiously towards the chopper, guns drawn, and dismounted. Mulligan shouted out another warning. Sensing real danger, she fired one of her cannons in front of the deputies. Several bullets hit a rock, which shattered and violently threw up dust and debris. The sheriff's cadre stopped in its tracks.

"Stop right there and nobody will get hurt!" commanded Mulligan. "This is official military business. I want to talk to whoever's in charge here? Keep your hands high and approach slowly!"

"I'm in charge here!" shouted Sheriff Sam Roscoe. He was 51, about 5' 6", stocky, with a ruddy complexion, pale blue eyes, and a mostly gray, somewhat yellowish unkempt midlength beard and mustache. He was sporting two six-shooters and carrying a long Winchester rifle.

"No . . . you're . . . not!!" the Mayor shouted back at him. "I'll handle this, Sam! Looks like we'd better try diplomacy, 'cause you just might be in over your head! Those looked like real bullets and I think that lady means business. Looks military to me!"

The Sheriff's face turned red with rage and he started stomping around and cursing. He was still in his cups from New Year's Eve.

The Lincolnesque man raised his hands and cautiously stepped towards the craft.

"Come over here sir and tell me what the hell is going on," said Mary Mulligan through the loudspeaker in a friendlier tone. She radioed the base and then slid her window open. "I'm Captain Mulligan, United States Air Force. Sorry to cause such a commotion but where's Carson City? Are you the Director of this movie?"

"This *is* Carson City. I'm Mayor Yarborough." He reached out his hand and Mulligan shook it, managing a smile. The other two men in dark suits, round collars and string ties edged a little closer. They were dumbfounded. "What kind of a rig is this?" marveled the Mayor. "This is *astounding*; you're *flying* in that incredible contraption! I've never seen anything like it!"

"Cut the crap, Mayor," Mulligan laughed good-naturedly. "*Cut!!* This is the real world. You're getting way too deep into your script."

Meanwhile a Times photographer and his assistant were frantically setting up their cameras 50' away.

The crowds drew closer. The Sheriff, stung by the firepower demonstration, regained his courage. His voice was slurred. "Get out of that contraption, woman! You're no more Army than my grandmother. *You're under arrest* for disturbin' the peace!"

"Shut up, Sam, and back off!" the Mayor shouted back at him.

The radio crackled. It was Colonel Pick. "Return to base immediately!"

"Well Mayor, Sheriff, you heard my orders," Mulligan smiled good naturedly. "I hope you're having a good time at my expense! Like I said, I think you're just a little too involved in your script." She started up the chopper. "Stand back now; I'm taking off. Tell that cowboy to control himself! I'll be back!"

The rotors began to turn, creating a dust storm. The mayor and his group ducked in panic. The Sheriff hit the ground and yelled. "Git back here; yer under arrest!"

The chopper lifted off, tilted, and headed southeast, and as it began to gain altitude, the sheriff carefully aimed and fired off his Winchester rifle at it. It was a lucky shot. The bullet hit a rare vulnerable spot in one of the hydraulics controlling the rear directional rotors, damaging it. Captain Mulligan flew on but the hydraulics were squirting out fluid. The craft began losing altitude and directional control. She radioed back to base that she was under attack. Security answered her call.

Major Wingard took the call and dutifully informed Colonel Pick, who immediately dispatched an AH-1 Super Cobra gunship to the scene with orders to shoot to kill if necessary.

"I got her!! I got her!!" shouted the Sheriff, dancing in glee.

"We'll teach them goddam anarchists a lesson!" echoed one of his deputies.

Barely five miles away, the wobbling chopper was forced to make a rough landing. Mulligan was shaken but uninjured. Some of the crowd headed out into the cactus desert at a trot; a few mounted their horses. When she saw people on horseback riding toward her in the distance, she radioed the base asking for immediate help, fearing that the Super Cobra might not arrive soon enough to protect her. Col. Pick immediately dispatched Lt. Bobby Wilson and his F-16 with instructions to locate the downed chopper and protect it.

He hit the afterburner a minute after he took off and flew at Mach 1.5. Minutes later, he had located Capt. Mulligan's chopper. Seeing several people on horseback riding towards the site, he swung around, flying at under 100', and buzzed the riders, about a dozen of them, then pulled up and came around for another pass. The horses spooked and four of the riders were bucked off. The rest hightailed it away from there at a full gallop. He came around for a second pass. Same result. Mary Mulligan smiled and flipped the radio switch. "Thanks, Bobby. That worked—they're spooked. Can you stay in range for a little longer? Ike Sizemore's on the way in a Super Cobra but it's over 300 miles. He won't be here for more than an hour."

"You got it, Mary! Wish I could land this thing. It's a bit of a gas hog, but I'm OK for now. *Turning out to be quite a day isn't it?*" He made a rapid, noisy climbing turn, making sure he was visible to the onlookers. Armed National Guard troops had mounted their horses and were heading toward Mary's downed chopper. Sheriff Roscoe was riding with them.

Bobby made a wide circle and came around again, flying at barely 200 knots. He saw the horses. As he flew near them he saw their uniforms, so he decided to veer off rather than provoke them more. Mary, meanwhile, turned her loudspeaker to maximum. But they were still too far away.

When he saw the cavalry formation Mayor Yarborough sensed trouble. He mounted his horse and rode toward them, waving.

"Stop. That craft is not hostile. But it is well armed. I have met the driver and talked to her. I can assure there is no hostile intent unless she feels she is being attacked. I know her; please let me go and talk to her myself."

"Too dangerous," replied their leader, a major. "We're under orders from General Trevelyan."

"At least wait," urged the Mayor. "She's not going anywhere, and it looks like they sent someone to protect her." As if on cue, Bobby's F-16 came into view, flying directly toward them.

"Turn around or somebody is going to get hurt or killed," Mayor Yarborough warned. "You're over your head!"

Bobby flew over them at 200', and half the horses reared up and bucked off their riders. They decided to follow the Mayor's advice.

"I told you," said the Mayor. "Now I know you're under orders. So why don't you wait while your horses settle down. If you think it's necessary one of you can ride with me to the Armory and I'll talk to General Trevelyan myself."

That satisfied their commander. They rest of the troops were very relieved.

Mary flipped the transmitter: "Thanks a million, Bobby! I owe you one!" *If you know what I mean*, she spoke *sotto voce*.

Sheriff Roscoe had regained his nerve. He and two deputies cautiously rode out, along with curious onlookers, photographers from the Times and others. As the Sheriff and his deputies came in sight of the downed chopper, they heard a roar in the distance and watched as the an enormous black bird with American insignia arriving and then hovering over the chopper, landing and blowing up a huge cloud of dust. The roar was deafening. Uncertain now, the Sheriff stopped and reloaded his rifle. He hid behind a cactus. The crowd was agape, fascinated and fearful.

Bobby Wilson radioed Mary. "I'm heading back. Major Sizemore is in the Super Cobra. You're safe now."

Mary dismounted from her Huey chopper and saluted Major Sizemore.

"Thanks, Ike."

The voice of the black commander, Major Ike Sizemore, boomed out of his Super-Cobra. "This is a military operation. United States Marines. What the *hell* is goin on here?! Stand back and nobody'll git hurt. Did you hear me? *Git back!* Git back a thousand feet or better. *Move it!* Anybody who violates that perimeter will be shot!"

He fired a cannon a hundred feet in front of the retreating crowd. The sound was loud and crisp. It splattered a cactus and sent up a cloud of debris.

The crowd quickly pulled back even further, falling all over one another. The Sheriff, realizing he might have acted hastily, backed up carefully from his cactus and then tripped, falling headlong into another large cactus. He screamed and cursed in pain long and loud, dropping his rifle. He grabbed it and ran, still cursing.

Major Sizemore turned up the volume to full and his voice boomed out. "Who fired at the chopper?! Drop your weapons and come forward with your hands above your head. You're under arrest!!"

Sizemore alighted angrily from the Super-Cobra brandishing an automatic weapon. Mayor Yarborough stopped, then began walking cautiously towards the scene. He stopped within a hundred yards, amazed to see a black man taking charge and issuing commands, wearing a Marine Officer's uniform. He composed himself.

The Mayor rode to the edge of the perimeter, a rusty barbed wire fence. "I'm the Mayor of Carson City," he shouted, cupping his hands. I need to talk to you."

"He's OK, Ike. I had a good talk with him when I arrived. He's the Director of the movie—or something. Calls himself mayor—that's probably his role, unless this is some other kind of spectacle."

"You sure?" demanded the Major.

"Yes, I'm certain," Mary reassured him.

"It's OK. Come on." He was using the loudspeaker. "But just you. Nobody else!"

The Mayor smiled and shook hands with Mary, then Major Sizemore.

"Yarborough's the name. You're welcome to our city. Sorry about Sheriff Roscoe taking a shot at your . . . your . . . vee-hickle."

The Major calmed down a little. "He has attacked a military aircraft and put one of us in harm's way. I want him arrested and handcuffed right now! Git him over here *now!!*"

The Sheriff, still a little tipsy, tried to hide behind another cactus.

"You'd better get over here right this minute, Sam," the Mayor shouted back. "I don't know what this is but it looks real enough to me." The Sheriff was now cowering behind another cactus, pulling the sharp spines out of his arms, neck and face, still cursing.

"Worse'n a goddam porkypine," he muttered to himself in pain. "Ow! Ow! I didn't mean nothin' by it, Mayor," he shouted. "Jes' tryin' to make it go away. Ow! I never seen nothin' like it!"

The mayor was now determined and angry. "Throw your guns down, Sam, and get over here right now! This man says he's a United States Marine officer, he wants you over here, and he's got the artillery to convince me!"

The sheriff cowered uncertainly, squinting, then looked hard. His jaw dropped. "My god, it's a *nigger!*"

"That may be, but he's got more firepower than we do. That makes him the boss. *Just do it!*" shouted the mayor. "*Get over here!.*" The Sheriff dropped his weapons on the ground, raised his hands halfheartedly and slouched toward the big chopper. "Give me your handcuffs." The Sheriff complied and the Mayor cuffed him. Major Sizemore stepped forward, grabbed his handcuffs between the wrists and threw him roughly into the gunship. He radioed the base, told them he had a prisoner, and asked them to set up a security perimeter around the downed chopper and Captain Mulligan.

Several photographers from the Times, including the cinematographer, edged closer and closer to the scene. Mulligan and Sizemore were on the radio talking to base. Sheriff Roscoe, moaning in pain, was sobering up very rapidly. Cactus spines stuck out of his neck, his legs and his back. He couldn't reach them because he was handcuffed. In vain, he begged Major Sizemore to free his hands.

After a long wait another Huey arrived to repair Captain Mulligan's damaged chopper. Major Sizemore took off in his Super-Cobra, flew through the bubble and landed. Security officers roughly pulled the Sheriff out and hustled him away.

They interrogated him for three hours while he sobered up completely, breaking down in tears. Some of the officers left the room shaking their heads. They took him to the brig.

A phone jingled; Benjamin Carmichael, editor-in-chief of the Carson City Times, clambered out of bed and walked into the hall to answer it. He had a hangover and was hoping to sleep in.

"Dad, You won't believe what I just saw and heard." It was his son Thad, a university student home from San Francisco for the long holiday. "Another flying mystery. Only this time I saw it plain as day—a silvery winged beast blowing fire out of its backside. You must have heard the roar!"

"Sounds like a real scoop. Yeah, I did hear *something*. Sure you're OK?"

"Sober as a judge, Dad! You know me."

"Uh . . . . Right . . . OK, meet you at the Times in 15 minutes." He shook his head clear, got on his horse and raced over to the newspaper.

A few minutes later, Thad rode up. Astounded, openmouthed, they stood outside watching the sky for a long time. Hearing another roar they saw, to their amazement, a chopper going over, flying slowly at 100', then disappearing over a hill. Benjamin sat on the steps and slapped himself to see if he was dreaming. He immediately dispatched his photographers, telephoned the Governor, then began sending teletype messages.

Governor Blaisdel rode up to the Times in a carriage with two of his aides; he had already been on the scene on the east side of town and had seen the F-16 go over.

"Any idea what's goin' on, Ben?" asked the Governor. "This is wild stuff!"

"Whatever it is, it's one heck of a story. Already got my camera men roaming city and countryside."

"I'm concerned it might be an act of war. I've already notified General Trevelyan over at National Guard. I'm telegraphing the President."

Barely an hour later, they heard a violent roar which shook the building; they all ran outside. It was Major Ike Sizemore's black Super Cobra helicopter gunship, flying even lower, then hovering, then landing just over the same hill. They all ran back into the building; Carmichael splashed water on his face, then rushed over to the teletype and again started pecking away furiously.

Over the next hour they watched the entire drama unfold. The Linotype operators were working furiously, entering text on their keyboards, dropping the matrices into the assemblers, and line by line, preparing one of the most astounding Special Editions in newspaper history. By noon the presses were rhythmically, noisily clanking as they cranked out page after page, copy after copy. To Benjamin it sounded more like a kitten purring.

Chapter 14

Stuck in 1900

Area 51, Nevada   January 1, 1900   2 PM

"Hold it right there!" Marine Capt. Peter Panic commanded as he and four other Marine security officers in two trucks, red and blue lights flashing pulled in front of a Land Rover followed by a pickup truck and stopped them in their tracks. They contained Dr. Sandor Rakoczy, his technicians Gerhard and Mikhail, two other assistants and a pickup load of electronic testing and other equipment.

"Get out of the vehicle and put your hands on your heads!" he ordered, his right hand on his sidearm.

"By whose authority?!" Rakoczy demanded.

"Lt. Col. Cassidy," came the reply. "Now get out of your vehicle and explain to me who you are and what you're doing in a restricted area of the base?"

"We're civilians and we're scientists, as if you didn't know," Rakoczy countered sarcastically. "Col. Cassidy has no authority in this matter. We're under specific orders from the General."

"Nobody informed us. All I know is you're in a restricted area and I'm under orders to protect it," Panic replied glibly.

"Call the General right now! We're collecting scientific data of the utmost importance."

"Sorry but I can't call anybody right now. Something's wrong with our communicators—they're all dead. Just get out of the vehicle right now and put your hands on your heads. You're under arrest!!"

Rakoczy and his team were exasperated. At that moment another Land Rover drove up: it was General Mills' adjutant, Army Major Philip Weir, who quickly sized up what was going on. He drew his 45 caliber pistol from its holster and held it by his side.

"Stand down immediately or you will be suspended from duty!" he shouted at Capt. Panic. "That's an order. These men are under direct orders from the General!" He spun the Land Rover around leaving a cloud of dust and headed back to headquarters.

Rakoczy and his technicians glared at Capt. Panic. "Is that sufficient?" Rakoczy shouted.

Capt. Panic, crestfallen, nodded to Rakoczy and signaled his men to back off. "At ease," he nodded.

"At ease my ass!" shouted Gerhard. "We're civilians and we don't take commands from the likes of you." Saying nothing, he and the other Marines drove off.

The General, who had been trying to reach Rakoczy, found out what had just happened. He was livid. He angrily summoned Cassidy to his office.

"Have you lost your mind?!" he demanded.

"These men were leaving the base with special equipment. They had no ID and they defied my officers. It was their duty to stop them."

"Colonel, you know damned good and well they were doing it under my orders and you know damned good and well who they are. They are going out there to make measurements to try to get answers to this mystery. Strike three. You are hereby relieved of duty and are under arrest! You will be confined until further notice. Major Wingard is now in charge of Security." The General notified Major Wingard.

Cassidy was immediately placed under guard. The General returned to Level 18. Rakoczy was already waiting for him, tight-lipped and gray with suppressed fury.

"You've got real trouble with that Neanderthal! He's a loose cannon! Please think seriously about discontinuing his activity and taking him out of the loop. He is putting us all in danger."

The General nodded his head. "He's run out of options and I've run plumb out of patience. He's decommissioned and locked up under guard." Rakoczy was relieved.

"General, Tom, let's go back to my office. I've got information of the utmost gravity and I need to tell you before I tell anyone else." They returned to the compound and took the elevator down to Level 14, Rakoczy's office.

"Please sit down, General." He sat and looked expectantly at Rakoczy. Moments passed before he spoke. "General, it's no longer speculation *We're in 1900!* There's no longer any doubt; there's no denying it. And we're not safe. There are some things we need to discuss as soon as possible. I have calculated that this phenomenon may reverse itself very soon."

There was a long silence while the General absorbed the full impact of Rakoczy's revelation. Finally, he spoke.

"Could it also be a kind of collective delusion—based on some odd natural cause?"

"That's brilliant thinking, Tom. We thought about that, too. If that's true, we've created an entire world out of thin air—or aggregate consciousness. Even so, we've calculated that it's reversible—same result, we believe."

Do you mean take us back to 2000?! When?"

"I don't know exactly when. And only *if* we're lucky. The variables have changed; we have, as old Doc Brown was fond of saying, tampered with the space-time continuum. The bunker shifted with the earthquake, for one thing. We could re-emerge right where we started, we could land ahead of the time or behind it, or we could be swallowed up. We could be entombed in rock, like those poor sailors found merged with the bulkheads on the USS Eldridge. As for when, we're working as hard as we can to calculate when this little time warp will bend back. Right now it looks like we're safe for about seven days—maybe up to ten, but that's a very rough calculation and I certainly may not have taken everything into account. For all of our sakes, we've got to find out as much as we can, keep looking and act accordingly. It's already very late in the game!"

"Do what you must," the General agreed. "I am behind you 100%."

Rakoczy's team once again proceeded north and set up their instruments at the five mile perimeter, where the transparent bubble still intersected the ground. They enjoyed a mixed success. Yes, it was a semi-sphere, a translucent green. Its mathematical center, they calculated was, no nobody's surprise, the time machine on Level 18. But it was still comforting to confirm it.

The closer they came to the bubble, the more transparent it became. As they approached it, several of their instruments' readings shot off the charts, particularly the tachyon detectors. The men could feel a bizarre tingling as they grew closer. Just as Mikhail was about to touch it, Rakoczy shouted that they were charged, and ordered them to stay clear of it. Mikhail was knocked unconscious, and his form momentarily faded in and out. He was quickly revived.

They then set up the receivers to listen for anything outside of the compound, but picked up only intermittent faint signals— some kind of very low frequency waves, but no coherent signal. Yet they knew it was something man made, not merely terrestrial waves. They knew about radio and telegraph from that era, but this was different. That set them wondering.

The knowledge that they had gone back in time had now became general within the science community at the base, and in mid-afternoon, Rakoczy, who now knew exactly what had happened and why, conferred again intensely and privately with General Mills, confirming to him from the astronomy, the nature of the experiment, the astro clocks, and the growing testimony from the pilots who had flown to Carson City, that they were unquestionably, if temporarily, back in 1900. The General was fascinated and astounded, but his military training and pragmatic nature prevailed, and he continued to refine his plans for dealing with the situation. Rakoczy and diGiovanni warned everybody in no uncertain terms that the effect might only last for just so long. And that it could be far worse than anyone had imagined.

As if by design, the bubble suddenly brightened, then turned a darker, bluer green. Mikhail fell to the ground unconscious. Something was happening. Rakoczy, diGiovanni and Gerhard could hear a loud shrieking and groaning sound coming the time machine as they headed for the lab.

"It's the time machine," exclaimed Rakoczy. "Look. A whole row of the simplex crystals has dimmed. That means they're burning out or they're not getting enough current."

"I doesn't take a lot," said Gerhard. "I think I know what to do." Meanwhile, Dr. Ludmila managed to revive Mikhail. As he returned to normal, the crystals resumed full operation. On a viewscreen they watched the bubble also return to its previous state.

"Whew! That scared the bejesus out of me," Rakoczy exhaled. "I have another concern: the matter-energy quotient here in our artificial environment. That may be an index to the stability of this phenomenon. How many people are outside the base? How much equipment?" he asked.

"A lot," Gerhard agreed. "Seven or eight people, three choppers, an F-16 and a lot of fuel and weapons."

"We will keep an eye on this," said Rakoczy. He called Colonel Pick and asked him if the situation in Carson City was resolved.

"Resolved!" Pick told Rakoczy. "They'll be on their way back in a few minutes. I've been informed that Captain Mulligan's chopper is repaired. They should all be here within two hours."

"Fine. If anybody else has to leave, please clear it with us. It's another variable and we don't want to take anything for granted."

"Roger. Over and out."

Security was ordered to stay out of the labs, and for the moment the base was sealed in and out, except for the aircraft. The hydraulics in Captain Mulligan's chopper were quickly repaired and she, along with the other two choppers, took off, flew back through the bubble again, and landed at the base. Bobby Wilson had already returned with his F-16.

When Captain Mulligan was debriefed, she couldn't believe her ears.

Rakoczy's phone rang and diGiovanni was on the other line. Something very strange was going on down on Level Twelve; Conch the Nommo had disappeared deep into his water tank. His ship, well guarded and hooked up to sensors on Level 20, had begun to emit a strange high pitched whine. The General was briefed. DiGiovanni spoke to Rakoczy authoritatively on another line. He covered the phone receiver with his hand and spoke low.

"Sandy, I've just talked to the General. I actually think we can trust him. He's surprisingly smart for a shit kicker." He switched to the General's line. "General, as far as Conch is concerned. I can tell you for certain that his ship is not in a condition where he can fly it. We've done all the reverse engineering we're capable of to this point; the propulsion devices are non-operational, and I don't think he's going anywhere."

The General had been connected all the time, unbeknownst to diGiovanni. "Shit-kicker eh? I heard that! Good thing you're a civilian! It's OK, Al; I take it as a compliment. You're pretty smart yourself, for a Yankee. Anyhow, what do you think your little spaceman is up to, then?"

"Sorry, General, I don't know. Maybe some kind of religious ritual. He and Puplampu, his African priest, are preparing something, and they're chanting. In fact, I'm now speculating against my better judgment that they could very well have had something to do with getting us thrown back 100 years and I don't want to interfere, because, deferring to Dr. Ludmila against my better instincts, she's almost certain of it. I haven't ruled out the possibility that he might hold the secret to getting us back safely."

"Wishful thinking, but let us hope! Do you still have full surveillance over what he's doing?"

"No we don't, and we're nowhere close to understanding it. Dr. Ludmila listens to him in a kind of musical language and some kind of telepathic energy exchange. She's confident because she translates it into tonal ratios—an actual language she claims Nommo has taught her!"

"Is he instructing us in how to get back?" the General asked. "I'm concerned about what's lost in translation! Our lives are riding on it! Is Rakoczy with you? Put him on."

Rakoczy picked up the phone. "Neither Al nor I are comfortable with mystical explanations, mind over matter. I don't know; but the alien is inscrutable. Sometimes I think there isn't anything he doesn't know. As far as surveilling him is concerned, yes, we do have live images of his area, and I know he knows it. But when he's underwater, it's very difficult to get a lock on him-30 feet below the surface. Then there's the dolphin, whom we know absolutely nothing about. Plus, even when we have him pinpointed in the water, we've never gotten any readings that told us anything new. I'm afraid we'll just have to trust whatever he's up to for the time being. And then get him in on the discussions as soon as we can. I'm certain he knows a lot that we don't know."

He pondered for a moment, then continued.

"I've asked Dr. Ludmila to go down there and try to talk to him; she's got the best rapport with him. She does this kind of Vulcan mind meld with him, as you know, and gets pictures and musical tones, and then draws them, plays them on her viola, records or transcribes them, and then translates them. She's quite an artist, too. We're hoping Conch can offer us some explanation of how we got into this. And how we might be able to get out of it intact. But I have a strong feeling we shouldn't interrupt his ritual. Right now, he's in his seawater tank, and Puplampu looks like he's in a trance. The only visible activity is the dolphin coming up for air every few minutes."

Chapter 15

Rough Riders and Time Surfers

A Union Pacific train pulled into the station in Reno, Nevada, shortly before 8 AM. Nikola Tesla and his assistant, along with two porters, began unloading baggage and equipment. He had pinpointed the longitude and latitude of the powerful terrestrial wave. They hired a carriage for the two hour ride to Carson City.

Tesla and his assistant strode into a general store and bought maps of the area, a rifle, a pistol, ammunition, tents, food, and other survival items. He then drove straight to the newspaper office to look for a rental. He was astounded when he read the headlines and saw the photos on the Special Edition. There they met the editor, Ben Carmichael, who knew of Tesla and his work and was both surprised and honored that he had come to Carson City. He quickly told him about the flying ships. They conferred for the rest of the day; messages began coming over the teletype and continued throughout the afternoon, some from as far away as Paris, London and Zurich. Governor Blaisdel had already wired President McKinley.

That afternoon, Tesla explained his theories and breakthroughs to a rapt audience. Carmichael offered him a large space within the building to set up his equipment, which fortunately had a large, well constructed rear porch patio, which allowed space for Tesla to assemble his tall generating towers. Carmichael also offered him and his assistant the hospitality of his large home. Tesla accepted gratefully.

Carmichael then summoned his friends, Nevada Governor Dan Blaisdel, and State Senator Jake Curran, an engineer and major contractor. Nevada's lone U.S. Congressman, Alvin McGrath, who was heading for Washington the next day, also attended the meeting. They convened at the Times, and Tesla told them of the anomaly he had discovered with his terrestrial stationary waves, while the Mayor, the Governor and several others continued on about the amazing flying machines and the near-violent confrontations. Tesla and his assistant listened intently, took notes, made some calculations, and all agreed on a plan to travel to the area in question—Groom Lake. He wanted to get going right away.

The Governor spoke. "I've sent President McKinley a wire explaining this as well as I was able. I don't even know if he'll believe me, but I've tried to tell him the best way I could what we encountered here in as much detail as possible. I've already put the photographs on a train to Washington with one of our National Guard officers."

Congressman McGrath spoke up. "The President's a shrewd man, but incredulous. He'll need hard evidence. Elihu Root is his Secretary of War, a very able man. *He'll* suspect some nefarious plot, maybe from Dixie. He thinks they're still fighting the Civil War down there, and he may have a point. Our hope is Governor Teddy Roosevelt—there's a man with intelligence *and* imagination!

McKinley has just designated him as his next Veep, since Vice President Hobart died." He paused, turning to Tesla. "My friend, that's pretty lawless territory out there where you're planning to go. Do you really think you'll find something?"

"I do, Mr. Congressman!" Tesla answered. "I'll find the source. The waves I told you about are stronger than I've even seen—or imagined possible—on this planet. Stronger than any earthquake. And different from any earthquake. By the way, you said you felt a little tremor about midnight on New Year's eve?"

"Matter of fact, we did. Nobody paid it any mind. It wasn't much; just a tiny jolt. Happens fairly often out here, you know. We've had stronger. A lot stronger."

"We should go. As soon as possible. It's *got* to tie all this together. We must know."

"Could be dangerous, Mr. Tesla. None of us knows what's behind all this, only that it's real. We saw it with our own eyes, and we're not dreaming."

The conversation went on for hours. Witnesses streamed in; it was like a town meeting, a Chatauqua. Finally, Governor Blaisdel made his decision. He issued an executive order and assembled a National Guard contingent to accompany Tesla. The Legislature and the Senate were still in recess for the Christmas holidays, so he wouldn't have to deal with *them*, thank God.

Compliments of the Governor, Tesla was also furnished with additional guides, horses, guns and camping equipment to make the 300 mile trek, the best Nevada had to offer. They calculated that the longitude and latitude pinpointed the event was somewhere in the area of southeastern Nevada, very near tiny, dried up Groom Lake and Tikapoo Peak.

"There's nothin' down there, Mr. Tesla." Senator Curran told him. "Just badlands and Indians, Pomos, mostly; some Miwoks. Don't tangle with any Miwoks; they're bad assed Indians, mean as a snake, especially if they think you're a government man. They're big and strong, too, mountain men. Usually they're only out of

Yosemite and Mono Lake to raid other tribes, or to rob and kill white men, but sometimes they range out pretty far. Pomos are different; they're more peaceful like."

The Governor spoke. "The military presence will be insurance enough. I'll send an entire platoon, well armed. Miwoks will leave you alone if you're showing strength."

That evening, every engineer, electrician, technician and politician in Carson City had met with Tesla at the Times. Theories abounded, and curiosity grew to a fever pitch. Dozens more volunteered to go.

Governor Blaisdel turned to Senator Curran. "This is pretty exciting. You know, Jake, this could put Nevada on the map, doing pioneering work like this." He turned and addressed the growing crowd. Nevada in the 20th century! Imagine what it might become!"

At daybreak Tesla and his contingent set out for Groom Lake.

Chapter 16

Incredulity

<u>Washington, D.C.</u>   The White House   <u>January 2, 1900</u>

At 5:30 AM on January 2, 1900, President William McKinley was awakened by his chief aide. He walked into the map room at the White House. A grim faced group of men including New York Governor Theodore Roosevelt, now the Vice President Designate, and Secretary of War Elihu Root, were waiting for him.

"Good morning, Mr. President," they all spoke, almost simultaneously.

"Good morning." McKinley grumbled. He turned to T.R. "What the hell is going on, Ted?" McKinley asked, "that I had to be awakened at 5:30 in the morning?!" He was visibly annoyed, his face was flushed, and he hadn't had his morning whiskey.

"Sit down, Bill!" Roosevelt told him. "You're not going to believe this!" They sat at the long mahogany table and Secretary Root laid out a large map and began to read from the transcriptions of the ticker tape that had been clacking all night long.

The newly enhanced map, very accurate map of the Southwest had been drawn up from an ambitious project of the U. S.

Geological Survey, completed only two years earlier. It showed an obscure point in southern Nevada with a small dried up lake, Groom Lake.

"This is where it's supposed to have happened?"

"What?" asked the President incredulously. "*What* is supposed to have happened?"

"We've had some very strange events in the last day or so. Here's the easy part: a huge stationary wave that wasn't an earthquake."

He produced the long typed transcript of a teletype from Governor Blaisdel of Nevada. The Governor was also sending photographs on the Union Pacific run to Washington, but they wouldn't arrive for several days.

McKinley cleared his head and lit a cigar ceremoniously, raising a cloud of smoke. The smell of tobacco and sulfur filled the room. A short man, he was almost lost in his huge chair. He smirked.

"Blaisdel is trying to get my Irish up. I got his teletype all right. I believe he might have had a little too much Irish whiskey New Year's Eve, and I think he's having us on. This is an elaborate prank if I ever saw one! Somebody's trying to make fools out of us, maybe Bryan and his stooges. You know we're facing an election in November, and I'm certain Bryan's going to take me on again."

Teddy Roosevelt spoke up. "It's no joke, Mr. President! At least part of it appears to be true. Whatever it is, we simply need to get to the bottom of it. Soon. It's very strange, but if any of it's true, then it's a security matter. And a military matter."

"Do what you feel you must. And don't involve me until you have something. No reporters. Understand? *No reporters!*"

"Unfortunately, they've already got wind of it."

McKinley's eyes flashed angrily. "How?! Not from here, surely! Has the ship of state now developed a leaky bottom?"

"Uncertain as to its origin. Probably from out West." said Roosevelt. "Anyway, Nikola Tesla's involved in it. We've got pretty good confirmation of that. And according to this latest cable, there's been an incident, and people are shooting at one another."

The President remained incredulous. He stood up. "Don't forget; it's still the Wild West out there. And what on God's green earth could Tesla have to do with it—he's an electric power man. Maybe it's not him either. *Maybe the circus is in town!* Sorry boys, I'm going back to bed. When you find the flying gunships and the winged firebirds, wake me up."

"Don't underestimate Tesla," Roosevelt observed. "A brilliant man. Unquestionably the world's leading inventor. Nothing would surprise me about him. *Way* beyond Edison. Fifty years ahead of our time, I've heard tell."

President McKinley put down his unfinished cigar, and, saying nothing, turned his back on the group and strode out of the room. He returned to the residence and crawled back into bed. The meeting continued.

Roosevelt spoke to Elihu Root, the Secretary of War. "Mr. Secretary, we've got what could be an unimpeachable source. The Tesla angle adds to the mystery."

"Governor, don't confide in anybody until we know with great certainty what is going on! If anything. The President could be right. It smells like a hoax. We're just going to have to find out more." The Secretary paused and then raised his head. "You know, if it *is* a joke, we'll all have a good laugh, but it'll be at their expense—whoever set this up."

"If this gets out to any of those nosey reporters, the laugh will be at *our* expense!" warned Roosevelt. "And we *are* going to have to tell them something. Anyway, Governor Blaisdel is one of my best friends and a very earnest man. And smart. I know him well. True, he is a Democrat. He campaigned for William Jennings Bryan in Nevada and California back in '96, but he's a fair man, a straight shooter. He's got a sense of humor, too, and this kind of prank would be completely out of character for him." Roosevelt suddenly sat up short and spoke rapidly. "Makes me wonder if someone's taken over out there in Nevada—you know, some kind of coup or something. There are a lot of disgruntled gold miners, old '49-ers and other misfits. I wouldn't put it past them!"

Root frowned.

"He said he's sending us photographs on the next train," continued Roosevelt. "Tell you what. Check the train schedules. I'll take a train in the opposite direction and meet them halfway—I think it leaves at 10 PM sharp. Tell the President when he wakes up. I'll clear the decks and go myself, maybe give a speech in Cleveland, maybe even Chicago, since I've now been announced as the Vice President Designate. That'll cut the time in half. Then I can wire him from—let's say—Des Moines. Maybe Omaha! If there aren't any photographs on the California train, then it's a hoax and I'll let you all know immediately. Meanwhile, I'll make a few pastoral calls in the Midwest in honor of the twentieth century! 'Bout time we kicked off the campaign!"

Governor Theodore Roosevelt, in his new role as Vice President Designate, could not resist the temptation to make a speech in Cleveland from the back of his train in the specially tricked out, luxurious caboose with an ample deck on the rear. Vice-President Hobart had died in office barely a month earlier, and Roosevelt, only 40, hero of San Juan Hill in the Spanish-American War, was the logical choice to succeed him. The nation's most famous war hero, he lauded in his speech the rising importance of America's entrance upon the world stage as the twentieth century dawned. A McKinley-Roosevelt ticket would be virtually invincible.

The multitudes cheered and Roosevelt waved from the flag-draped, luxuriously appointed car as the train slowly pulled out of Union Station in Cleveland. The train chugged through America's heartland, next stop, Chicago. Roosevelt waved at crowds which greeted him in Toledo, Fort Wayne and Gary and a succession of small towns as the train passed slowly through the stations. In Chicago he gave the same speech at suppertime and the crowds were even greater and more enthusiastic; he gave another at Des Moines late that evening. At 3:30 AM he arrived in Omaha, briefly addressed the small group assembled there, and then took a carriage to his hotel for a few hours rest.

The eastbound California train was due in Omaha a few minutes before eleven that morning. When it arrived, Teddy was ready. He anxiously boarded the train and met the young Nevada National Guard Lieutenant who had been dispatched to deliver the photographs—along with several copies of the day old Special Edition of the Carson City Times with a picture of the U. S. Marines' Super Cobra helicopter gunship and Mary Mulligan's Huey chopper.

Saying nothing to the gathering crowd of dignitaries and curiosity seekers about his mission, Roosevelt gave a short speech and rushed off to the Presidential railroad car, which had been pulled off the westbound train and sat on a sidetrack next to the roundhouse, awaiting attachment to the rear of the eastbound train from San Francisco, which he would ride back to Washington with the Lieutenant. Before getting underway, he studied the photographs with mounting excitement and amazement. He then sent off an encoded telegraph message to President McKinley that the photos were real, and that, so far as he could tell, most or all of the story was true.

Forty-two hours and several messages later, Roosevelt, the Lieutenant and the photos arrived at Washington's Union Station, where they were met and hustled off to the White House, amid considerable consternation. Now a dozen reporters were hanging about asking pointed questions. They were told little.

In the White House, skepticism no longer reigned, though it had not died. Many more wires had come in, some from Switzerland, France and England, and a team of scientists and journalists were preparing to set sail for the United States. The entire military had been quietly placed on alert status, an event which was not lost on an ambitious young reporter from Emporia,

Kansas, William Allen White. The notorious yellow journalists, William Randolph Hearst and Joseph Pulitzer already knew about it. The tabloids were licking their chops. The Washington Post had already run a story on page four, and the White House feared it would soon erupt into front page headlines.

Chapter 17

Cassidy's plan

Lazy tropical fish drifted across the computer screen in Lt. Col. Miles Cassidy's office, where he remained under house arrest. Guards stood on sentry duty outside his office. He had been humiliated by General Mills and was furiously angry with him—and with the scientists—whom he believed had put him up to it. It had been a long day. The General had been merely angry, then cold and businesslike with him, but the scientists obviously thought he was beneath contempt. He deeply mistrusted all of them, especially Rakoczy and diGiovanni, and believed the General was a patsy—gullible and indecisive. To Cassidy, all intellectuals were pseudo-intellectuals, dupes, part of the New World order—and this is their big move! *Mills is awed by those eggheads and will do anything they tell him to. This is a national emergency if there ever was one, and somebody's got to take decisive action; somebody's got to take charge. J. Edgar was right! The entire world is in danger.* He scratched his head. *And we certainly couldn't have traveled into the past. Could we?* He leaned back further.

But what if it's true?!

Stripped of of his power and assigned to meaningless paperwork, Cassidy leaned back in his straight wooden chair, deep in thought. His dog Mitt, a nine year old Westie, lay quietly at his feet.

Cassidy had time to orient himself to 1900 if indeed it was true. *Who's the President?* He accessed the Cray and found William McKinley and Theodore Roosevelt. He downloaded detailed information everything he could find about America in 1900. McKinley was to be assassinated—but not until 1901. The Spanish-American War was just over—less than two years, and we had not only annexed Cuba but taken over the Phillippines. Hawaii had been annexed. He read about Admiral Dewey, Teddy Roosevelt, and William Jennings Bryan, and McKinley's veep, renowned financier Garret Augustus Hobart, who had just died in office. But now it was peacetime; the Army had been reduced to unacceptable minimums. Why didn't Admiral Dewey take over Indonesia, Okinawa, even Japan—a future war could be averted.

Out of the deepest curiosity he wondered if the time travel journey was recorded in the Cray's vast memory banks.

It wasn't.

It was time to sleep. Marine Guards accompanied him and the dog to his bachelor quarters and returned them early each morning to the office.

Captain Peter Panic, third in command at Security, picked them up on this morning, January 3 at 5:45 AM. Cassidy was in his exercise room performing a strenuous workout. Panic knew the routine well and finished it up with him, Cassidy quickly showered and dressed in a clean uniform.

"Got something important to share with you, Captain," Cassidy said as they got in the Captain's Jeep Cherokee. "You're a smart Marine, and you have a military mind. A Marine knows when opportunity presents itself and knows how to capitalize on it!" Panic was immediately interested. "You know about this time warp we're supposed to be in. Well, it's not science fiction; somehow it may have really happened!"

"Looks that way," replied Captain Panic.

"Aren't you curious about this?" smiled Cassidy crookedly. "You're a Serbian. I know how you think! Why do you think I hired you?!"

A number of the Marines were sympathetic with Cassidy and with his ideas, and felt that the General and Col. Pick had overreacted—after all, he was only trying to protect the base, and above all, the United States of America.

Cassidy knew well how to play on those sympathies, and, as he studied and learned more and more about the time period they were in, ideas began to form in his mind, ideas as to how he could change history, avert World War I and teach the Kaiser to respect the United States of America, perhaps avert the coming Communist threat by warning the Romanov's, and tell the Archduke not to travel to Sarajevo in 1914. And find eleven year old Adolf Hitler in Austria and shoot him. He was starting to love history, especially that which hadn't been written yet and might possibly be averted and altered. It was intoxicating for him. America still had a formidable military machine under McKinley. Cassidy intended to commandeer it and use it. He was sure he had the ordnance and the manpower to take over. *They'll never know what hit 'em!*

Without doubt, Area 51 had modern weapons at their disposal that no government in 1900 could withstand. The idea became an obsession with Cassidy. He found a virtual Rosetta Stone of information on the Cray—maps, names, elaborate, precise facts on events, places, people, and above all the movements, management and personnel in the U. S. military—a 100 year old history that was now oh, so current if it was really 1900!

All the following day, Col. Cassidy's closest associates conferred with him: Lt. Moore, Capt Panic and other officers and enlisted men whose loyalty and unquestioning obedience he knew he could count on. The plan began to take root in their minds and they began plotting and mapping out exactly the logistics of carrying out the plan.

It was still something of a game between them, and for Cassidy, an intense way to pass the time, but the idea was beginning to take hold. The thing he would need the most of was aviation fuel.

At 7:30 AM, the morning of January 4, a sharp military single knock came on the door. He was startled; his chair leaned back too far and he fell back noisily on the floor, striking his head on the corner of the desk. He scrambled up, rubbing his head. The General entered the office. They saluted.

"Colonel Cassidy, I've been thinking this over. I've looked into the matter, and I feel that you were acting, however inadvisedly, in what you believed was in the best interest of the United States. I believe you're a loyal officer."

"Thank you sir," said Cassidy. "And I'm very sorry I lied to you when this all began. My desire was to protect, not to deceive."

"I'm inclined to believe you. I'm going to release you for now and restore you to limited duty. We are in a very bizarre and even dangerous situation with this time warp, so you must respect our science team; we're counting on them get us back to normal. Also, I should tell you that Reverend Luna survived the surgery to remove the bullet, though he's still critical."

"I've been praying for his recovery, General, and yes, I know he came through the surgery. I've been following up on it."

"This is now the fourth day since the event, and I think you now realize the time period we seem to be in, and the fact that we've not been under attack by anyone."

"Yessir." said Cassidy, still rubbing the rising bump on his head where it had struck the desk. "It is a contingency none of us were trained to anticipate. I know that now and I deeply regret that I overreacted." They saluted. As the General turned to go,

Cassidy spoke up. "Sir, what about Sgt. Mel Daumer? I can attest to the fact that he felt he was acting in the line of duty, and if it's anybody's fault, it's mine."

The General hesitated, then spoke. "Colonel, I appreciate your candor. I will release Sergeant Daumer to your and Major Wingard's custody for the duration of this crisis."

Cassidy nodded and saluted, smiling inwardly with great satisfaction.

Now restored to duty, Cassidy did his best to make everything appear normal. He even apologized to his deputy, Major Wingard for his actions on the Airbus and feigned concern for Rev. Luna, still barely clinging to life. Major Wingard was incredulous at this atypical behavior, but shook hands with Cassidy and accepted his apology, with some inner reservations.

Early that afternoon, Cassidy, still a rated test pilot with valid credentials for flying the V-22 Osprey, called the General's office and requested permission to access it and possibly test it. There were still problems with the Osprey and the pilots from Boeing, who had been testing it in early December, were due to return a few days after the New Year holiday.

The General gave him the green light.

Cassidy immediately called his closest associates—his would-be co-conspirators—together. He had a plan. For America. There was opportunity. They could change the future. Not to take advantage of it with all the power at their disposal would be to disrespect the Powers who had placed it in their reach. Their destination was Washington, D.C., the White House.

With the downloaded topo maps from USGS, they put together a route for stashing fuel at 500 mile intervals for the Super Cobras. They chose to take the southern route and avoid hazardous updrafts and downdrafts over the Rockies.

146

Armed with tacit permission from the General, they first collected several dozen steel drums and pillow tanks to store the fuel; then they drove to the hangars where the Ospreys sat. Cassidy chose the MV-22—M for Marines—V/STOL (vertical and/or short takeoff and landing) Osprey in Hangar M-13 for the mission. Its 16 fuel tanks, capacity 1,700+ gallons were nearly full and only needed to be topped off—and the range was nearly 2,000 miles. And this Osprey had already been exhaustively tested only a few weeks earlier.

They arranged the 55 gallon drums and 100 gallon pillow tanks in the large passenger section (capacity 22) in the Osprey, then pushed it to the fuel dispensers next to the hangars, filling the drums with JP5 fuel for the Super-Cobras, and the pillow tanks with the special JP8 fuel for the Osprey. Pretending to be refueling the Osprey, Sgt. Russo and Corporal Rodriguez, Cassidy associates and co-conspirators, carefully filled all the tanks.

"This Osprey will be a flying gas can," observed Lt. Moore to Col Cassidy. "And we have to stash extra fuel in the Cobras." Cassidy nodded and grinned. They had made all the calculations. Additional pillow tanks were loaded into each of the two Super Cobras, extending their range to about 550 miles, possibly 600, since they would be a thousand pounds short of their 14,000" pound maximum gross weight. No sense in pushing the limits.

Nobody had noticed, and the first and most important preparation for the invasion of Washington had gone off without a hitch

Chapter 18

Cassidy meets Tesla

Carson City, NV   January 4, 1900   5:30 PM

Free at last, Cassidy walked to one of the hangars and readied another AH-1 Super Cobra for flight. He threw in some extra weapons, spare fuel and ammo, along with a few exotic surprises. He pulled down the maps and carefully calculated his course. He gritted his teeth and took off toward Reno, flying through the green bubble, which he noticed but refused to speculate on. He detected nothing on radar, radio or satellite, and no VOR signals. Only the base. But there was no devastation visible anywhere and the atmosphere seemed crystal clear. He began to doubt that a war had begun, that America had been attacked.

He looked at his Nevada maps and then turned towards the capital, Carson City. During the nearly two hour flight, he studied the videos the other pilots had taken, found the city, and soon made up his mind that it definitely wasn't the year 2,000. He scouted out the area where Mulligan, Sizemore and the other gunship pilot had landed.

A dozen uniformed men from the Nevada National Guard, patrolling nearby and on high alert watched him land. He set his craft down and sized up the area. They could hurt or kill him if he wasn't careful—they were well-armed and they could shoot. He got on the horn.

"Keep your distance and put down your weapons and nobody will get hurt. This is United States military business!" He had decided not to identify himself.

They heard him. Several of the guardsmen climbed on their horses and headed back towards the city at a gallop; two remained. They laid down their weapons and cautiously walked to within about 50 feet of Cassidy's chopper.

"State your business and stop right there!" Cassidy ordered threateningly. He quickly alighted from his craft brandishing an automatic weapon.

"We're from the Nevada National Guard, sir," shouted one of the officers. "We need to know who you are, why you are here, and what you want."

"Who's your commanding officer?" Cassidy snapped. "Where is he? I want to talk to him right now!"

"General Trevelyan. He's in the Governor's office right now. Why don't you come with us? You'll have to leave your weapons, though."

"No fucking way!!" shouted Cassidy at the National Guard lieutenant, who was shocked at the strong language. "Get on your horse and bring him here to me right now! *Do it!*" The lieutenant headed for the Capitol Building at a gallop. The other guardsman, a short, mustachioed corporal, remained. He made friendly overtures to Cassidy.

"Say, that's an amazing contraption you've got there, Major Cassidy—or is it Colonel?"

"Lieutenant Colonel." Cassidy looked down and realized he had forgotten to remove his name tag.

"Well, Colonel, we're all pretty excited. Bet Colonel Roosevelt would've loved to have had a machine like this when he took San Juan Hill down in Cuba. Guess we've been too far out in the sticks to know what's going on. We had no idea!" That was putting it mildly. Cassidy listened politely but impatiently. The corporal continued. "You know, we've got a world famous inventor here, an electrical engineer. He just got here yesterday. Name of Tesla. Now he's headed south to check something out. Got photos of him in this morning's newspaper. Wanna see it?" The corporal pulled a newspaper out of his jacket pocket and handed it to Cassidy.

"Here, sir. You can have it. I bought several copies for souvenirs."

"Thanks," said Cassidy, unfolding it. His eyes widened. There was the date: January 4, 1900. On the front page were two photos—one of Captain Mulligan's chopper, the other of Tesla. He read the detailed stories, including a brief recounting of Tesla's accomplishments.

"Where is he?" Cassidy asked, suddenly feigning friendliness. "I'd like to meet him in person."

"Well, he headed south this morning with a platoon of men from our National Guard. I wanted to go myself, but everybody volunteered at once. He's headed way down to the south end of the state to check out something important, something to do with electric waves that came from there. I don't understand it, but he thinks it's big. It's right there in the paper."

Cassidy turned to page two and read about Tesla's planned trip to Groom Lake and Tikapoo Peak with the Guard. It was obvious that they were headed for Area 51.

"When?" Cassidy asked, suddenly acutely interested. "How far? Which way?"

"South by southeast, I'm purty sure. Don't know why they'd go there; there ain't nothin' but cactus, dried up lakes and Indians. Purty much the same way your flying machines were headed." He pointed to the southeast. "I seen all of 'em and they all went thataway till they were outa sight. That's all I know, sir, but they started out at daybreak yesterday and they move pretty fast; it's easy terrain mostly. I think they'd have covered better than 150 miles by now."

"OK. I've got to go now." Cassidy smiled insincerely, glancing at his watch. "I'm late to an appointment. Tell your commander, General whoever, that I will return. Stand back." Cassidy took off in the Super Cobra and headed southeast. In less than an hour he spotted the caravan. He circled over the incredulous group and landed a few hundred yards in front of them.

Nikola Tesla was flabbergasted. The guardsmen crouched and took their positions, aiming their weapons at the chopper. They had been expecting Indians, not flying machines.

Cassidy was being extra cautious. Maybe he could communicate with them, on his terms. Maybe not. His voice boomed out.

"This is United States military business. You are not under attack. Send your commanding officer over here right now! Unarmed!"

Tesla looked over at Captain Kilroy, who nodded to him. In mixed fear and fascination, they both walked cautiously toward the Super Cobra. The radio was chattering.

"Who are you?!" he demanded of Tesla. "I asked for the Commanding Officer."

"My name is Tesla; I'm the project engineer." he answered matter-of-factly, instinctively mistrusting Cassidy.

Captain Kilroy, the officer in charge, nodded to Cassidy. "I'm in charge of the platoon but he's the man to talk to. We're just a contingent the Governor sent along to protect him."

Cassidy was stumped; then an idea flashed. He saw no threat here and decided to be friendly. "Well, it's an honor, Professor. If I'm not mistaken, you're headed for our base at Groom Lake, because that's where all this happened."

Tesla couldn't argue with that. *Base? Our base?! All this happened? He must know something.*

Cassidy continued. "Look, Professor. Why don't we all just settle down and relax. I know you've got a million questions, and I've got a few of my own. Plus, I just might be able to save you a trip. Or *fly* you there!"

Tesla's eyes widened; he quickly assented, and nodded to Captain Kilroy. Everyone was relieved including Cassidy. Tesla desperately wanted to have a look at the chopper, especially the radio equipment. He walked to the Super Cobra and looked inside. He was astonished beyond belief. Cassidy grew suddenly hostile and ordered him to keep his distance. He had General Mills on the horn.

"Everything is under control, General. I'm going to spend the night here with the Nevada National Guard. And they've got an engineering type named Tesla with them, a foreigner. Apparently, he's some kind of famous inventor. I'll find out as much as I can and radio you tomorrow morning."

He lowered his tone and turned to Tesla. "I'm sorry, professor, but you'll have to back off. Orders are orders. This is top secret and it's military business."

They pitched camp near a dry arroyo with a few stunted salt cedars growing around it. The sun was setting. It was getting cold. The soldiers built a campfire, pitched the tents, and began preparing food. Cassidy joined them and relaxed for the first time since the whole thing had begun. They sang songs and swapped stories. Cassidy took a portable fluorescent light out of the chopper and lit up the entire area where they were cooking and eating, to everybody's amazement, especially Tesla's.

Tesla questioned him incessantly about the lights, the chopper, the radios, and wanted to know who had invented them. Cassidy didn't know much. He slipped and mentioned Juan de la Cierva, a helicopter pioneer from back in the 1930's. Tesla, a fan of Jules Verne, heard "1930" and began to suspect that all this had indeed come from the future. He felt, correctly, that he, above all, sat at the pinnacle of the technology of his own day.

One of the Guardsmen began spinning yarns around the campfire. They ate, drank and relaxed. Soon the fire was spent and all retired to their tents, except for Cassidy and Tesla.

Cassidy, a Wyoming native, was almost gleeful. Opportunity was at hand. He had accepted the fact that they were back in 1900. *I'm in a Western,* he thought to himself. *And there's a new Sheriff in town!* He now knew what he had to do.

Tesla walked quietly over to Cassidy's tent by the Super Cobra. Cassidy was ready for him as he came into range and fired a stun gun at him, rendering him unconscious. He would be out for two hours. He dragged him into the chopper, and took off noisily.

Guardsmen poured out of the tents. But by the time they realized Tesla had been kidnapped, the chopper was out of sight.

Tesla awoke with a throbbing headache. He was alone in a windowless room with a small fluorescent light in the ceiling—part of a brig that was attached to Security Headquarters. Tesla examined the fluorescent light. Is that Edison's work? He looked around; there were strange connectors in the wall. There was a chair and a cot. Am I in jail?

He got up slowly and checked the door. It was locked. He called out loudly. There was a response from a nearby room, but it was unintelligible. He thought he heard sobbing, but then it stopped.

He found another door; it was a small lavatory with a fluorescent light, a sink and a water closet. He wondered if he was dreaming. First he examined the light. *Plasma! Alternating current! Mercury?* The bathroom also had a fluorescent light above the mirror over the sink. Turning one faucet on in the sink he was surprised that hot water came out of it; cold water came out of the other. There was a towel. He splashed cold water on his face and made up his mind that he wasn't dreaming. He sat down, put his head in his hands, and tried to think. Then he threw his head back and began to laugh.

Back at the base, Cassidy met with his loyal associates. He had convinced them that General Mills and the scientists were conspirators and had caused the crisis, that they were high officials in the New World Order, and were carrying out an elaborate plot to take over the United States of America. There would be only one chance of saving the base and the country, *saving the world,* and they would have to act now.

He then opened the Cray and learned about the 1900 military chain of command, and the Spanish-American War. Assuming that they were primitive, he glossed over the armaments and ordnance. He knew that airplanes hadn't been invented yet, the roads were virtually non-existent, and he figured the artillery was of Civil War vintage. On that point he was mistaken.

It was a bit sketchy and he knew he'd have to have a local to fill in the blanks, someone from this time period who really knew what was going on. And who better than Nikola Tesla. He spent the rest of the night in exhaustive research on Tesla and was astounded at what he found—an authentic genius.

Now his obsession to take over the government intensified. He could begin by capturing and either killing or sequestering Army Chief of Staff, General Donald Quarters and then kidnapping President McKinley. A fairly methodical man, he knew he needed much more than that. He now thought seriously of recruiting Tesla to carry out his plan—a plan to change the direction of the United States government, build its military to make it an invulnerable super power, all with his encyclopedic knowledge of future events. He could even stop Communism in its tracks and he had 17 years to do it.

The General wouldn't expect to hear from him until morning. Four more men and a woman, all Marines, who fully sympathized with his ideas, were summoned. Two of them were Gulf War veterans and rated chopper pilots; one had just returned from patrols over the no-fly zone in Iraq. Cassidy told them to get there on the double. In a few minutes, they arrived, and Cassidy began laying out his plan. They had to carry it out right away or all would be lost.

They spent hours with the USGS maps, calculated how much fuel and how much ordnance would be needed, what each Marine's function would be. It was intense. Jaws clenched, eyes solemnly intent, adrenalin pumping, the team prepared to execute Cassidy's orders. They would save America from the future New World Order.

Chapter 19

Killing time

Cassidy called on Capt. Peter Panic, and fully briefed him on his fellow Serbian, Nikola Tesla. Panic, of course, knew who Tesla was by reputation, but little else. He was instructed to visit Tesla, now locked up in the brig for a day and a half, though to nobody's knowledge except Cassidy and Panic. The brig now had two prisoners, Sheriff Roscoe and Tesla. The jailkeeper, a Marine PFC, had no idea who they were and didn't ask questions.

Cassidy instructed Panic to apologize, make amends and plausible excuses for kidnapping him, and to bring him to Security to meet with Cassidy; above all to try and make friends with him.

At 10 AM, Panic called the jailer at the brig. He ordered him to check Tesla's and Sheriff Roscoe's cells, be sure they had food and drink, and bring them fresh fruit and bottled water. The jailer called him back. The Sheriff was still agitated and unhappy but Tesla had eaten his breakfast and seemed in fairly good spirits. Panic then walked to Tesla's cell, unlocked it, opened it, and introduced himself—in Serbian. Tesla was pleasantly surprised, but quickly evaluated Captain Panic as a lesser mind and someone not to be trusted. He did not let on.

"*Dobro jootro. Zdravo.* I am Captain Panic. I am deeply sorry you were confined here, Professor Tesla. Our base was under threat and we have very strict rules of engagement when we meet someone we do not know—we have to treat them as a potential enemy."

Tesla looked at him suspiciously. After a long pause, he nodded. "*Razoomyem.* I understand," he said quietly.

"Please come with me, Professor. Colonel Cassidy also wishes to apologize to you, and has invited you and I to go to lunch with him. Let's go."

Tesla nodded again and followed Capt. Panic to Security headquarters, where Lt. Col. Cassidy was waiting. He would play along—better than sitting in a cell not knowing where he was.

"Professor!" nodded Cassidy, holding our his hand. Panic had taught him a couple of Serbian words, which he mangled. "*Molim! Izvini.* I'm terribly sorry about what happened. And inconveniencing you. There was something very strange going on at the base, and we hid you in that room to protect you."

"*Razoomyem.* Tesla nodded once again, wondering what Cassidy was about to spring on him.

"You must be starving," Captain Panic told Tesla. "Come eat with us."

It was getting on towards 11 AM. They walked the quarter mile to the officer's club portion of the large, low, beige brick mess hall and sat down to order their lunch. They were a little early, they were told.

"We will wait," Cassidy told the waiter. "Bring me a brandy."

"Remy-Martin, Colonel?" he asked.

"Yes. A double."

The waiter looked at Captain Panic. "Please bring glasses for me and my guest." As the waiter set the six ounce shells before them, Captain Panic reached into his satchel and, smiling broadly, pulled out a bottle of Rajica, a 110 proof Serbian plum wine, and placed it in front of Tesla, who was surprised.

"Re-hee-ka! Slivovitz! Hvala! What a surprise, *Khvala ti!*" Tesla nodded with satisfaction as he removed the cap and poured Captain Panic's glass nearly full, then his own. Deeply suspicious of Panic and Cassidy, he had read them correctly and continued to play along.

"*Nyema naa chyemoo!'* Panic told Tesla. "You are very welcome!" He turned to Cassidy. "Like to try it?" Cassidy nodded The waiter brought an extra glass with the brandy, and Captain Panic poured it half full of the Rajica, He knew Cassidy could drink.

Cassidy, too, was surprised and was caught up in the moment. He raised his glass, proposing a toast. "To the future!" he proclaimed as the three clinked their glasses together.

Tesla's eyes narrowed and he looked intensely at Cassidy. "You appear to be welcoming me now. Why was it necessary to render me unconscious and then lock me in a cell. For all I knew, my life was forfeit. I cannot quickly set that aside. I wouldn't consider that very hospitable, Colonel."

"I am deeply sorry, Professor. We have been on the highest military alert, and the rules of engagement are very clear. Without certain knowledge, everybody is to be considered a potential enemy. We know who you are now, and we will try our best to make it up to you. In fact, we are honored. Trust is earned, and we will try our damndest to earn yours."

"Indeed!" said Tesla. After a long pause he looked long and hard at Cassidy, across from him at the table, and then at Panic, to his right. "In any case, Captain Panic, I am grateful to you for the Rajica." Tesla had missed his favorite drink from his homeland, and sipped the Rajica, savoring the delicate fruity flavor as the alcohol nicely warmed his tongue, his gullet and his heart. "*Zivyeli!*" he nodded as he raised his glass. "To your health." He looked intensely at Panic and Cassidy, briefly raised the glass, tipped it up and drained it dry. They followed suit.

The waiter returned and took their orders for lunch.

As they walked back to Security Hq., the Rajica kicked in, enhancing the sounds around them and brightening the sunlight—a little too much.

Col. Cassidy informed Headquarters that they had picked up Nikola Tesla and that he was their guest. Major Wingard entered, walked over to Lt. Col. Cassidy's office and stuck his hand out; Cassidy shook it and introduced him to Tesla.

He spoke in a conciliatory tone. "Glad you're back in the saddle now, boss. The General told me about it. Very strange things are going on here, like being sent back in time for 100 years. I can't believe I'm saying it and I still can' t really believe it's really happened!" He turned to Tesla, shaking his hand enthusiastically. "Mr. Tesla. It is a great honor. Since it appears that we are from your future, we want you to know you made a great mark on our lives. As a scientist you must be deeply interested in the unprecedented events that have taken place here."

Tesla was surprised but flattered. He nodded back to Major Wingard, whom he liked instinctively, and squeezed his hand hard. "Indeed it is! And thank you, Major. It is an honor for me, likewise."

Cassidy went along. "It's strange, very strange, Major, but you know, we're Marines, and we're trained to survive in all environments. This one just wasn't in the manual!" They both smiled. "By the way, we've got orders from Bell-Boeing to run several more tests on those V-22's before we deliver them to San Diego. While there's some time to kill. We can get a head start. You know, the V-22 is my baby; I've been with it since '88, and I was on their first team of test pilots."

"Yes, I know it," said Major Wingard agreeably. "Sounds good."

"I'll clear it with the General this afternoon," said Cassidy.

"Major Wingard shook Tesla's hand again and smiled at him. "Welcome to Nellis Air Force Base. Our commander, General Mills and our chief scientists want to meet you this evening, if you wish. We will have a dinner in your honor."

Tesla nodded in acknowledgment. "Thank you Major. I look forward to it." His all-ranging curiosity had returned; he wanted to get his hands on all of the amazing technology that surrounded him.

Cassidy got his clearance to test the Osprey. The plans were now beginning to jell. Lt. Col. Miles "Mad Dog" Cassidy and his team of tough, disciplined Marines were prepared to act. He and two of his Marine associates took their electric cart over to the hangars where the Ospreys were kept. Lt. Tabatha Moore, a stately 5'9", buxom but not fat, with lively green eyes and auburn hair took Tesla into an empty office. He sat down in front of the live computer terminal on the desk.

"Can you teach me how to use this, Miss Moore?" he asked, reading the name tag protruding outward from her ample breasts, which overfilled her blouse. Tesla could not help looking at her breasts.

Tabatha smiled at him, putting her hand on his shoulder. She sat down very close to him and leaned over the keyboard. One button was open and Tesla could see all the way down her blouse. He took a quick breath as Lt. Moore patiently showed him how to press Enter, how to access the databases on the Cray 940, and how to surf. Here you are, Professor. This is easier that you might think."

"Thank you."

"Sorry, Professor Tesla, but the Internet is down; otherwise I'd show you how to use it. You could tap into an infinite number of websites, databases on any subject. Just remember, when you press Enter, you've exercised a choice and you can't take it back."

Tesla nodded and smiled, enjoying the moment. "Forgive my ignorance," he replied innocently. "What's a website? Also, what's a database?" She explained as best she could.

"I'll try to find an instruction manual for you. I know this is all new to you. You've got quite a learning curve to deal with. I have to go to the hangars; sorry I can't help you now."

"You've been a great deal of help!" Tesla acknowledged. "More than you know. Thanks very much."

For the next three hours Tesla pecked away, surfed, searched, and quickly mastered the essentials. He learned everything he could, finding astounding scientific facts, blogs, formulas, things even he had never imagined. He was like a hungry dog in a meat market, a kid in a candy store. In a word, he was hooked. *I wonder; could it be possible?* he asked himself. With hesitation, he slowly typed in "Tesla." There was a short delay, then the deluge. It was overwhelming.

Cassidy's favorite warplane, the V-22 Osprey, a Marine tilt-wing aircraft, was a first class gift, a rare gift to the Marine Corps, whose aircraft were usually hand-me-downs from the Navy. The Osprey could take off and land vertically, swivel in horizontal position and become an airplane, and fly at more than 300 knots. It was heavily armed. And it could fly 2,000 miles without refueling. Perfect! Even if some of the newer testing data had been fudged just a bit. It would also carry up an additional 10 tons of weapons, supplies and personnel. He needed the twin engine AH-1 Super Cobras too for his operation, but they were gas hogs, with a limited range—barely 500 miles. That presented a logistical problem. He almost wished there were single engine Cobras available on the base, which were much more fuel efficient, but there weren't.

Nevertheless, to carry out Cassidy's plans, they would need the AH-1's, and lots of fuel. The Super Cobras were strong fighting vehicles with a large variety of offensive weapons: cannons, missiles and other surprises the 1900 Army would have no defense against. *If* they could steal them. The gas consumption required that the small renegade group set up fuel storage in advance, at strategic locations along the way for the choppers, say every 500 miles or less. The Osprey could haul most of the spare fuel, and the weapons and ammo. Plus a few surprises. More than a few.

Testing had begun on the prototypes of the Osprey back in 1988, and Cassidy had been one of the early test pilots. But President George Herbert Walker Bush, a Navy man of course, ostensibly from the advice of his Secretary of Defense, Dick Cheney, had scuttled the program under the pretext that it was too costly. *Yeah, right!* thought Cassidy. *Trilateral Commission! We know who he's really working for!*

Now, quite surprisingly, under Bill Clinton, purportedly the New World Order's most passionate advocate, the program had gotten back on track, and testing was nearly complete. Nearly but not quite. Two Ospreys sat in hangars on the north side of the base, ready for additional testing and then for delivery to the Marines in San Diego. Further tests were not due until early January, and only two of younger test pilots from Bell and Boeing were present. The mechanical team would arrive around January 10. Cassidy knew there were still some problems, mainly the deadly danger of VRS—vortex ring state—upon descent—dangerous and difficult to manage, which could cause a very hard landing or even a crash. But Cassidy was confident he could handle them, as he had done in the early days when he was testing the Osprey.

The co-conspirators swiftly began their preparations, and Cassidy gave them their instructions. They would commandeer the two AH-1 Cobra gunships. And the *pièce de résistance* would be one of the two Bell-Boeing V-22 Ospreys on the base. Cassidy dearly loved the Osprey. It was a dream; it had always been. And it was improved now; it was safer. He was supremely confident that he could handle the glitches.

On this go-round he had been up in it several times with the new test pilots, and had studied it meticulously. The tilt rotors had been reworked; now the vertical takeoff seemed much more efficient and safer. The rotors would switch in 30 seconds or less and there were more intermediate positions, which, for this round of testing, were the Boeing engineers' main concern.

He had already carefully calculated where the fuel would be cached. The first storage site near Silver City, New Mexico, the second near Pecos, Texas, and the fifth and last in a field near the small village of Springhorn, Ohio, where the rest of the spare fuel would be stored. They would fly over very rural areas and few or no towns to reduce the risk of being seen. From Springhorn, they they would improvise, but would be in range for the main event—taking President McKinley by surprise. They had little doubt that it would succeed—the element of surprise accompanied by overwhelming power—a supreme strategic canon etched upon the mind of every Marine. Only a matter of time.

Col. Cassidy, Lt. Moore, Sgt. Russo and Corporal Rodriguez loaded dozens of empty tanks and barrels into both choppers and pushed them into the fueling area. Master Sergeant Anthony Russo, a co-conspirator, who was head of the security detail in that area, helped to allay suspicion from the two guards, and ordered them into other areas to perform tasks he improvised on the spot. They filled the polyethylene bladder tanks and barrels with several thousand gallons, loading the Osprey and two AH-18's nearly to capacity. That took the longest time and was risky. They would transfer most of the load to the Osprey at the first cache point in western New Mexico near Lordsburg, and each succeeding fuel deposit would lighten the load.

Top speed for the Osprey was just over 300 MPH, so that flying to each point would take just under two hours and then rest while the choppers caught up. They allowed another two hours for selecting the exact spot and unloading. The fuel tanks and barrels would be covered up with large tarps away from curious onlookers and prying eyes. The Super Cobra would use up about twelve hours of actual flying time to Springhorn, Ohio site, and four to five hours to refine the site selections, hide the fuel and unload. Only the Osprey, loaded to capacity, would make the first run, depositing fuel and spare ammo at the five locations.

Cassidy, Lt. Tabatha Moore and Master Sgt. Anthony Russo, with fuel to spare, took off in the Osprey and headed over Lordsburg, New Mexico, towards Silver City. Meanwhile, Captain Panic, a naturalized Serbian-American, Captain Rynning, an Estonian American, also a rated pilot, loaded a large cache of weaponry and ammo on the two AH-1 Super Cobras. Five sites were chosen from the maps, and were confirmed during the actual run with only minor variation. They chose the southern route to avoid high peaks and dangerous updrafts and downdrafts.

The fuel run was a complete success. They left at dusk and returned a little after 2 PM the next day. They had also photographed the entire route in detail noted where population areas, Indian reservations and small towns were and how to avoid them to the maximum degree.

Area 51, NV   10:45 PM   January 6, 1900

It was now nearly 11 PM. "It's now or never!" Cassidy announced to his team. All the aircraft were in their hangars and under guard until morning, orders of Major Wingard, whose suspicions were aroused.

Refusing to be deterred, Cassidy, the only pilot among them capable of flying the Osprey, set out with Lieutenant Tabatha Moore, the only woman in the group, to steal it. They quietly approached the hangar with special weapons for silently disabling the guards. There would be at least five and possibly more.

Cassidy and Moore, in full uniform, drove quickly to the north mountain hangar complex on the base. At the first hangar, only two guards were present; they recognized them. The first one, alerted earlier by Colonel Pick to keep an eye on Cassidy, challenged them, while the other stepped around the corner of the building and quietly called Major Wingard. Cassidy engaged him in conversation and Moore stunned him. He collapsed silently. She then shot a lethal dose of Black Leaf 40 nicotide into his carotid artery with a pen syringe. He died instantly.

Major Wingard, knowing there might be trouble but completely unaware of the violence that had just occurred, came around the corner in his Land Rover, and got out.

"Colonel Cassidy. Wait! I've got something important here you need to know." Cassidy turned and nodded, while Lt. Moore quietly stepped into the first hangar. Cassidy kept his cool.

"What is it Major? I'm a little busy here; checking on the Osprey. Nobody knows the Osprey like I do; I'm checking the maintenance logs. You know me; I have to see for myself."

Wingard didn't question this because he knew Cassidy was authorized to test the Ospreys. "I'm the only one who can fly it!" Cassidy added. "By the way, you're not a pilot, are you; one of the few."

This disturbed the Major as if Cassidy were feigning friendliness but couldn't fully restrain himself. His mistrust of Cassidy returned.

"OK, Colonel. Gotta be on my way; the wife's got dinner on the table."

Wingard walked around the corner. Cassidy couldn't see him but heard the car door close and the car drive off. Wingard's suspicions rose and he pulled the Land Rover over a hundred yards away. He quietly walked back towards the hangars.

As Cassidy and Moore approached the second hangar, two guards, who had not witnessed the attack, asked them why they were there. Moore surreptitiously fired a powerful stun charge at one and then quickly killed him, while Cassidy, fearing discovery, fired a crisp, silenced round from his sidearm into the other guard's forehead. He crumpled lifeless to the ground. Two to go, on the inside. They met the same fate. Cassidy and Moore quickly dragged the five bodies to a dark corner in the hangar. As Major Wingard quietly rounded the corner, Lt. Moore spotted him and waited for him. When he stepped towards the hanger, she shot him with a silenced round, and dragged him inside with the corpses of the guards they had murdered. She thought he was dead. He was seriously wounded but the bullet had passed through his abdomen, miraculously missing the vital organs. He had not bled profusely, but he fell unconscious.

Inside the hangar, Cassidy reached Panic on a secure frequency. Tesla, unaware of what had just occurred, had secretly armed himself, was already inside one of the choppers where the weapons, fuel and supplies had been loaded. It was now 3:15 AM; a shift change would take place at 5:00. He had to act very fast.

Giving the signal to the already fully loaded Super Cobras to take off on his mark, he opened the hangar door, towed the Osprey out into the yard, fired it up, and took off vertically, and very noisily. Seconds later the two Super Cobras lifted off almost simultaneously, and they headed east as the entire base almost instantly came awake and alive. But it was too late.

In the panic of the escape, they did not miss Sergeant Russo until they were well into southwestern Arizona. Too late to go back for him.

General Mills was awakened immediately. Within a few minutes, they discovered Major Wingard, still breathing, and the corpses of the murdered guards, as well as the thefts of the Osprey, the two AH-18's, and the weapons. He suspected Cassidy and soon found out who else was missing. They soon deduced that they had taken Tesla with them.

The remaining Security personnel were summoned and assembled. Sergeant Russo recanted at the last minute, and informed the General of Cassidy's entire plan to capture the White House and take over the U. S. military. He was arrested on the spot and thoroughly debriefed as the countermeasures were contemplated. They could court martial him later, but if he was telling the truth, he would be indispensable. For the time being he remained under house arrest to be constantly accompanied by two officers.

An urgent military meeting was convened. "You are all aware of what has happened; it is tragic but it is also an act of war, deadly, mutinous and treasonous. We must act now. Time is of the essence," announced the General. "It's nearly 4 AM. We already have actionable intelligence, a full record of Cassidy's use of the Cray, notes, and direct information from Sgt. Russo, who is cooperating."

"We will assign teams to conduct these operations," added Colonel Pick.

The General continued. "Their choppers can't get to Ohio until late tomorrow afternoon; they have to stop to refuel four times before Ohio. The Osprey will have to refuel at the East Texas or more likely the Mississippi site Sgt. Russo told us about. If they refuel and regroup in Ohio, they've got several more hours before all three of the craft can possibly start the last leg of their journey—Washington D.C. We'll catch up with Cassidy provided he follows the route they planned. They really can't change it because the choppers have to refuel in those five places. Our aim, if possible, is to capture them alive and bring them back. But we have to warn Washington this morning, no later!"

The adjutant, Major Ike Sizemore, was told to assemble the team, prepare a plan the pursuit and analyze the contingencies. He met with several officers and enlisted men to his office on Level 3.

"We'll meet in one hour, Major, then we'll solidify our plans and put them into action. Meanwhile, prepare the Osprey, test it if necessary. Who can fly it?

Major Michael Crosby, Area 51's top bomber pilot, raised his hand. "I'm rated for the Osprey, Sir. But I don't really trust it. There are still some issues; that's why the test pilots from Bell and Boeing are here."

"Understood," said the General. "I didn't know it still had those serious problems. With all the people that died tonight, we don't need more casualties."

Col Pick spoke again. "I may have a better idea. We have their plans, and Sergeant Russo, who was left behind, has told us everything he knows. Let's consider the B-2 Stealth Bomber. It has a range of nearly 7,000 miles, more than enough for the round trip without refueling plus some exploring. When they see it they'll know we're coming after them, they'll know the game is up."

"That is an excellent idea," remarked the General. "It's good strategy. I though generals were the strategists! The idea makes perfect sense, however, and whenever and whatever equipment we actually send after them. I'm not optimistic about their cooperation because they're already facing a general court martial for murder, mutineering, treason, grand theft and God knows what else. Who can fly the B-2?"

Major Crosby raised his hand once again. "I can fly it, sir, and I love that airplane! It's maneuvers like a fighter, flies at nearly Mach 2, and leaves no footprint. The B-2 has state of the art cameras and we can make a fully detailed and comprehensive photographic record of every acre we cross."

The General nodded his head and spoke authoritatively. "Major, I've made the decision. Deploy the B-2 as soon as it has been checked out thoroughly and fully fueled. It's past 4 AM; you should leave at the crack of dawn so you can spot the fuel sites, the Super Cobras and the Osprey in full daylight. Carry a reduced crew of four. Get 'er ready, Major!"

"Roger, General, Colonel! I'm on my way." They saluted and he left.

Chapter 20

Sheriff Sam Roscoe

Carson City, Nevada   January 7, 1900   4:30 AM

The General was prepared to adjourn the meeting. "Wait. One more thing. We don't know if they know about this in Washington, so they've got to be informed, and reliably. Somebody will likely spot the Osprey and for sure the choppers because they're flyng lower. But the military won't know what to make of it. We need to have the Nevada Governor contact President McKinley officially and tell him what's going on, including the fact that more aircraft will be in their skies when we go after them." He turned to Col Pick and whispered, "Wally, I can't believe I'm saying this. President McKinley! 1900! Are we in a group hallucination?"

He whispered back, "Maybe a group dream, General. And how will we know when we're awake?!"

The General turned to the group and resumed. "We're trying to stop a war, such as it is, not start one! After our little foray to Carson City, I'm sure someone notified Washington, though they may not believe in what they're seeing anymore than we do! We *must* contact the Governor again and make damned sure Washington is alerted"

"Absolutely correct," said Colonel Pick. "It's crucial. Shall I send Bobby Wilson, or better yet, Captain Mulligan? They're already been and Captain Mulligan met the Mayor. Perhaps I should go along."

The General pondered this for a moment. "Whoever goes needs to be very careful. They may not consider us friendly, and I'm sure somebody in their Guard or the Governor's office is fearful of the power we already demonstrated."

"How, then?" asked Col. Pick. "Leaflets?! Maybe as a last resort. I think we should test the waters very carefully."

Captain Mulligan spoke up, almost shouting. "Well don't forget we've got their Sheriff right here in the brig—the one who took a shot at me! Why don't we talk to him?"

Everyone nodded assent. "I was just coming to that," said the General.

Sheriff Sam Roscoe of Douglas County, Nevada, sleepy and still in a state of bewilderment, was awakened in his cell and brought to the large ante-room adjoining the General's office suite on Level 3. He was in handcuffs and leg shackles. He had been alone in his cell for four days, with visits only from those who brought his food, and from Major Laura Schenk, the social worker, who was allowed to speak to him only from outside his cell, since he was considered dangerous. He had refused to speak to her. Now he was *really* scared. Dragged from his cell in the middle of the night, he was sure he was about to face a firing squad. He stood, staring vacantly; finally he was pushed into a chair. A chickenhawk bird colonel sat before him in a strange blue uniform. And now a general! General Mills and Captain Mary Mulligan walked over to him and sat down.

"Welcome, Sheriff," said Colonel Pick. "I hope you've been comfortable. I believe you remember Captain Mulligan."

"Good morning, Sheriff," Mulligan smiled.

"This is our Base Commander, General Thomas Mills," said Colonel Pick.

Dazed and confused, the Sheriff nodded in awe, not knowing what to expect next. The General pulled his chair close to him, looking at him intently.

"Good morning, Sheriff, I'm General Tom Mills." He turned to the sergeant who had brought him in. "Sergeant, there's no need for these restraints."

"No sir," said the sergeant, removing the handcuffs and leg shackles. The Sheriff took a deep breath.

"Sheriff," the General smiled, "If I were to say you were just a little confused, that'd be putting it mildly, wouldn't it?"

The Sheriff nodded, but couldn't bring himself to speak. He couldn't focus his eyes. General Mills tried to put him at ease. "What did you say your name, was, Sheriff?"

He had to force himself to speak. "Sam," he answered in a wavering voice. "Sam Roscoe, sir."

"O. K. if I call you Sam?" The Sheriff nodded. He breathed a little easier.

"Sam, we're almost as confused as you are, but we've figured out what's going on. You see, we're from a time when people were inventing all kinds of amazing machines, and one of our scientists invented one thet could travel 'way back in time."

The Sheriff's jaw dropped and he became glassy eyed again. The General got up and put his hand on his shoulder, and spoke slowly.

"Really, Sheriff. It's something that people from your time were writing about, like Jules Verne."

"Who's Jules Verne?"

"He's a man from your time who wrote about traveling in time. Only in the year 1999 *they really invented one*. Trouble was, it was so new that they couldn't really control it. One of those machines, right here on this base, went haywire and the whole lot of us got sent back to your time. We didn't know it ourselves until we started flyin' around the base and then visited your town, Carson City. The reason you're here is that you took a shot at one of us."

"I didn't mean to hurt nobody," he stammered.

"We all know that, Sam." smiled the General. "We figured out that you were just doing your job. So we've dropped all charges and were going to take you back home!"

"When?" The sheriff was visibly relieved. "When, sir?"

"Today. Matter of fact, I'll be going with you, along with some of my men—and women. But meanwhile, we'll show you around our base, let you get acquainted. Kind of a trip into the future. Now: the people of Carson City need to know that we're not their enemy, so we're going to need to talk to some of your neighbors. You can help us. I know Carson City's the capital, so we'd also like to talk to your Governor. And your National Guard people. They need to be convinced without a doubt that we're friendly."

Captain Mary Mulligan spoke consolingly. "Sheriff, I'm the one you fired at. I was a little upset at the time, as I'm sure you can understand, but it's OK now; I know you were just trying to keep order. Nobody got hurt. You couldn't have known that we were friendly." She smiled at him.

"I'm sorry, ma'am; I'm really sorry," he blurted in a broken voice. Tears came to his eyes and his lip trembled. He needed a drink.

"It's OK" said Captain Mulligan, getting up and patting him on the shoulder. "Luckily, nobody got hurt. By the way, I already know your Mayor. Yarborough, I think is his name. Seemed like an awfully nice fellow!"

"Yes ma'am, he is," the Sheriff assured her. He was finally starting to loosen up.

"You know, we'd like to meet him again. I'll be going along when we take you back home today."

Two AH-1 Super Cobras and two single engine Air Force Hueys, with General Mills, Sheriff Roscoe, Captain Mulligan, and a dozen Marines, arrived at the site of the old State Fairgrounds in Carson City and hovered. As they prepared to land, they heard shots in the distance. One round struck but didn't do any damage. The helicopters retreated several miles and landed in a flat stretch of desert behind the low hills to the east of Carson City.

Fifty National Guardsmen, half of them on horseback, who had been on high alert since Colonel Cassidy's visit two days earlier, took up defensive positions. Tesla's accompanying National Guard platoon had returned to Carson City and informed the Commander of Tesla's kidnapping at the hands of a rogue officer. They were now definitely hostile.

"Plan B!" lamented Col. Pick. It was too dangerous there. They prepared to return to Area 51.

"Aren't you gonna take me home?" Sheriff Roscoe asked timidly.

"Of course!" reassured Col. Pick. "They seem to think *we're* the enemy but they're not going to shoot at you!"

"Why do they think you're the enemy?" Roscoe asked.

"We're not sure., but I think you know some of the reasons why!" He raised one eyebrow.

The Sheriff nodded. "I'm really sorry. It's all my fault!"

"No, not your fault! Tell you what, Sheriff Roscoe," Col. Pick continued. "You tell us a safe place to drop you off. Be sure you tell the Mayor, the Governor and everybody else we're not hostile, and have your Governor inform the White House if they don't already know something is up."

They then proceeded to tell him in detail of Cassidy's murder of his Deputy and several guards, and his theft of the three aircraft. "We're think he's headed for Washington, DC. We need to notify the President and the Army Chief of Staff of the danger, but the Nevada National Guard and everybody else thinks we're a hostile force."

Col. Pick quickly wrote a detailed letter to the Governor, which the General signed, and Mary Mulligan wrote one to Mayor Yarborough.

"Sheriff, it is crucial that these be delivered, and that you tell them what is really happening. Remember, you were only locked up because you shot at one of our aircraft. That's past now; you've been forgiven and we've moved on to more important matters. Col. Cassidy is going to try to kidnap President McKinley; they've left the base with three powerful war machines and they have to be stopped. Our country is at stake and the President needs to know!"

Sheriff Roscoe was himself again; he saw how important his mission was, and his mind was working. "Are you sure they'll believe me?" he asked.

"They know who you are," Col. Pick replied. "As to whether they believe we are what we say we are, that's an open question. But in all cases, this must be in the Governor's hands and he must inform Washington!"

The Sheriff undersood. "I'll do it."

"OK, let's get you home." They had downloaded a detailed USGS county map from the Cray. The Sheriff showed them where to drop him off. "Don't you worry about a thing!" he said with determination.

Chapter 21

The War Room

It was unusually cold and nearly a foot of snow had fallen. Temperatures had dropped to near zero. Reporters were milling around outside the White House, rubbing their hands and noses, scarves around their ears. Daylight was just beginning to break in the east.

In the War Room inside, President McKinley, Secretary of State John Hay, Secretary of War Elihu Root, and Theodore Roosevelt were briefing Army Major General Donald Quarters, who had just arrived from Fort Alger, Virginia. They were still looking at the photos Governor Roosevelt had brought home. The General was skeptical.

"Can't they fake these photographs? How do we know some model builder didn't dream up these monstrosities?"

"They're real enough," said Roosevelt emphatically. "I studied them very carefully during the long train ride with their National Guardsman. He saw two of them flying into Carson City and watched it when one of them took to the air again with its rotary

175

propellers. He also saw a big gray one with fixed wings flying over their town at an unbelievable speed. He's available if you want to talk to him. I think I can tell a fake photo from real, and I certainly know when someone's lying to me!"

McKinley lit a long Cuban cigar, then spoke up. "Representative McGrath of Nevada will be here Friday on the train, on the 7th. He's bringing new photographs of some of the individuals involved. We've got names: Mills, Mulligan, Sizemore, Cassidy. One of our guardsmen took notes from the radio in the rotary wing craft when it was on the ground, and he has more names."

"They've got armaments," said Secretary Root. "They picked up some of the shells and spent bullets. Ballistics tell us there very real. Alloys they've never seen. Unlike anything *I've* ever seen. Their insignia are red, white and blue, with an American flag—with 50 stars on it! And U S. Marine insignia."

"That's impossible!" shouted General Quarters. He controlled himself quickly. "Excuse me, Mr. President! Sorry for the outburst, sir. But we're the United States Army and you're the Commander-in-Chief! Wouldn't you be the first to know about it? And is whatever this is really a Navy operation? The Marines haven't got anything remotely technical, much less a flying machine. And you don't mean to tell me those things were really flying!" As ever, there was little love lost between the Army and the Navy.

"Apology accepted," McKinley frowned. "Yes, it is all quite fantastical. But yes, it would appear that they were."

Secretary of War Root broke in. "Look, General, we're just as mystified as you are. Fantastical indeed. But we have genuine evidence. Yes, they were flying. Not only flying but high and fast. Now General, I am aware that you, Admiral Dewey, and the Navy aren't on the best of terms. This is *not* Dewey's doing; he's a loyal officer; he has his hands full in the Philippines, halfway around the world. But we have photos of airships with Marine insignia. Our Marines *are* under the Secretary of the Navy John

Long and myself. These are *decidedly* not our forces, so they must be imposters. Way out west and way inland."

"I cannot believe this," said General Quarters, agitated. "I need evidence, not doctored photographs. Something is going on that we cannot ignore!"

His boss, Secretary Root, raising his voice, rebuked him. "General, *we* will provide that evidence. Do not overstep your bounds!"

Quarters looked intently at Root but said nothing. The Secretary continued. "Now, except for a few ships in Hawaii, and Admiral Dewey's fleet in the Phillippines, there are no significant Naval operations in the Pacific at present, much less a project of this magnitude!"

"Gentlemen, gentlemen! There is no need for contentiousness." The President sat up straight in the oversized maroon leather armchair and leaned forward. Everybody who knew him well knew what to expect.

"I am your Commander-in-Chief," said McKinley decisively, flicking his ashes. His high voice began to rise and fall musically; his speech began to sound like his familiar oratory. "The General is correct in that there is far, far too much here to ignore here. We have no idea what they are up to, but they are obviously a force to be reckoned with, and we have sufficient reason to take serious precautions for the safety of the United States, its sovereign citizens, and its precious legacy. Whoever they may or may not be, and whatever else they may have done or not done, we have incontrovertible proof that they are impersonating American military officers, to what end I do not know. But the one thing we do know is that they have already committed serious crimes—crimes against the United States of America which must be dealt with quickly and severely!"

The oratory and its ringing echo in the huge room ceased momentarily. The President was still under the spell of his own eloquence. There was a long pause. Finally Secretary of State John

Hay stood up, put both hands on the table and looked directly at McKinley.

He spoke thoughtfully. "Mr. President, it might be just some crackpot inventor, maybe that Tesla fellow. But it could also be the vanguard of some kind of invasion—Spaniards or the Germans. The Spaniards are still smarting from Cuba and the Philippines; they've got real issues with us. My best guess is the Kaiser, whom I have never trusted. He is an imperialist of the purest waters—he has boundless territorial ambitions. His military machine is *very* advanced and he is a known Spanish sympathizer. And he has neither love nor respect for the United States of America; in fact, I have been told that he is openly contemptuous of us. That concerns me gravely."

They all listened intently. The President set down his whisky glass and replied. "Yes, John, your surmise is most logical. We're all still speculating. They *could* have brought this force into the United States through Canada, where we have no control over anything that goes on. Canada possesses a modern coast to coast railroad."

The President stopped, took a long breath, placed his right hand under his chin, pondered for a moment, then nodded. He turned decisively to Quarters and Root. "I am ordering that our borders and that all our Army installations be placed on full alert." The General nodded to his aide, who began taking notes. "They are also to inform the Governors of the respective states and coordinate their efforts with their Natonal Guards."

"Yessir," said Quarters, who waved his aide over, then turned to his boss, Secretary Root. Root nodded.

McKinley continued "All the bases under your command must be in a state of full readiness. If the Secretary of State's surmise is correct, it is possible, however unlikely, that we may be facing a German invasion force. Mr. Secretary Root, you are to alert all our northern borders and all our military bases from California to New York. If you are asked why, you are to tell them that is top secret and top priority, and an executive order from the President of the United States!"

"I shall attend to it immediately," replied the Secretary, nodding to his aide. McKinley's jaw was set and his face was flushed. He sat back in his chair and drew deeply on his cigar. The General nodded to his aide, who quickly left the room. There was a long, silent pause.

"If there are no further questions, this meeting is adjourned. Report back to me personally at noon when your orders are carried out."

Quarters and Root left hastily; Roosevelt remained. He and the President walked into the elaborate paneled dining room. An elaborate breakfast of fresh fruit, juices, toasted bread, eggs and country ham, was served by the immaculately dressed and attentive dining room staff.

McKinley quickly dismissed the servants and told them that this was a private meeting. They ate quickly. McKinley lit another cigar, then poured himself a water glass full of whiskey from the crystal decanter. He quaffed half of it, sat back and exhaled.

"Ted, what frightens me most about this thing is that we don't know anything. You're the country's biggest hero, and you may be President sooner than you think. You and I have an election in November to face. We may have a serious military threat here. Let's get to the bottom of . . . ."

At that moment a sharp knock came on the door. It was Secretary Root.

"Mr. President, I've just received a wire from the commander at Fort Dodge in Kansas. Less than an hour ago, they witnessed three of those flying machines just south of their base. One of them was a massive craft with fixed wings, two of them with the rotating blades like we saw in the photos. They were flying directly east. And we've got what looks like another cable from Governor

Blaisdel, but it didn't come through properly. We're cabling him back."

McKinley's eyes widened, but he quickly gained his composure.

<u>Washington, DC</u>   <u>January 7, 1900</u>   <u>7:15 PM</u>

The nation's capital was on a war footing and nobody was sure exactly why. Wild rumors swept Washington and reports kept coming in about military preparations. The press was in a frenzy. Some were certain that the President had gone mad.

General Quarters had carelessly let a few facts slip out at home, and his teenage daughter Annie told all she had heard to a local reporter down in Fredericksburg, Virginia, a friend of the family, including her father's concern about a German invasion. The reporter made light of it to Annie but immediately boarded a train to Washington and headed to the Post's new church-like E Street building next to the National Theater, where there was a frenetic buzz of activity.

The previous night, an ambitious Post reporter had gotten hold of some of the photos from Carson City, and the Post ran a huge banner on the front page complete with pictures. 'TESLA'S FLYING MACHINE'

The New York Times ran another, more disturbing article. The header ran: AIRBORNE GERMAN INVASION? It was written, on page two, with a touch of whimsy, but it was disturbing nevertheless. The Times had been scooped by the Post today, but they planned to run both stories on the front page tomorrow. The Times and the Post also knew that the tabloid kings, the yellow journalists, William Randolph Hearst and Joseph Pulitzer were about to leap into the fray. And the Police Gazette was due out on Saturday.

The new German ambassador, Baron Peter von Moltke, who had presented his credentials only weeks earlier, was summoned to the White House. The son of the German military genius and hero of the Franco-Prussian War, Helmuth von Moltke, he was automatically suspect. Secretary of State John Hay questioned him for two hours with great care and diplomacy. Hay then met with the President.

"Nothing, Mr. President. Either he doesn't know anything or he's the best liar I've ever known. And as to any resemblance to Baron Helmuth von Moltke, there is none whatsoever. This one is a popinjay and a dilettante, and decidedly not of the highest mettle, either militarily or intellectually. My guess is that, if there is a German invasion, he has not been informed. He thinks the Times article is a joke."

McKinley nodded rhythmically as he listened. He was visibly relieved. "I will send a new message to Sir Wilfred in Ottawa and ask him to summon the German ambassador."

"You've cabled the Canadians? I thought . . . ." McKinley raised his hand and then rested it on Hay's arm. He spoke gently.

"John, I have thought this through and I am now certain that it's not the Canadians, certainly not the government. As you know, I have known Sir Wilfred Laurier for many years. He became Prime Minister back in '96, the same time I was elected President. We are fast friends, even though he is a Liberal. I have just finished exchanging a series of quite candid correspondences with him and he has assured me that there are no alliances between his country and any foreign power, and that he is aware of no military activity in the western part of his country. Frankly, I am now inclined to believe him, because I am also certain he would not betray the United States of America, especially in military matters. In fact, I now feel it is quite unthinkable."

"Well, he was very critical of our actions both in Cuba and the Philippines, and he has called us Imperialists."

McKinley smiled. "That was for local consumption, his fellow Canadians, not for us. He's a politician just like you and I. And he needs us far more than we need him." He lit his cigar carefully and deliberately, nearly allowing the match to burn down to his fingers. He raised his head, looking directly into Hay's eyes. "Whatever the case may be, John," spoke McKinley thoughtfully, drawing on his long cigar between pauses. "I have no intention of confronting him without evidence. You have already spoken with the Canadian ambassador. I am also well acquainted with Earl Grey, who will undoubtedly be the next Governor-General. England is our ally and Canada is one of the brightest stars of the Commonwealth. If there were trouble with Germany, Canada would leap into the fray—on our side." He nodded and placed his cigar carefully in the huge ceramic ashtray. "In any case, John, we have more immediate matters to deal with. I have no intention of risking an international incident, and I am far more concerned about immediate tactical preparedness."

"Where else, then, might this threat have originated?" Hay asked peremptorily.

"Canada *was* the most logical choice; and there remains a remote possibility that the Germans, Spaniards, whoever, could have launched a sneak attack, landed on a remote coast such as Labrador, and quietly commandeered the railroad. But this is January and all those Canadian bases are frozen solid. And all without detection? Their railroads have a sophisticated, modern telegraphy system; there's no way it could have been achieved without someone being alerted somewhere." The President stubbed out his cigar, sipped his whisky and lit another. "As to your question of where else? Well, of course, there is the other border—Mexico. They have no love for the Spaniards, to be sure, but their western coasts, especially on the lower California peninsula, are sparsely populated and unguarded. But where might such a thing have originated if the Pacific coast is involved? Admiral Dewey is busy in the Phillippines and is in full control. We have prevailed and the Stars and Stripes are flying over Manila. *They* have no technical expertise. Any European ships bearing arms and men would have had to sail halfway around the world—around the Cape of Good Hope and clear across the Pacific, or worse, around Cape Horn. Whom else, then, might we suspect, the Japanese!?"

Hay chortled, spluttering his whisky. "Japanese indeed! But, Mr. President. You forget that they are *flying*!" The President reacted visibly. He shook his head, half-smiled, put down his cigar and laid his hand heavily on Hay's shoulder. "I'm glad you have a sense of humor, John. It has helped to sustain me through many difficult hours." He poured a liberal amount of rye whiskey out of his favorite crystal decanter into John Hay's glass, then poured four fingers into his own glass.

"Drink with me, John. For moments like this, God gave us alcohol. Thanks be to our Lord and Saviour for this blessing! Before another word passes between us, drink; let us test our tenuous reality; let our true selves rise through the vapors." McKinley clapped both hands on Hay's shoulders and shook him affectionately.

Hays grinned, relaxed, leaned back slowly and inhaled deeply He tilted his head and looked intensely back at McKinley. His eyes twinkled; a single syllable guffaw broke loud and staccato— "Hah!" and he exhaled audibly.

They lifted their glasses and quaffed their whisky with celerity. McKinley immediately refilled them. The mood had changed; their bond of friendship was cemented. The moment had drawn them close. They drank in silence, pondered, breathed the new air. Time slowed down.

Suddenly a loud knock broke the spell. Elihu Root entered. He was clearly shaken. "Good morning, Mr. President. Good morning, John. Please excuse the intrusion but I have some additional news and it is not good. Two of the flying craft, the autogiros, still flying east, were seen landing near our fort at Dayton. Shots have been fired. It's causing quite a stir, as you might imagine. If they follow their present course, they could be heading for Washington."

McKinley's private secretary knocked and entered. He handed a teletype transcription from Governor Blaisdel of Nevada to the President, who perused it and then read it to Hays and Root.

Mr. President:

I have some astounding news which you will find difficult to believe, but which I assure you is completely true. You may be in great danger. There is a base in my state which houses a large number of flying craft, perhaps 100 or more, which are so technically advanced as to overwhelm the rational mind; I would not have believed it myself had I not seen it with my own eyes. There are war machines in that place of such terrible destructive force that no force on earth could withstand them. I have received notification from their Commander, Brigadier General Thomas Mills, and I must tell you that they claim to be loyal Americans, and that I believe them. It would seem that a catastrophic accident to some unimaginably advanced device has landed them back in 1900 from 100 years in the future.

A renegade colonel, a villain named Cassidy, has murdered a number of men on the base and has stolen three of the craft, armaments and fuel, and kidnapped Nikola Tesla. All three of the craft they stole are formidable military machines, beyond anything I have ever imagined. One of the renegades, left behind, has recanted and has informed us of his plans, which include the possibility launching a surprise attack on the United States military and taking you, Mr. President, as a hostage. General Mills has assembled a force far greater than that of Colonel Cassidy and will be pursuing him with a number of those flying gunships, a fact which Colonel Cassidy, we fervently hope, is not aware of. The plan to intercept them near Dayton, Ohio.

Meanwhile, you must exercise all available precautions to protect yourself.

Our Governor has also informed the Ohio National Guard and was assured they are well armed. And confident they can deter the renegades. I pray he is right, but at least they will have the element of surprise.

I strongly advise that you remove yourself and your family to a save haven and allow your military to prepare a strong defense. Help should arrive within a day of the arrival of the renegades.

I must warn you, Mr. President, that however fantastical this may seem, it is quite real.

I remain, sir, as ever, your obedient servant,

JAMES BLAISDEL, Governor of Nevada

There was a pause as the men absorbed the full brunt of the news.

"We will convene a full meeting of the Cabinet at noon," announced McKinley gravely. "It is time to act."

Army Chief of Staff Donald Quarters was summoned urgently to the White House and briefed. He wired the commander of the Army post near Dayton in Montgomery County to assemble an artillery batallion and infantry, proceed to Springhorn, coordinate their strategy with the Ohio National Guard, and be ready to fight.

Chapter 22

The Invasion

Springhorn, Ohio   January 7, 1900   4 PM

In 1898, second year of the McKinley era, the shrill war cry, *Remember the Maine*, echoed in newsrooms, bars, in homes and on the street, throughout the country. America, everybody was sure, had been attacked without provocation by the warlike Spanish Navy, stationed at their Cuban base, whose people merely wanted independence from their Spanish masters. The Maine was sunk, hundreds of American lives were lost, and Spain was blamed. America was faced with a choice: either respond to this outrage or lose face and be condemned and ridiculed by all, especially our Pan American neighbors, as being the most spineless wusses on the planet.

America now had a new idol—the 38 year old hero of San Juan Hill, Colonel Teddy Roosevelt. Vice-President Hobart, a financier who envisioned a vast industrial empire in Hawaii and west, would never live to see this dream realized. He suffered a heart attack and died on November 21, 1899. Immediately upon Hobart's untimely death (the sixth veep to die in office) the public began to acclaim

186

Teddy Roosevelt as his replacement. Though he wasn't announced until June, 1900 as the Veep Designate, TR became a member of McKinley's inner circle only weeks after Vice President Hobart passed away.

McKinley, with the help of Teddy Roosevelt and his Rough Riderrs, had won the Spanish-American War, vastly expanding America's sphere of influence in the Caribbean and the Pacific, and had, in fact, officially designated Hawaii a Territory on July 7, 1898. But by the turn of the century, America's army was no longer a formidable force, and they were thinly spread out between the Caribbean and Cuba, and nearly halfway around the globe, Hawaii to the Philippines. Lt. Col. Cassidy was keenly aware of this fact, as his V-22 Osprey and the two AH-1 Super Cobras, loaded for bear, crossed the Ohio line, seeking the final fuel and weapons stash they would use before the attack on Washington.

But it was to be a short campaign. Informed by Washington, Army units and the Ohio National Guard were on high alert. Members of the Guard, following up on reports of flying machines landing near Dayton, had discovered the fuel and weapons in a snow covered wheat field next to the tiny town of Springhorn. Despite the fact that they had no radar, no missiles, no anti-aircraft, the 1900 ordnance was more modern, more accurate, and longer range, than Cassidy and his Marines had counted on, for all his military research.

The 1900 military were determined to fight, and, expecting Cassidy and his companions very soon, camouflaged what remained in the open, and hid their horses and their exploding shells, and their long range artillery including the Hotchkiss cannon, a formidable weapon even for 1900. It was accurate to 2,000 yards, and able fire their 40 mm. shells at 43 rounds per minute. The Army unit's commanding officer, an engineer, had already modified the cannons to fire high in the air at flying machines, though he was met with incredulity when he gave the order. Nearly 400 armed Federal and National Guard soldiers were laying low in nearby horse and cow barns and sheds. They were ready and anxious to engage the enemy.

Earlier in the day, Major Sizemore and his colleagues had come up with specific plans. The *pièce de résistance,* the B-2 Stealth bomber, was nearly ready. They calculated that it was could reach Spinghorn, Ohio in well under two hours if they flew near top speed. That would be hours before Cassidy and his cohorts could get there.

They decided to slow it down. Then it would carefully duplicate the route that had been mapped out and confirmed by Sergeant Russo, try to locate the three aircraft, and report whatever else was going on with the American military and possibly the state militia—the National Guard units—with highly detailed photographic records from the B-2's powerful cameras. They would hear from the General shortly and plans would then be discussed and solidified with all possible contingencies taken into account.

The B-2, after a thorough maintenance check of all systems, was finally able to take off at 9:15 AM from Groom Lake's white sand runways. It flew through the bubble and streaked eastward at Mach 0.6, just over 400 mph at their altitude.

Tesla, riding with Captain Panic, pretended to grow increasingly enthused over the plan to take over the White House. He cursed McKinley as an incompetent, Chief of Staff Donald Quarters as a drunkard and an egomaniac, and shared his hopes for a powerful position in the Cassidy administration, inventing a new Cabinet post as Secretary of Electric Power, even prophetically suggesting the brand new post of Secretary of Energy.

Lt. Col. Cassidy was waiting for them to catch up with him and then refuel at the eastern Illinois fuel site on the Indiana line. They met on the Osprey, studied the maps, and flew in unison towards Springhorn, Ohio at 12,000', the Osprey flying slowly, only a little above stall speed. As they crossed the Ohio line, Cassidy activated the Osprey's tiltrotor, converting the nacelles from airplane mode to helicopter mode.

A little before noon, the Army and National Guard could hear the insistent, penetrating beat of the choppers approaching from the west. The Super Cobras also came in high, and as the Osprey descended to their altitude, began their descent, in formation, towards the field in Springhorn, Ohio. The militia hid behind a low hill less than three miles from the field.

As Capt. Panic's Super Cobra approached the battlefield-to-be in Springhorn, Ohio, less than 1000 yards behind Cassidy, Tesla got the drop on him. "Turn around or you will be killed—either by the Army or by me. You haven't a chance! Everybody knows you're coming!"

"Then you'll die too," Panic fired back. "You can't fly this chopper."

Tesla fired a round a millimeter from Panic's nose through the window and laughed derisively. The noise was shocking and deafening. "I can fly it!" The air whistled tremulously through the bullet hole as they flew.

Panic complied and headed away from the Dayton field, but he was still visible to the militia, who began firing their long rifles and the Hotchkiss cannon.

The rifle bullets whined past the chopper, several missed, and they were nearly out of range. The Hotchkiss cannon then fired several of their 40 millimeter cannon shot in fairly rapid succession at Captain Rynning, now only 500' from the other Super Cobra. Rynning's was hit but not damaged, but he guessed that formidable forces were ranged against them, so he immediately changed course and headed back for the fuel site he had just left.

Panic's chopper was not so lucky as three of the shots found their mark: one struck below the lag hinge—the vertical hinge pin on one of the blades in the rear. Another struck the blade grip attaching the blade to the hub, and the third the outside of the left fuel tank, where it lodged. JP5 fuel began leaking. Panic, relieved to escape the line of fire *and* to distance himself from Capt. Rynning, could not freely maneuver the chopper. Though it held its altitude—at about 1000'—it pulled slightly to the right, a problem he could not correct. He could only fly forward in wide clockwise circles to make any progress, so he tried to fly west. Quickly grasping the technique, he flew in 10 mile successive spirals west-northwest towards central Indiana until Tesla ordered him to land, still holding the gun at his head. Fuel was running very low. "The fuel tank is empty." Panic warned. "We have no nitrogen and it's an explosive mixture! We've got two 100 gallon bladder tanks; we'd better land and get them out in case the fuel tank ignites."

As if it had been choreographed, they began to smell smoke.

"Here!" exclaimed Tesla. "That looks like a good place. Land in that field." Panic nodded, descended rapidly and began hovering over a campground in Chesterfield, Indiana, a few miles northeast of Indianapolis, looking for a place to land. It was cold and there was an inch of powdery snow on the ground. But people were everywhere. It was, in fact, Camp Chesterfield, which was holding the annual nationwide Psychic Fair, a week long meeting of Spiritualists, theosophists, astrologers, psychics and mediums, and even some Quakers who were devotees of their clairvoyant founder, George Fox.

Seeing the hovering chopper and hearing the powerful beat of the blades, they were flabbergasted, amazed, elated, fearful and ecstatic, all at the same time. Tesla grabbed the PA microphone and announced loudly to the group to clear a space so they could land. They scattered in all directions like frightened sheep. It was just in time, as the chopper ran out of fuel at just eight feet of the ground, and stirring up a huge cloud of snow and dust.

They landed noisily and hard. "Stand back!" shouted Tesla. The rotors, like a ceiling fan, were slowing to a stop. They could still smell smoke. "We're here," shouted Tesla to Panic in Serbian over the noise. "Let's get the hell out of here! No time to remove the bladder tanks!"

Tesla grabbed the microphone an shouted. "Get back! Get back! It's not safe!" As everyone backed away, Panic and Tesla jumped out of the chopper and ran to a safe distance. Tesla had left his gun on the seat in the chopper.

For the crowd of Spiritualists and turn-of-the-century new-agers, fear was trumped by enthusiasm and excitement and they were mobbed. Everybody was jumping up and down, cheering and whistling. In spite of himself, Captain Peter Panic was caught up in the flood of emotions from the crowd. He was already relieved that he would now survive this expedition, and not be going to war with the United States and the State of Ohio.

They spoke in Serbian. "It's over," said Tesla matter-of-factly. "The General knows your route, your fuel dumps, and is now on his way. President McKinley has been informed and both the Army and the National Guard are on full alert, and are waiting for Cassidy's V-22 and yours and Captain Rynning's Super Cobras. Before we took off, while you thought I was sleeping, I was sending out messages informing Col Pick of the entire plan."

"What about Col. Cassidy, Captain Rynning and Lt. Moore? They are walking, that is flying, into a trap."

"They are in deadly danger," agreed Tesla. "But they have chosen that path, as you did. You are fortunate. They may already have been killed. Do not forget that this is my time, and I know that the military has become inactive, sleepy and bloated during the last two years after our string of global victories. These events have changed that overnight. A sleeping giant has been awakened! And they are more advanced than you think!"

"What is to be done with me then, Professor?" Panic said humbly.

"I am not sure. But let us not speculate on that now; we are very welcome here. You are intelligent enough to know you cannot escape, so this time you are *my* prisoner." Panic, resigned to his fate, keenly felt the irony.

"They will try to capture them alive, provided the 1900 military has not already killed or captured them."

"They might be better off dead!" lamented Capt. Panic.

Many of the guests at Camp Chesterfield recognized Tesla and thought this was his latest invention. As Capt. Panic watched, they picked Tesla up and carried him on their shoulders into the camp's central building, which was also the dining room. Capt. Panic followed along meekly, also surrounded by admirers, who peppered him with one question after another. He accepted it all because he knew there could be no escape.

There were dozens of small cabins on the campground. "We can put you up in our Presidential cabin!" said 22 year old Edgar Cayce, one of their most gifted psychics. "We are blessed and we are honored, Mr. Tesla. Welcome!"

They heard a great roar from above, getting louder by the second. Everybody looked west, but only Captain Panic knew what it was. "Oh shit," he murmured to himself. It was the B-2 bomber flying at under 5,000'. The rest, including Tesla, were shocked and amazed.

Captain Panic stopped, faced the crowd and raised both arms high. "It's all right," he shouted. "It's from the future and it is a great warship. We call it B-2!"

"*The future!*" the crowd echoed audibly.

Tesla hadn't seen the B-2, but he quickly figured out why it was there, and knew where it was heading. In seconds the B-2 was out of sight.

Edgar Cayce fell on his knees, bowed his head and folded his hands. "It is a blessing beyond imagination, beyond imagination! Pray to your God, our God, whatever name you have given him, that we may receive this blessing in its full measure, and that B-2 will complete his divine mission." Cayce walked to the softball field behind the cabins, a quarter mile from where the chopper had landed. Everyone followed Cayce's lead. "Here is where we pray—and celebrate the gift of spirit!

Suddenly there was a loud explosion and a huge fireball. It was the end of the Super Cobra, its fuel tanks and its weapons. Everybody watched in amazement as the craft burned furiously and debris, blown sky high, fell and clattered to the ground. The last to hit the ground was a severed chopper blade, which spun crazily downward and fell near the softball field.

Earlier on, Lt. Col. Cassidy, flying at under 1,000' selected the fallow, snowy farmer's field in Springhorn, switched the Osprey to vertical flight, and began circling the site for landing. He located the spot and began to descend. Alarms went off, detecting approaching aircraft. *Where the hell are the Super Cobras?!* He looked at the clock and a fearful adrenaline rush nearly overcame him. *Did they send the other Osprey?* The detectors read out: B-2 bomber . . . *Oh shit! I'm dead!*. He rose and flew toward a small, heavily wooded hill to the south. As he flew over it at 400', his co-pilot, Lt. Tabatha Moore he saw the footprint of the B-2 on the screen. It was headed straight at him.

"It's the B-2 from the base," she screamed. "Let's get the hell out of here."

They flew over a small, thickly wooded hill to a cornfield. He selected a flat spot to land near a barn as the B-2, flying low, buzzed him at 350 knots, missing by less than 300'. Their radios were silent. He tried to accelerate the landing, but in seconds the wingtip vortices in the wake of the B-2 enveloped the Osprey, now at nearly 100'. Miraculously, he was able to crash land the Osprey without seriously damaging the craft or badly injuring himself beyond a sprained leg.

He leapt out of the plane and walked-ran limping and hopping to the nearby barn, hands on his sidearm. Suddenly he was surrounded by a platoon of Ohio National Guard troops on the highest alert, who had hidden in the barn awaiting the arrival of the invasion force. They were only yards away, their powerful 30-40 Krag rifles pointed straight at his head.

"Drop your firearms!" commanded the Lieutenant in charge of the platoon. They had watched the B-2 fly over and were now in a near panic. "We know who you are! We know what you're doing!"

Lt. Moore turned around defiantly, handgun still in her right hand. In a fraction of a second, eight rounds crashed through her head and body; she was dead before she hit the ground. Cassidy, dropping his sidearm on the ground, did not move fast enough. Two rounds passed through his chest and abdomen. He fell to the ground in agony, twitching, screaming, but still alive. He knew he was mortally wounded if his only chance was 19th century medicine. Darkness descended upon him, and his final conscious desire as he fell into coma was to be returned to base.

The B-2 climbed to 1,500' swung back west for another pass. powerful surveillance cameras telescoping to a virtual distance of under 10' or less from the scene, playing live on the 12" screen in the cockpit. They saw the assembled troops and artillery, then Lt.Tabatha Moore's riddled body and saw Cassidy on the ground wounded and lying still, not knowing if he was alive or dead. As they banked into a climbing turn to the southwest, they saw a flash from one of the cannon. Seconds later, to their amazement, a 40 millimeter cannon shell moving close to *Mach 2* grazed the tip of the left wing, throwing the navigation slightly off. Two more cannon flashes were observed but by this time they were well out of range.

The now returning B-2, spotting Lt. Rynning's Super Cobra in western Illinois, dropped to a low altitude and buzzed it. It landed immediately. Now they had to account for Captain Panic's Super Cobra, and they correctly surmised that Tesla was with him. They circled twice, attempting to guess its last trajectory, but didn't find it.

Their task complete, they headed back across the United States of America toward home base at 35,000'. In less than three hours, the B-2 Spirit had landed at Area 51, its emergency mission fully accomplished, having flown nearly 5,000 miles, with fuel to spare. The General was there to greet and congratulate them.

The other Osprey on the base was loaded with spare fuel, tanks of nitrogen to fill the ullage in the fuel tanks with inert gas, as well as a lot of spare parts, in case the first Osprey needed repairs and could actually be flown back.

Osprey number two was to be deployed about an hour earlier than the B-2—at 4:30 AM, carrying two enlisted Marines, the base's top aviation mechanic and the one Navy Seal stationed at Area 51. Fuel deposited at the sites by Cassidy and his co-conspirators would come in handy, but they would be returning two Ospreys and two Super Cobras all the way to Nevada, so fuel—JP5 and JP8—would be at a premium. And if the first Osprey couldn't be flown, they would blow it up.

But knowing the second Osprey would likely encounter hostile forces in Ohio, the General and his staff agreed to postpone its departure indefinitely. He drove onto the runway, got out and boarded the Osprey, carrying the filmed record of the B-2's joiurney. The crew were surprised and delighted.

"Gentlemen, this is almost over, and time is on our side. The Army and National Guard in Ohio have already confronted and possibly killed Col. Cassidy and Lt. Moore, and fired artillery rounds at the B-2. They're a tough, determined lot, and I don't intend to challenge them while they still think we're the enemy. President McKinley has already been informed, so we'd better wait until the news gets to Ohio that we're their friends. Lt.

Moore is definitely dead; Col. Cassidy may still be alive. Then there's Captain Rynning's Super Cobra in Illinois, and the other Super Cobra that disappeared. Captain Panic flew and Tesla was either his passenger or his prisoner. We have to find them, but we believe they can take care of themselves until we do. They will be concerned about survival now, not carrying out Col. Cassidy's insane plot!" He stopped and took a deep breath.

"Like a drink, General?" asked the pilot, a personal friend of General Mills. "That was a long speech!"

The General nodded and smiled. "Maybe that's a little premature, but we've won a major victory. So no champagne yet. OK!"

The civilian mechanic, Don Guidry, a Cajun from south Louisiana, opened the cooler, filled a tall glass with ice cubes, produced a bottle of single malt scotch, opened and held the bottle over the glass. The General nodded, and he poured first an inch, then two inches of whisky. "General, this is for you. Nobody deserves it better! We've got a little work to do, so we'll postpone our celebration!" He passed out plastic cups to the rest of the crew and filled them with Pepsi.

The General nodded and smiled, took the glass and raised it. "Men, I consider it an honor!" He drank, sloshed the whisky in his mouth and swallowed. "I hate to admit it, but I actually think I needed that drink!" The crew smiled, downed their Pepsi, and relaxed. Each one got up and shook the General's hand.

Day had dawned and the day wore on as the B-2 left and returned. The had decided to take the Osprey after all because there was another rated pilot on the base who could fly it—a civilian—Ian Barnes, who was a dead ringer for Harrison Ford. Barnes, in fact, liked the Osprey far better than Major Crosby, who had flown the B-2 instead.

The men in the Osprey relaxed, napped, ate their dinner and continued to study the photos. In late afternoon, the General called.

"Mr. Barnes, it's time. We have confirmation that President McKinley now knows the whole story. The U.S. Army and the Ohio militia are standing down. Tesla, Capt. Panic and the chopper are in Indiana, near Indianapolis. Captain Panic is repentant and is Tesla's willing prisoner. And Lt. Col Cassidy is dead, may God rest his soul."

There was a moment of silence, then Barnes replied. "We are well rested and ready, General. We've studied the B-2 photos in detail all morning."

"Good luck and Godspeed!" The General signed off and the Osprey executed its magnificent vertical takeoff as the entire base watched and cheered.

"*We're gonna need it,*" Barnes sang to Guidry, with a swashbuckling grin. "Let's hope this piece of shit holds together!"

Chapter 23

Seeds of Time

Area 51, Nevada   January 8, 1900   5 AM

It was their first night of deep repose and intense sleep since the event. Ludmila Ivanova and Sandor Rakoczy awoke in their spacious quarters refreshed in body and lucid in mind. As Sandor arose from the water bed, Ludmila put her hand around his neck and slowly drew him to her, kissing him softly and long.

"Something's happening in my body, Sandor," she whispered. "Something lovely, something different I've never felt before."

Sandor relaxed and climbed fully back in the bed. He pressed her soft, body gently to his lanky frame, enveloping her, kissing her gently on her full, moist lips. "You are so lovely, Ludmila," he breathed. "You are the very essence of womanhood." He drew her to him more tightly.

She kissed back. "Wait, Sandor. Whatever is happening, it is not quite there. It is unfolding in its own time. Let us wait to make the moment perfect!"

Rakoczy nodded and smiled. "Yes, love. It's time. Don't forget you're 100 years younger!" As he was climbing out of the bed, Ludmila suddenly took a deep audible breath.

"Sandor! I must visit Nommo. Now. He is calling me."

They both dressed quickly and climbed into the high powered, magenta colored electric golf cart that was their transportation around the base. They arrived at the compound and descended, Rakoczy to Level 18, Ludmila to 21. News arrived that Ian Barnes' Osprey had just returned with Tesla and Captain Panic. Panic was taken to the brig; Tesla joined the others, recounting his adventures in Indiana.

"We're going to have to divert events on to a different course," Rakoczy told the General. "Timing is crucial. Not only the time of departure from here, but the time of arrival." They began adjusting, programming the Dybbuk. "The fried insect that returned in the carrier is emitting much radioactivity."

They began to analyze it. It was the same kind of radioactivity that was emitted by the organic object—the carbon based bit of plant life that they had sent forward a day farther into the future. When that object had returned, the bubble had contracted just a little—they could tell because it was more intense, and began registering higher on their instruments. When the insect was brought back a day *closer* to their departure time of 1-1-2000, the Bubble altered again, moving slightly farther out to its original position, only a few hundred feet from the five mile radius. But they had constant instrumentation on it now. They began to ponder the consequences. Then something clicked in Rakoczy's brain. He turned to Gerhard.

"If the bubble contracts when we send an object a little before the departure point, what do think will happen if we sent it a little ahead of it?"

"Are you thinking what I'm thinking? A control experiment. Calibrate the variables as closely as you can; make your calculations with the greatest possible precision. Make sure it's as close to the exact mass as possible, and exactly as far ahead as the last one was behind."

They decided to send an object into the future which was only a few hours *before* midnight 1-1-2000. They calibrated the small payload to arrive at that exact moment—noon on 12-31-1999, then launched another organic parcel with identical mass to arrive a day earlier.

The results seemed promising. Sure enough, the bubble returned to its original position. It was as if the moment of departure represented a crucial point in the continuum, and that the Bubble's expanse could be precisely calibrated by relating both time and mass proportionately to that exact moment.

This excited all of the scientists. Hope rose and morale along with it. Rakoczy, diGiovanni and Rose all began theorizing on what could have caused it, but they realized they had to put that off until later because they needed to get back in one piece.

Suddenly the room lit up. A palpable wave surged through the room, through the bodies. Everyone shouted or moaned. In an instant it was gone. All eyes moved to the monitors focused on the bubble, glowing bright greenish white, like the inside of a giant eye that was just lit up. The bubble continued to brighten

The skin of the bubble monitored from outside glowed and softened. It was whiter, like freshly fallen snow. Everything in the laboratory began to glow, seemingly from within. Everybody braced themselves for whatever was to follow. In seconds it was over. Everything appeared to return to normal.

"Oh shit!" exclaimned diGiovanni. "I'm afraid it's beginning. It's changing. Something's happening." He sat down at the Cray terminal; his fingers flew." Rakoczy watched over his shoulder. The east door opened and Dr. Ludmila walked in.

"Gentlemen, rest your sphinxes. Nommo has caused this; he is preparing us for our journey back. He has also told me that

Professor Tesla must go first; his is a new energy that has never entered the time stream. The Dybbuk is aware of him; it knows. It may help all of you to know that Nommo has been an inseparable part of all these manifestations, like the bubble, all along."

Robert Rose was not consoled. "I hope to Jesus you're right! But this scares the living shit out of me!" He turned to Rakoczy and diGiovanni. "Can you make it go away, kill the reversion," he whined. "I'd rather live here than die there. We're still in the Now, whatever number the calendar shows—our future is still our future whatever year it seems to be, whatever direction it travels in. I'm still me and I presume you're still you, singular and plural. Plus, we have certain advantages—technological—that nobody else has. How about us getting outside the bubble and letting it collapse on its own. You know, take all the computers we can, take the specs, everything that's not nailed down. We've already seen people outside of the bubble, talked with them, interacted with them."

"Don't know," mused diGiovanni, who was partially captivated by that solution. "We might be part of the bubble; we might be taking the bubble with us."

"Not an encouraging speculation. Here we could be executives, sages, kings, gods, full professors! Still scares me out of my mind. The idea of being entombed in a bulkhead, or a rock, or waking up just in time to die a horrible death. I still get nightmares about what happened to some of those poor devils in the Philadelphia Experiment."

"I get your point, Robbie. Do what you must. You can jump ship if you want to," said diGiovanni. "*Unless* we find out that there's some kind of critical mass where the entire life-mass has to revert at once. And there's one thing certain about bubbles. They have to burst."

Rose frowned, then nodded. "OK," he said. "Let's find out. How do you propose to do it?"

"I've got some ideas," observed diGiovanni. He turned to Rakoczy. "Sandy, *are we part of the bubble?*"

"Yes indeed, I believe its some kind of singular phenomenon, though not a singularity as we usually think of it. But yes, more of a probability than a possibility that indeed there might be a critical *organic* mass—like all for one and one for all, I don't know! But remember that the DYBBUK is the dilating isotropic *biophase* converter. It's hair trigger sensitive to energy variations within biomasses; it was invented taking carbon based life forms into account; part of its magic is sending bio-phases into the future through those virtual 4-D crystals—the tesseracts. Imagine an individual being able to focus the energy of his entire collective, making it take any shape and direction it willed it to. That's the ultimate Independent Variable. You know, we've suspected all along that Conch is doing this—for reasons of his own"

"I hate not knowing," lamented diGiovanni, "and I hate that word. Robby may be right. But it doesn't feel right. I somehow think we won't be in the same body, or we're not in it now. Our best bet is to control the reversion. Maybe a few people can opt to leave; nothing happened while we were scrambling F-16's and choppers. We've had up to twelve people away at one time, and the bubble didn't move. And what universe are we ending up in? The next one over?"

By now, from the evidence of the organic matter and lifeforms that were sent forward and retrieved, it had become clear that at anytime from New Year's morning 2000 on, the area within the bunker had been flooded with destructive radioactivity, and they could only conclude that it had been nuked.

"The species is insane," Ludmila would repeat in her more cynical moments. "Who could blame our great Mother—Gaia— for wishing to survive and taking steps like removing the ozone layer, *killing off the human cancer with radiation treatment!*"

Now, down to business. Realizing that time was growing dangerously short, Rakoczy reviewed the events of 1900. *The Cassidy invasion was averted. Cassidy is dead, as are all but one of his co-conspirators. Will his death be cancelled if all reverts to 2000? That is something to ponder. Will another present seamlessly form around the road not taken until now, a time in which Cassidy would never have existed. A time in which the hard lessons will have to be learned all over again.* He fervently hoped not.

They realized they were on a different track now. Somehow, they also realized that they were all the same people, and they wouldn't return to find replicas of themselves in some parallel universe. They knew that had to avert this catastrophe, *save the world.*

Rakoczy returned to his lab and told Ludmila he would be there all night with Mikhail and Gerhard. Tesla was with them. They were close, very close to the solution now. There was nothing she could do tonight.

Tesla left early and encounted Ludmila as she was getting off the elevator on Level 18. The connection was instantaneous. They slipped back into the elevator before the door could close and pressed 21. They fell into an embrace and kissed each other hungrily as the car descended. Her nipples, totally erect, protruded from her blouse. They fell to their knees as Tesla buried his head in her ample breasts, seeking and finding. She pressed his head tightly; he could scarcely breathe.

When the elevator door opened on 21, they danced, kissed and wrestled each other over to the empty apartment across from the pool. Two steps beyond the front door he took her into his arms. Her body arched toward him in response; her breathing was audible; she squeezed his flesh hard as she straddled his leg and pushed hard. He could feel the bone. The kiss unbroken, he grasped her buttocks and drew her to him. They sank to the floor on the carpet as he touched her vagina; she was very, very wet. Tesla's penis was marble hard, and, lifting her skirt and moving her loose panties aside, he eased himself inside her and then gradually plunged to the hilt. She hooked her feet around his legs and pushed up hard, moaning louder with each breath, timed with each stroke, then rhythmically pushing down hard as if to force it out.

"Fuck me, fuck me hard!" she blurted, over and over. She was good. Within a minute she had found the steely ridge at the root of his penis and straddled it with her clitoris at the full penetration of each stroke, skillfully, rhythmically. As the first of three climaxes overwhelmed her she drew her legs up to envelop him further, to draw his entire body into her. "Yes, yes" she screamed as the fire coursed through her innards, down her legs, squeezing Tesla's flesh until it hurt, though it actually helped, because he was striving mightily to hold back. He now knew she could climax again and again—and again. At her third, he finally let the passion overwhelm him, his spasms shooting, filling her to overbrimming with his semen. Ludmila took a final deep, audible breath and let herself go limp. She looked deeply and lovingly into his eyes, exhaled and smiled. Tesla was still rock hard. They lay there, nailed, taking longer and longer breaths, relaxing.

"I knew it would be like this!" she exhaled, touching him playfully; he laughed gently.

Chapter 24

Into the Maelstrom

Ludmila Ivanova walked as if floating on air to Conch's compound on Level 21, semen dripping from her, still full of his presence, his live seed radiating surprisingly powerful energies throughout her virtual body. She more than glowed. She also knew that she was ovulating. Tesla lay sprawled on his bed in passionate exhaustion, in total euphoria.

Tesla's time-binding live seed was expanding her sensibilities so vastly so that she could now receive Conch's pictures, his impressions, directly without physical contact, ever easier to translate them into precise language. Ludmila knew it, now understood why this liaison had to take place. The pictures now translated themselves into words, into formulae. She was able to transmit the data with great accuracy both to Rakoczy and to diGiovanni.

Conch, for reasons that were now becoming fully clear, brought about the entire incident. Now she received a shocking image. Conch the Nommo was to be sent a certain number of days ahead—beyond the holocaust date—presumably into the very heart of the destruction. He stated the exact time—the images flashed in her mind. But how was he to survive this? She agonized deeply, for she deeply loved him, perhaps more than she loved herself.

In order to return, they now had to duplicate the collapsing field in some way without causing destruction. That meant taking another precise laser measurement of the radius of the field to confirm that it had remained constant. It turned out to be a highly coherent multiple of an irrational number: $4\prod^4$ – four *pi* to the fourth power, or 24,936.7 feet, about 7,600 meters. Everybody knew that if the pulse were calibrated at the precise radius, they would arrive at the time they left. They also knew that someone, one or all, would have to arrive a little early to attempt to change the disastrous events that were set to occur, and avert a world war. The question was, how early, and what conditions might change if they didn't quite complete the reversion. Plus the fact that they were moving towards the 2000 present on a different tangent—an alternate time vector, probable but still shrouded in theory and speculation. This also implied that the backward-forward time axis wasn't merely a one-dimensional line but *at least* a three dimensional cylinder, like a cosmic tube with a virtual diameter of more than nine miles. In fact, the cylinder's locus in spacetime was the luminous star trail that wound back to the exact spatio-temporal address approaching the first moments of 1900.

Ludmila, in a virtual trance, played and recorded Nommo's precise tones on her viola—fretless and able to convey them nearly to perfection; areas of her brain had effortlessly and seamlessly evolved, or rather, *eased*, into perfect consonance. But one vital key seeemed to be missing. Rakoczy could partially understand it but his intense musical training as a violinist and highly sensitive ear helped him to bridge the gap. And there was no room for error.

One imperative was clear. Tesla's role was crucial, and he would have to travel forward.

Crisis! Time was running out. Many on the base were thinking seriously about jumping ship, staking their claim to existence right there in 1900, in the Old West, like old Doc Brown. "Access every brain cell in the compound," Rakoczy and the General had agreed.

The Airbus passengers were now being gathered up and prepared for the time jump. Rakoczy, Gerhard and diGiovanni questioned each of them in detail. The educated ones were too literal minded. Dolly Klein showed an aptitude but was constantly translating them into Yiddish and adding punch lines. Marta was too conventionally Catholic and kept translating the images into the Virgin of Guadalupe, popular saints, Jesus and the Pope. They thought of the Mariachis, who were more than happy to perform, hoping to cheer everybody up. During their first number, Puplampu and Conch appeared. The mariachis were tapped for command performances on Level 21.

Still no tangible results.

They were finally down to the Rastaferian Ian Marley, who still insisted that his 'tobacco' be returned to him, that it helped him to think. General Mills and Colonel Pick relented after much argument, but finally with good humor, did so. As he lit up the pungent sweetness of Jamaican weed pervaded the room. Jesse Maxwell and Vanessa entered; Jesse loved the smell and inhaled deeply. His abstract thinking was stimulated and he amazed the scientists with the ease of his mastery of both abstract mathematical symbols and subtle concepts. He speculated on parallel universes and especially on return vectors, which was both impressive and reaffirmed some of the theories that the scientists and techs were coming up with.

"Definitely the scion of James Clerk Maxwell!" Gerhard exclaimed. Rakoczy and diGiovanni nodded in agreement.

Most of the younger scientists and techies found all of this both promising and humorous, but Conch was indicating clear approval, so they began taking it very seriously. Ian Marley joined Conch, Lantos and Puplampu and began working closely with Dr. Ludmila. It was nearly midnight.

At the 7 AM meeting on January 9, there was a surprise. Smiling broadly, Dr. Narayan Singh and his nurse appeared in the doorway pushing two wheelchairs, one containing his much revived patient, Kitty Schrödinger, followed by Reverend Luna, who had miraculously survived the gunshot wound. Kitty had been having vivid dreams, and upon awakening, had seen Conch at her bedside, through Dr. Singh had not seen him, and thought she had become delerious and was hallucinating. Then she had gone into trance, and had begun speaking to Dr. Singh first in his native Punjabi, then in ancient Sanskrit. Simple things. Her entire lexicon was recognizable to Dr. Singh as coming from the Mahabharata, especially the Bhavagad Gita, which he knew well.

Highly energized, Kitty threw off her blanket, got out of the wheelchair and smiled, and bowed to the assembled scientists and military men. They applauded.

Tesla spoke in his heavy Slavic accent. "We have neglected certain realities. We do not have the all information we need."

Rakoczy shook his head slowly. "Yes. We are flying blind; we are hunting a black dog in the night. If I were religious, I would pray! Sure you want to come back with us?" Rakoczy interrupted. "Could be risky!"

DiGiovanni chimed in. "That's putting it mildly!"

"All of you except myself carry a huge negative potential that has to be neutralized," Tesla warned.

"We have an ally from another world, a powerful being. Can he not help?" diGiovanni replied.

208

Rakoczy spoke up. "Ludmila knows how to communicate with him, we'd like to return a few days early to try in every way to avert the computer malfunction, the electrical disaster that brought this about in the first place."

"That's where I come in! I was born to tame and harness electricity," Tesla smiled. "I think I have what you call bragging rights!"

Rakoczy nodded and half-smiled. "I suppose pessimism now is a waste of energy since we're going anyway."

"If you all die, I will die, too. You are correct, Sandor," said Tesla. "I must be the first to venture forward to your present. I am a new traveler, not a returning one as all of you are; my full life force carries the positive potential. You carry the negative potential; half of your life force is suspended in the time stream you forded, the time womb from which you emerged here. If they are not balanced each of you will return a stillbirth."

"But what if we are in a parallel world—what if the vector we traveled back on deposited us in an alternate 1900?"

"I have thought of that. But I think the vector you traveled on has a homing instinct." Tesla replied. "It has already blazed a new trail through forbidding obstacles; that trail is now the path of least resistance."

"Yes!" quipped the General. "You mean, *run home to mama.*"

Tesla laughed aloud. "I love your English language! It's like clay; you can mold meaning into any shape. It follows your intent!"

He paused and took a deep breath. "It is nearly time; we will resume when we arrive."

Ludmila and Tesla walked back into the room to where Rakoczy was sitting. She stood between them, enfolding them both in her arms. "This is group hug!" she smiled. "We three, we are one. I am lucky woman; I share you both. In every way you can imagine! Nikola, you are part of us! You must return with us to our present and stay!"

Tesla winced. "Perhaps. But I will be returned just as you are returning! If I survive it in either direction. Still, I am part of you as you say; perhaps I will be needed—in some small way. I warn you that many will forget and then begin to disbelieve. Your brains are not wired for a real time journey; they are more efficiently wired for dreams. *Nommo has done something like this for me.* Is it rewiring my brain? I'm not sure. But if I travel to your domain, I must make certain none of this is forgotten. For me and for all of you."

Ludmila, eyebrows raised and an enigmatic grin on her face, began to speak, then stopped. Her lover, Sandor Rakoczy, was looking directly at her, mouth agape.

Ultimate sacrifice

Area 51, Level 21   January 8, 1900   4:40 PM

"It is time. I will go first, then Ludmila, then Nommo. Then the rest." said Tesla.

"Why Ludmila before the rest of us?" Rakoczy asked.

"She is a doctor," Tesla lied. "I need to survive for all of us— myself least of all. If I am hurt or damaged perhaps she will be there to save me."

Dr. Ludmila, still at the pool, walked over to Nommo and put her hand on his left shoulder, near his neck. She closed her eyes; they were obviously communing. Then she walked back to where Rakoczy and Tesla were standing.

"Yes," she said. "Nommo has confirmed it. Begin now to prepare your instruments. Nommo will give the signal." They walked up the stairs to Level 18.

"We will begin in one hour," she announced to all. "Prepare yourselves physically and psychologically."

The bubble was already doing odd things; strange blips emanated from it. It would disappear for an instant, blink out of existence, hold steady for seconds or minutes, then undergo a strange dimensional shift to 4D, like a sector of a hypersphere. The scientists were in a nightmarish panic. Rakoczy and diGiovanni wanted to do the reversion now. Robert Rose was a little calmer; he almost seemed fatalistic about it.

The alien, Conch spoke, rather, communicated through Dr. Ludmila. In shock and deep sadness she informed Rakoczy and the other scientists that Conch would be sent three days ahead to January 4, 2000, into the eye of a thermonuclear holocaust.

But not everyone derived optimism from the alien's seeming unconcern; a collective being wouldn't concern himself about the fate of individuals because it would make no difference whatsoever. Could such a being even conceive of a solitary human being's dire need to preserve himself? For such a being, it would not be an issue.

Nevertheless, Conch's and Puplampu's presence began to be felt ever more intensely as the preparations were finalized for the near 100 year time journey. Images played in the minds of all.

"Do you know when it will be completed, when we will be out of danger of a nuclear war?" the General asked Ludmila. "Has the alien told you what will happen? How, what order? When life will resume a normal pace?"

"We are in uncharted territory General. Arriving safely and resuming our existence there and then seems to be a reasonable certainty. Nommo is a benevolent being—and a powerful one. I believe we are protected. The instant in spacetime we supposedly vacated will seamlessly form around us. It will be as if we had never left. But I do not know what we will experience by returning early."

"We must assume that risk," said the General. "We are attempting to avert a world war. Even if the odds are low that we will succeed, low is preferable to nonexistent any time."

"Indeed," Rakoczy agreed.

"Perhaps we should only send one or two to the early date."

Ludmila closed her eyes. "No. The answer from Nommo is very clear. Everyone will return early."

"Can I presume we'll be returning one at a time?" he asked.

She closed her eyes again and said simply, "No General, we will not. And we will not be conscious during the return."

"How do you know this?"

"It is part of the certainty that Conch has filled my mind with. We are not even returning to our so-called present. I have no insights on what it will be like. Perhaps because *return* means returning to the precise point in spacetime that we left."

It was time for Tesla to travel forward to 1999, December 28. Ludmila led him to Nommo, who placed his right four fingered hand on his head. Electricity surged through him, electricity even Tesla had not known, theorized or experienced. Everybody shook hands from the scientists and techies, to the military men, to the Airbus passengers. Surprisingly, he placed his left on Ludmila's head. Power surged through her, orgasmic power but more bliss than pleasure, more rapture than bliss as it intensified through every cell of her body.

Tesla was led to the "hot seat." "Indicate when you are ready, Nikola. And the best of luck." Everybody in the room applauded and cheered. When the cheers died down, Tesla clung in a deathgrip to his waking consciousness. ***Nommo, the alien, stands behind the time machine. He is looking at me intently, and I think he is smiling, through it would be difficult to tell. His shaman,*** *the young Dogon, Puplampu, standing beside him, is smiling broadly. I am suddenly calm. And I am ready.*

He sat down. Ludmila kissed him on the forehead, her hand on his arm. He smiled and waved to the assembled scientists, then nodded. Unexpectedly, Rakoczy threw the switch at that moment.

They both disappeared.

WHOOOOOOSH

As he had promised himself, Tesla's consciousness held fast; it was a supreme act of will, every detail permanently etched upon his mind, the symbolism more intense, more real than so-called reality. He saw the connection, felt it, exulted in it, saw the order of things: reality flowed out of the symbols, and he knew his mind would record the entire journey down to the tiniest nuance.

I have entered a waking dream.

I am in the Bahnhof, the main railroad terminal in Berlin. It is eerily silent. The terminal is the present—my last known present, 1900. In a dynamic symmetry trailing off at the edges, gigantic clocks loom before me everywhere I look; there are nine levels joined by moving escalators splayed out crazily in all directions; four are underground; some appear to go nowhere. The clocks are alive; their concave faces swirl in and out of focus. They mock, they ignore, they glower, they stare; they are watching my every move.

The train tracks are time vectors; they run in what appear to be straight lines on four separate and distinct axes, not three. It is difficult to visualize, but each of the four axes is perpendicular to each of the others—identical except for their innate curvature.

Hundreds of trains arrive and depart, every one on its own track, every track a separate and distinct time vector. Some of the trains run backwards on Negative Axes One and Two.

*I am drawn to a vertical elevator train called Axis Negative Three;
I step into a cubical car with mirrored walls, floor and ceiling, and am
suddenly in free fall; I am weightless; my stomach is on the ceiling. In
a Doppler blur, downward acceleration, the walls of the cube begin to
inflate outward, expanding into a sphere; the mirrored walls are now
concave; I see myself reflected as in a funhouse mirror, and has gone
from a hypercube to a hypersphere, its maximum natural expansion.
This is clear 4-D viewing! It burgeons forth from my inner eye.*

*I now have the eye of Brahmin—a perfect sphere seeing in all
directions at once. The spherical boundaries of the universe contain
the Eye; the vault of heaven is the socket! I am an Eye. I am Zero, the
junction point of all.*

*Now strobe-like halos of sharp, brilliant light, travel from bottom
to top, flashing rhythmically through the car. They accelerate as the
elevator drops. There is connection; there is electricity. I wonder. Does
the current alternate?! It must. Other elevator trains are running
parallel to this one; I suddenly realize that I must sidestep into the next
one, and I do so effortlessly. Ludmila is there; she is not conscious, but
she glows; I step into her light and we suddenly become one; we are
fused; we throb as one. From her center a pinkish-mauve glow pulsates
ever brighter, oscillating, penetrating the walls of the car. Pulsing
through the universal gaze of the omnidirectional Eye of Brahmin in
brilliant haloes, the energy grows in strength and penetrating power
as it draws ever nearer to its goal, illuminating the soft boundaries
between the nearest neighboring parallel universes. It is a driving
human force; taking on a human cast, all is burgeoning with new life.
Like Kirlian symbols, every seed was seen in its full maturity.*

*We are at Level Zero. Axis Negative Three is now changing sign;
it is now Axis Three. As we bottom out, a fissure in brilliant white
light appears in the mirrored sphere, sundering into dazzling flashing
mirror images which revolve in contrary directions like a gyroscope.
They climb the walls of my car, a black flood of darkness in stunning
contrast at the border of the light, rising from below, threatening to
engulf all. Once again I am alone.*

*Then utter blackness, blackness beyond blackness. Dead silence—
an eerie silence unlike any I have ever known. For the briefest moment
all moorings are lost; utter uncertainty. Time has ceased; I am on the
verge of dissolution. Eternity in an hour. Hope of finding my way
back is fading fast.*

*Suddenly I am recaptured with a vengeance; I enter Axis Four;
it is a river of time with a furious current; sound has returned—ice
glissandos in accelerating tempo played by a mad xylophonist, rushing
wind like a hurricane, thunderclaps to rival the primal explosion of
creation. My astral sphincters are relaxed and the powerful shock
waves pass through me without terrifying me; there is no impulse to
defend the physical body that is not present—an unexpected gift! It is
as if I have passed an important test.*

*The current becomes a whirlpool around a tiny island; the water is
icy cold but exhilarating. I realize that the island is my cardinal self,
and that in this life I am an eddy, a paradigm of standing waves as
the endless stream of universal energy flows past the island. the I-land.
Those icy currents: I must understand them; I must learn to control
them, ride them, navigate in them, turn them, even reverse them! I
have never felt so intensely alive!*

*This partially awakens me in the dream; I am motionless at the
still point at the center, the eye, but I can now feel the whirlpool
spinning around a polar time axis. The sphere begins to contract into
a cube; now there are six curved sides.*

*In this vision I learn a new skill—how to slow time down at will,
how to focus on a scene and enter it, and how to find the subtly moving
boundaries within the space I am alloted. The car has now become a
tetrahedron. I can see into the surrounding space in 60° and 120°;
space is triangulated; there are no right angles. What a difference!. My
vision is tetra-scopic—and as the tetrahedron burgeons into a sphere,
the four sides encompass all space. I slow it to a leisurely pace, and
for a very long time I accustom myself to four spatial dimensions, one
dimension per panel, strangely interchangeable dimensions, no up, no*

215

down, no left, no right. My comprehension—my share of universal intelligence—unfolds to levels beyond my imagination.

Then my curiosity awakens, my obsessive need to know how and why. I try to focus on the source, the basis, the mechanics of the whirlpool, the river, the Bahnhof, the car, but the center cannot hold.

I see ahead and I see behind: the time vortex is open on both ends!

Suddenly the multiple images collapse and merge into one. I am fully awake, out of the dream vision. I have arrived. Somewhere. Somewhen. A single thought pervades my entire consciousness.

I am to save the world."

Everybody was holding their breath. Tesla's form faded in and out for several seconds, then he disappeared, not instantly but over a full minute, beginning with his feet. His face still moved; he glanced back at the audience, closing his eyes hard as he and Ludmila were engulfed in the vortex.

Gerhard shouted to Rakoczy and diGiovanni. "Look at the bubble!" They stared at the monitor. The bubble was skewed; it had expanded and taken on a mottled cast, and it was brightening and dimming in rapid succession. It looked unstable. Something was happening. All eyes were upon it; people were taking shallow breaths; their hearts were pounding. Some were praying. It looked like it would collapse, and then what?

Mikhail looked carefully at the image, then at his watch. "I am timing. Wibrations are slowing, but pace is not irregular, just slowing."

It was now Conch's turn. With large ties, Conch was fastened, hands and feet, to a x-cross of graphite/titanium alloy, while the Dybbuk, the time machine, was carefully calibrated to January 4, the counterpart to December 28. Puplampu gave the signal.

It's now or never!" shouted Rakoczy. "Remember Maxwell's demon!" Jesse Maxwell smiled knowingly, proudly. Everybody was intently focused. They braced themselves. He threw the switch.

For an instant, Conch's teal body became a glowing emerald, then he disappeared. The time currents, the river of time, suddenly opened into a vast collective ocean, opalescent, an immense singularity. Sound flashes vibrated everything and everybody, like a mini-earthquake originating in the core of every being.

Puplampu, frowning, raised his hand. Everyone knew to restrain their applause.

The collective consciousness of the travelers wavered; the flow of time seemed to stop; then it slowly resumed. Seconds were like minutes. Minutes were like hours. A wave of anxiety swept through the room; a universal frown and stare, as if the group were being controlled as one.

Suddenly a flicker from the Dybbuk; seconds later, another, stronger. A hush as everyone held their breath. The LED's on the time machine came back on, strongly and brightly, and Conch's image began to reappear, top of head first. There was a hush. He was charred, smoking, horribly disfigured, hunched over revealing huge gashes in his teal body. He must have been in excruciating pain. It was heart rending, heart stopping, a shared pathos, a horror. Eyes filled with tears; a deep sadness overcame all. It had failed.

But it wasn't quite a solid materialization; something else was happening. No heat could be detected; then the smoke, which gave out no odor, simply faded and his figure, which had not moved at all, became translucent, then disappeared again.

The sacrifice . . . .

All eyes were once again on the monitor showing the bubble There was a long pause, an absolute silence.

"Look!!" Gerhard and Mikhail shouted. The bubble was shrinking. Its normal green had shone forth once again. Within minutes, as everyone watched with bated breath, it had returned to normal.

It was time. Puplampu nodded to Rakoczy, who set the collapsing field around the time machine to the precise dimensions that would return them to December 28, 1999 and sat in the hot seat, the mathematical center. "Everybody inside the circle!" he commanded. Except for Puplampu, they were already there. He looked around at the gathering; hands were joined; everybody was looking intensely at him.

"It is time," he said simply, in a low voice. "Bon voyage to all of us!" He nodded to Puplampu, who threw the switch. They all glowed momentarily and quickly disappeared. The expanding and collapsing field in the DYBBUK was then set for the full return at midnight, December 31, and the interim return on December 28. Puplampu gave the signal and threw the switch.

Brief unconsciousness. The collective eyes opened and then shut tight as the blinding light pervaded the bunker, filled the bubble.

It was a sheet of sun.

PART TWO

Back to the Present

Chapter 25

The journey home

In immeasurable time the blinding light was gone as quickly as it had appeared. Now warm, moist, gentle darkness replaced it, softly engulfing every modicum of every consciousness—timeless darkness, the womb of time. A tunnel that was not a tunnel, a stitch in time, beyond the demon's lair.

A gentle glow, mild, dilated, seemingly aware and responsive appeared and grew from a small seed of light, filling the space and bridging the time gap: a sweet cone, a cream horn with a shimmering, rich photon filling coming out of each end.

Tesla, disoriented, arrived first. He did not know where he was. He staggered to the nearest doorway and saw the elevators—Level 18. He got on. Enough of his memory had returned that he knew he should go to Level 21. He got off, walked uncertainly to an open door across from the elevator, and saw a bed. He flopped on the bed and fell unconscious.

Dr. Ludmila was next. She opened her eyes and urgently looked about. Three were missing: Nommo and Puplampu and—

and . . . . She lost the train of thought. She immediately ran down the three flights of stairs to Level 21, and cautiously opened the door into the pool area. She received a huge shock. And she knew one thing with certainty. *This is not over.*

But there they were, the three of them, intact, as if nothing had happened. Puplampu smiled broadly; suddenly everything was all right. She saw Conch and Lantos surface and disappear on the other end of the huge pool. A wave of joy and relief flooded her mind, body and spirit.

It was soon replaced by a sober assessment of the situation and her duty. *I must concentrate; the world is in deadly danger. Difficult, nearly impossible tasks—I must perform. Nommo has bought us a little time. The world will not end in three days. But it will end.* These were deeply disturbing thoughts for the usually optimistic Ludmila. The thought reverberated; she tried to flush it from her mind. It was in a loop, like an irritating melody that doesn't go away. It brought forth clear thoughts, unambiguous, specific. *But it will end . . .*

Puplampu was there, unchanged from the present, his 120 year old self intact. He smiled and took Ludmila's hand and whispered softly to her. He had not traveled with the group but had taken the long way home, lived out the entire 100 years in a normal earth life He had miracuously returned to Mali with his Dogon tribe, joining Nommo at the pre-Area 51 base in 1948.

Ludmila felt much better. As if on cue, Lantos the dolphin and Conch the Nommo came up simultaneously from the deep water, and swum over to where she stood in amazement. The dolphin twittered in a high clicking glissando, up and back down, and Conch stood on the surface of the water, as if it were a solid platform. It was a moment of supreme joy and triumph for the four beings in the room.

Conch waved her over. She sat at the corner of the pool, her usual place, and placed his left hand-fin on her forehead. *The word, a place, an island. The words are so clear; this is unusual. Yes, in Russia. I have it. Novaya Zemlya—yes I know it, the atomic test range. A lone missile with an atomic warhead. In three days. In Russia, flying, over Russia, exploding over Russia.* Conch quickly withdrew back into the water *I must tell the General immediately. This is crucial.*

The rest arrived almost simultaneously. The team stood momentarily in the same circular formation as when they left, still holding hands. Now, for all, it was both familiar and strangely unfamiliar. Had they really arrived? Everyone in the room was re-awakening.

The General and his staff materialized. Robert Rose opened his eyes and looked around. There was the atomic clock, shining forth in readiness. He watched the second hand move for nearly a half minute as he reoriented himself. Then he saw the date. There was external power. There were working satellite signals; the GPS's worked. The lines to NORAD were intact, and there was TV.

"December 28, 1999!" he shouted. Intense energy filled the room; sighs of relief burgeoned into cheers. It was a long, blissful moment. People embraced. Waves of audible relief swept through the room, then more cheers. "We made it, we made it, we made it!"

"We're early," "Hopefully early enough. This is not over. We have work to do."

"It's Tuesday the 28th," Rakoczy said. "We know there will be a huge surge and collapsing field on Friday night at midnight the 31st. We're at the terminus of the entire multi-state system. We don't want to go back again. I've theorized that we will have changed the corridor as well—subtly or massively. All the variables fell into perfect order then; it's almost a certainty that they will not on Friday night. But we can definitely change an important event, that is, if the world we've arrived in three days early is real enough to disconnect a 750,000 volt power line. *That will prevent us being sucked into an endlessly repeating time loop!"*

"It still feels unreal," observed Mikhail. "Like I felt when I accidentally touched bubble—when I woke up, that is." Nods and grunts of assent emanated from the rest.

Rakoczy raised his head, speaking to to all his colleagues. "That's because we're not quite home yet, everybody!"

"Of course," observed Gerhard. "We are still traveling on the return vector. We've already learned that time vectors are not freeways with two way traffic any more than a triangle is like a cube Or are they? We got off on Exit 12/28. The road terminates at the last instant, first instant: exit 12/31, 1/1."

"Indeed!" confirmed Robert Rose. "We'd've never done it in the first place ; no offense intended Sandy, Al, Gerhard, but we just don't know enough. We're lucky to be home!"

"No offense taken," Rakoczy affirmed. "If we *are* home. But the fact is, Gerhard is right. We haven't truly arrived yet. Our vector is close to the departure point but still moving. Every hour of the next three days should intensify the reality we're feeling."

"I can't wait until fat lady sings!" Mikhail quipped.

"Well put," said Rakoczy. "Gerhard, you and one of your assistants please go up to Level One and look north towards Tikapoo Peak. The bubble is not on the monitor. We must know where it's still there, or if there's any residual. Bring some instrumentation. Do it immediately."

Gerhard and his assistant Hans Peek gathered up the detectors and headed for the elevators.

A few minutes later Gerhard called Rakoczy. "We still detect the bubble, although it is dark now and we can't see it."

"Thanks, Gerhard. I'm not happy about it but we needed to know. Get all the readings you can, activate the sensors if they're not active, and we will proceed accordingly. Don't forget, we're three days early, so in a way we've not fully returned. We will monitor the bubble and see if it phases out as we approach the witching hour on New Years' Eve! Physical events of that magnitude leave a signature on the time-space matrix, a residual."

"Incidently, Sandor, speaking of residuals, we have a guest from the past. In case you've forgotten, Mr. Nikola Tesla,"

"Where is he?! And don't call him a residual, Gerhard. How about, let's see, a *resident.*"

"Whatever! I don't know but if he is here I will find him."

"Right," said Rakoczy, deeply concerned. "Look for him in the guest quarters on Level 21. If he's not there, find him and take him there. If he's sleeping, don't disturb him. We all need some rest and we can continue tomorrow morning."

Ludmila returned to Level 18 and shared the news for the scientists, techies and their military colleagues including the General, Col. Pick and their aides. She took the General aside and whispered in his ear.

"Tom. I have just seen Conch. He is fine as I said. But he has given me some startling news, information that may be crucial and may change the course of events!"

The General nodded, then turned and addressed the group. "Go home and rest, all of you. You've earned it," he announced to the assembled time travelers. Everyone was strangly tired, sleepy, disoriented. Nobody was talking. They nodded to the General and left. Soon the labs were empty.

The General and Ludmila took the elevator up to his office.

"Sit down, Ludmila. I need to reorient myself and take a few deep breaths."

Wondering if the entire five mile radius of the base had been returned to 1999, his mind only registered absurdities and contradictions. *Were here. So it must have. But it won't be done for three days . . . . I must be exhausted. I can't get my head around it.* He sank into his desk chair as full realization of events, of past time, present time, his own time, and all the paradoxes, coursed through mind and body.

He nodded his head to Ludmila, who explained Conch's message in full detail: a Russian missile in Russia, to be launched from Novaya Zemlya on December 31. The doomsday machine, the *fail deadly* broadcast had not been disconnected. The world will be in deadly danger if that nuke is detonated, and Yeltsin will be powerless to stop it.

"I must call the Pentagon now" he exclaimed. "Excuse me, Ludmila. It is classified. Thank you, Ludmila."

Surprised to be dismissed, Ludmila prepared to leave. As she got up, the General extended his hand, an amused grin on his face. "Ludmila, you know everything anyway! This is security training that was beaten into my head at Colorado Springs!"

"Colorado Springs?"

"Air Force Academy! Class of '68."

They shook hands warmly and Ludmila left. She wanted to hug him.

The General picked up the red military phone. An aide, Lt. Col. West, answered. "This is Brigadier General Tom Mills at Nellis . . . . One of my operatives has brought me some intelligence on events in Eastern Russia . . . ." Immediately General Shelton's aide, Major General Goldfein came on the line. Without revealing the participation of Conch, General Mills related the details of Novaya Zemlya and the potential missile launch. Goldfein listened with great interest and sent an urgent memo to General Shelton, who convened an emergency meeting of the Joint Chiefs.

The General leaned back in his chair, closed his eyes and breathed deeply. He dozed momentarily, then realized he needed to sleep. He closed the blinds on the windows and stretched out on the plush black leather couch in his office, and fell into the deepest sleep of his life.

Chapter 26

The Time Being

When he opened his eyes, something had changed, something was different. Never a shirker, the General looked at the time. Eight o'clock! It's late! His attention then shifted to the papers on his desk and began rifling through them Atop the pile was a paper, and a name scribbled; Security—Lt. Col.—Carmody? Canady? Looks like—Cassidy? He immediately called Security. Major Wingard answered.

"Major Wingard, Security." He recognized the extension. "Good morning, General!"

"Good morning, Major. How are things going this morning?

"They appear to be going fine, General. I slept like a baby and just woke up a few minutes ago. Some odd things have been happening around here, like a power outage, some kind of electrical malfunctioning. Communications were down. I'm figuring it came from our mad scientists down on Level 18! Doesn't seem to present any danger, though. Pretty routine. By the way, what day is it, General?"

General Mills looked at his calendar clock. "Wednesday, December 29. Strange I had to look!" he laughed.

"Same feeling, General. I wonder if the Russians are flooding us with with mnemonic gas! It's December 29. Well, Y2K isn't due for two more days!"

"Maybe it's a senior moment," observed the General, concerned. "I'm going to make an inquiry. In our business, even temporary psychological states are grist for the mill. I think you'll find them interesting." He picked up a paper from his desk and examined it curiously. "Now wait. I found a note on my desk regarding Colonel. Uh, wait a minute, Lt. Col . . . . Carmody, Cassawary—sorry, I scribbled it and I can't read my own handwriting."

"Sounds vaguely familiar, General. As I said, I woke up in a strange state—after a very vivid dream—a compelling dream. But now I can't remember it."

"Indeed!" agreed General Mills. "I slept as if I'd been up for a week. I tried to remember, but I got very sleepy suddenly and I had to close my eyes for awhile.

"You know, you're right. It may be those boys down in the labs with their weird experiments. Bet that's what it is. It's like grasping at an elusive dream that's fading by he second."

"Wait, Major. There's something else; let me read it. Ah, *here it is*. Your promotion came through! Congratulations, Lt. Col. Wingard! It so happens I have your silver oak leaves right here on my desk!"

"Thank you, General. "I'm speechless! Karen will be delighted!"

"We'll have a little ceremony. It's about time: the Chief of Security should be at least a Lieutenant Colonel—or above! Unless you have other plans. We'll have a special honorary dinner for you and your family tomorrow night at the Officers Club."

"That's fantastic, General. It's a great honor."

The General glanced down at a paper on his desk. "Wait, Colonel Wingard. That name. There it is: *M. Cassidy, Lieutenant Colonel.*"

"Who?" asked Lieutenant Colonel Wingard. "Never heard of him."

"*In fact, neither have I,*" said the General.

Brigadier General Mills smiled with satisfaction at the small envelope containing Major, now Lieutenant Colonel Wingard's shiny new silver oak leaves. *He's a good man. Trustworthy. A good Marine.* He moved the package and noticed it was heavier than expected. Inside he found another sealed envelope. *More oak leaves?* He opened it. His jaw dropped. Inside were two sets of the two star insignia of a Major General. Quickly, he looked up the most recent orders. There it was! His promotion.

He immediately left the office and drove home. Smiling broadly, he told his wife. They embraced joyously.

It was now nearly noon. Tesla awakened, his mind clear. His memories were fully intact. He entered the pool area. His heart leapt: there was Ludmila. He hurried to her side to embrace her. Ludmila stepped back, surprised.

"Hello. Are you new? I don't believe we've met."

Tesla thought she was joking. "We returned together!"

Ludmila looked at him blankly, then smiled. "I don't know you sir, but I'm sure you belong. I'm Dr. Ivanova, and you may call me Ludmila. Please excuse me; I must tend to another patient." She left the pool area.

Puplampu walked over to him and took his hand. "Welcome back, Professor," he said with great warmth and a twinkle in his eye.

Tesla now began to understand. *Have they lost their memories?* He spoke urgently to Puplampu. "We returned three days early. There is a world crisis and it must be averted. Has everyone lost their memories?"

"Not I," Puplampu repied in his deeply harmonic bass voice, "not you, and not Nommo. One more there is, Gerhard. Knows you are here he does, and your living place he will arrange. With him in touch you must remain. Important tasks you must perform; that is why you are here. And keep Professor Rakoczy awake and aware we must; a paradox he senses, so try to forget he will. All others fell into deep sleep; memories they have not."

"Will I return to my own time?"

"Yes."

"When?"

"Returning you are now. But have need of you we do; we borrow, then return. In two of our days, in the womb of time, know this you will. During next two days, in both times you are living."

Tesla was silent.

Puplampu smiled inscrutably and took his hand. "With me you will come; from my companions a gift receive." They walked to the edge of the pool. Nommo rose above the water while still standing on it. Lantos, the speckled dolphin blew a geyser of water in the middle of the pool, submerged and came up next to Nommo. She clicked and gurgled and a musical voice, nearly human, emerged with words nearly comprehensible. Puplampu placed his long, dark bony hand on Tesla's right shoulder, Nommo placed his left four-appendaged hand-fin on Tesla's head.

"The most important work you have done; now listen you must, think you must, commune with all of us you must. Too easy it will seem, but for now, simply *be* you must, here in our time and space. Sleep for all the others, like a dream, their memories will carry away except Gerhard. When fully return you do, forget all you will as well, except for the lessons. To your companions some of these lessons you will owe; helped you they have! And helped *them* you have!"

Tesla was humbled. *What is it they want of me?* he began to ask himself, but Nommo's powerful and loving energies filled him with understanding.

"To bring balance you are here," answered Puplampu "Balance to this group it will bring; balance to their minds it will help to bring. Though know it in their minds they will no longer, feel it in their hearts and souls they will. Changed forever will they be. Faith shall you find once again, of a mustard seed, of your seed carried in the fertile soil, seed of your earth mother and your mother earth. Man of God your father was. From him you learned most important lessons—and in your heart still Christian you are.

"I am understanding," mumbled Tesla, almost in trance. "But I am tired. Seed carried in my earth mother Djuca, seed has touched my beloved Ludmila. I am understanding but I cannot find words. Same seed; seed of light binding time."

Puplampu smiled broadly; Nommo lifted his hand-fin from Tesla's head. "Enough it is. With us, in both worlds are you now. Nearly completed your task is."

It was a silent but powerful blessing.

He returned to his quarters and fell into a deep, dreamless sleep.

Area 51   December 30, 1999   5:30 PM

"Wake up, Professor!" Gerhard gently shook Tesla awake; Rakoczy was with him, his memory of past events still intact. They had brought food and drink, and when Tesla saw the food, he was hungry. They ate and Rakoczy and Gerhard reviewed the entire time journey. He had forgotten nothing.

"The General called us and informed us that he had notified Washington."

"Notified him of what?" Tesla asked. "Have I forgotten something?"

"No!" said Rakoczy. "This came from Nommo: a rogue Russian general is preparing to launch a missile from their old testing site—at Novaya Zemlya, and make so much noise with rockets and explosives around the base that the missile launch won't be positively detected. It looks like our government has informed Yeltsin in time; apparently they've detained a Colonel Kassidian and a rogue general, whose name we do not know. So the launch may have been aborted"

"Let us hope so," smiled Tesla. "It could start a war! But seriously, this could be good news."

"I want to go outside," Tesla told them "I need to breathe the fresh air. Would you like to go with me; we could take a walk."

Rakoczy frowned. "I'd like you to postpone that. We're getting strange energy readings and you could be at risk. We'd like you to stay put until the full reversion—midnight tomorrow night. And we are going to have a New Year's party and music. Al and I, Ludmila and the Nommo are a string quartet, and we're going to play Schubert."

Tesla was unhappy but he didn't show it. "Yes, I like Schubert," he said.

"By the way," Rakoczy added. "If you come up to Level 18, please take the stairs. You're in a different situation from the rest of us. In fact, let me know, and Gerhard or I will go with you. We'll monitor you with our detectors, just to see if you're being affected."

"Are the labs in operation now?" Tesla asked. "Isn't it a holiday?"

"No, they're not, and it should be safe. But after all this we don't want to take any chances. I will have Dr. Ludmila give you a physical examination tonight."

Tesla's eyes widened. "And run some tests if she feels it necessary. How do you feel?"

"Not well!" he exclaimed, almost too quickly.

"Welcome to our world, Professor!" Gerhard smiled. He knew about Tesla's and Ludmila's liaison, at least strongly suspected it. "Rest up. Things should return to normal soon, normal for here at least, whatever that means!"

"Get some rest," said Rakoczy. "By the way, here's a portable telephone if you need to call me or Gerhard. I've set it: press '5' for me and '6' for Gerhard."

"What about Dr. Ludmila?" he asked, singlemindedly.

"We'll call her right now. It's dinnertime but she should be free soon." Tesla smiled broadly.

Area 51, Nevada   11:58 PM   December 31, 1999

It was the New Year's eve celebration on Level 1 in the large, formal dining room, which served as a ballroom on this historic night. It was festooned with garlands of flowers and lavish holiday decorations and illuminated by the massive crystal chandelier in the center of the 12' ceiling. The string quartet finished their encore, the final movement of Mozart's Dissonant Quartet. From the shadowy corner where he was standing a dark, slightly built man unobtrusively walked over to the bar, picked up a goblet and poured it full of bubbly. It fizzed audibly. He took the bottle with him back to the corner.

The best looking couple in the room Lt. Bobby Wilson and Captain Mary Mulligan eased themselves under the center of the crystal chandelier. The minute hand on the large clock on the north wall moved to 12:00 and its electronic bell tone, modeled after Big Ben, began to peal loudly. They kissed ardently, arms enfolded around each other, then threw their arms wide open, prolonging the kiss. Everyone applauded.

The crystal champagne glasses were filled again, and Alfonso diGiovanni, the putative Master of Ceremonies, raised his glass and flicked it with his thumb and third finger. It rang out a perfect high C, and the audience, now silent, waited in anticipation.

He proposed a toast.

"To the New Year and the new millennium!! And here's to the Y2K that never happened. The Big Fizzle!"

As the champagne glasses clinked musically, Ludmila looked over at the dark man and smiled broadly. She winked. Nikola Tesla began to laugh. And laugh.

Above Reno, NV   12:55 AM PST   January 1, 2000

Capt. Deukmejian was now talking to Reno Air Traffic Control. The high winds had died down and had shifted and the air was as smooth as glass.

A high note from Gabriel Alcaraz's trumpet set the key for Auld Lang Syne, and the passengers on America West flight 2849 burst into song for the second time in an hour. They sang two choruses.

The movie was ending. Hill Valley, Doc Brown and lovely Clara, their boys Jules and Verne, and Einstein the terrier, back to the present in 1985, stood smiling in their gilded black carriage on the railroad tracks before the transfixed Marty and Jennifer. "Your future is whatever you make of it, so make it a good one, both of you!" he beamed.

"How long to Reno?" Gabriel Alcaraz asked Vanessa.

"We should be landing in just over 30 minutes," she replied cheerily. "Are you going to play another song?"

"Si si!" he laughed. The mariachis proudly got up and played El Rancho Grande while smiling Marta flashed her skirts and pranced energetically. Nano Brown called for another beer. Reverend Lazaro Luna smiled broadly and began to sing in Spanish—in a rich baritone: "Alla en el Rancho Grande, allá donde vivíiiiiiii-ahh . . . ." Brigham Romney kissed his mother and his sister, who giggled. Ian Marley, laughing, eased into the restroom, ripped the smoke detector from the wall in a flourish, stomped on it, and lit up. He emerged, laughing uncontrollably, dancing, his knees practically touching his chin. The Whipples pried themselves apart and joined in the song. Kitty Schödinger, in motley, turned perfect cartwheels in the aisle while Dolly Klein, arms in the air, danced behind her. Happiest of all, Jesse Maxwell, still miraculously cured, leaped out of his seat, grabbed Vanessa, kissed her hard and long, and twirled her around the aisle.

Palpable joy, excitement, a supercharged current of loving bliss pervading every movement, touching every atom, pouring out the fingers and toes in streams of light, exalting the bodies, the surroundings, the sound, the light, the air. Every breath brought the essence of life coursing through the bodies of the beings.

As Captain Ani began the descent into Reno, Monica and Bubba, holding hands, emerged from the cockpit smiling. "Look out your windows!"

The sky glowed as the waters of Lake Tahoe and the splendid, garish lights of Reno came into view.

"Looks like one helluva party!"

Tesla awoke at ten o'clock with a burgeoning hangover. The champagne bottle was empty. He felt an emptiness in his heart; missed Ludmila acutely. He rolled out of bed, stood up and keeled over, knocking his head hard on the corner of the headboard. He struggled up and sat on the bed, rubbing his left temple which was swelling quickly. The room was lit only by a 5 watt night light plugged in the wall. He felt the bump; it was wet with blood.

But something was wrong; something was unreal, which disturbed him profoundly. *It doesn't hurt! I can feel the tingling, the pain, but it doesn't hurt! The pain—it's as if I'm knowing it, observing it, but not really feeling it!"* He reached for a tissue, wiped it and tore off a piece, placing it on the wound like a piece of gauze. He fell into another profound sleep; then a strong image of Conch stirred him.

He awakened at noon and immediately touched his temple. The tissue had dried on it; it was still swollen but the swelling had receded. He was now fully awake and refreshed. He drained the plastic water bottle on the nightstand, and sat on the side of the bed. He realized he was still fully dressed; his shoes were still on. He slowly got up, walked to the doorway and flipped the light on. There was fresh fruit on the small coffee table and bread.

Hoping to see Ludmila again, he walked over to the pool area. Puplampu opened the door as if anticipating him, and led him to the edge of the pool. Ludmila was not there.

"It is time," Pupampu spoke to him gently in his deep baritone. "In your own time always be with you we will. Helped to save all in this time you have; now enrich your own time you will."

Conch's body arose fully from the water and he and Lantos glided to the corner of the pool where Tesla and Puplampu stood. Tesla bowed, and Conch placed his hand-fin on his temple, healing the wound. Then he placed his hand on Tesla's forehead and spread his long fingers on top of his head.

Tesla, in a virtual trance, came fully awake and aware. Something was different. Something had happened. His determination to leave the compound returned. He grabbed some fruit, stuffed it into one pocket and pushed he plastic water bottle into his pocket, then he boarded the elevator. His mind raced. *Readiness is all. Something is happening. I going to sneak out there right now. Oof! The elevator is like a rocket; my stomach is on the floor. But it's exhilarating. Real sensations—real!! The alien restored them! Where are you, my darling Ludmila? Now I am ready for you.*

Here at the top level; nobody is noticing me. I wonder if I'm even visible! But I am vibrating with those energies.

He ran into Gerhard, who was coming in.

"Professor! We didn't want you to go outside until we were sure it was safe."

Tesla smiled crookedly. "Sorry, I forgot! But I am fine, as you can see."

"Oh well, no harm done! Looks like you passed the test!"

"My dear friend, I am a man of nature, an outdoor man. I must feel the sun on my face, breathe the desert air!" He threw his head back and inhaled deeply through his nostrils. "Smell it. The desert perfume, even in wintertime! I am so happy, Gerhard, so happy!"

Gerhard smiled. "I'm happy for you!"

"I am going to for a walk now, my friend. It has been days, weeks in both centuries! Goodbye, my friend."

"Goodbye. Enjoy yourself. I'll see you later!" Gerhard entered the building.

Tesla walked towards the open desert, only a hundred paces from the compound. It was a warm day for January. There was a long east-west fence, but he found a gate and walked out into the desert. He sat down and took off his shoes and socks, breathed deeply and began to stroll northward. It was one of the happiest moments of his life. He didn't stop for nearly an hour.

Sky! Sun! Clouds! Earth! Trees! Fresh air, desert air! I'm miles out in the desert now, and I've kicked my shoes off; my feet are planted in the earth.

Ouch! I've stepped on a bit of cactus. It hurts! Hallelujah! It hurts! I can feel the pain, the glorious pain. I'm restored!

Power is surging up through me from that ground! I am Antaeus! The desert is alive. I humbly thank the Power and the powers for granting me this, for granting me myself. For saving me, for saving the world, my world. Dear Spirit, dear Nature, I am your liege man, your priest, your knight, your fool; I surrender my will to Your greater Will.

I am the God—intoxicated man!

It was now late afternoon. He reached a strikingly grotesque Joshua tree, beautiful in its own way, close to the five mile boundary and stopped to examine it. He sat down to rest, pulled out a large clean handkerchief, took a swig of the bottled water, and took the orange and banana out of his pocket and placed them on the handkerchief. *It's a picnic! I'd wish I had some of Panic's Rajica now!* He carefully peeled the orange and ate it slowly a section at a time. It was luscious. Then he peeled and ate the banana; it was surprisingly sweet. *Food tastes so much better in nature.* He then ate the banana in small nibbles, savoring every bite. It was delectable.

The Joshua tree was special; he wished he could photograph it. *I will take Ludmila here; we will have a picnic,* he thought innocently. He stretched and yawned, stood up and looked at the horizon. The sky was starting to turn; the sun was setting.

Gerhard was in his lab. An hour and a half earlier, after briefly seeing Tesla, he had entered the building. A disturbing thought crossed his mind: *Tesla's goodbye felt more like a farewell.* He tried to dismiss the thought as he boarded the elevator and rode to

Level 18. It persisted. He entered Rakoczy's lab to check the time machine, then into the adjoining room to check on the Sprague-Dawley albino lab rats. They were scurrying about happily and their eyes were no longer glowing green.

Forty-five minutes had gone by. The thoughts returned; something was wrong. Then it hit him. "The bubble!" he shouted. *We can't see it, but it could still present a danger.* He switched on the detector and received the shock of his life. There were unusual and powerful energy readings emanating from the bubble, and it was visible again. Adrenalin pumping hard, he took the elevator to Level 1, ran out the door and looked for one of the electric carts. There were none to be had. He then followed the path he thought Tesla had taken into the desert—north. The bubble would still be 4 ½ miles north. He called Tesla's name as loud as he could. No response. Heading due north, he broke into a run. In good physical condition, Gerhard ran nearly a mile, but then had to slow down to a fast walk. He kept it up until his side ached, then sat down to rest for a few minutes. His energy returned and he started running again. "Second wind!" he exhaled aloud. He loped more than a mile this time before he had to rest.

Tesla was exhilarated as he got up from his little picnic and walked around the Joshua tree. Suddenly he heard Gerhard's voice shouting from a distance.

"Nikolai! Teslaaahhh. Nikolahhh! Turn around. Turn around!! You're too far! Turn back!"

Tesla hesitated and looked back. Then he sauntered past the Joshua tree. Gerhard, running as hard as he could, reached the Joshua tree, still shouting. Tesla saw him and started to shout back. But it was too late. Suddenly a brilliant green flash burst forth, temporarily blinding them both. When Gerhard's sight returned seconds later, he watched Tesla's body glow, then fade and disappear as he was enveloped in the powerful wave.

He was gone.

Chapter 27

Postscript

Hand in hand, Ludmila Ivanova and Sandor Rakoczy stood together in silence facing east, enchanted in the pre-dawn stillness as they watched the horizon lighten ever so gradually. Pristine desert scents subtly pervaded the expectant air. The day promised to be a perfect one.

Tesla had disappeared only three days before, and Ludmila, though she did not witness his parting, knew well the gift that he had bequeathed to her; her memory had restored itself fully the instant he left. A powerful awareness of his legacy to her now flooded into her mind and body. She could only presume, only hope he had returned to his own time, returned safe and sound to 1900.

Something old . . . .

She knew, she had known, she had been known. It all stirred in her.

240

Something new . . . .

Rakoczy touched her cheek, then gently kissed her soft, full lips. Time ceased its forward motion; lost its moorings. They were an island in time; a baby universe. The currents eddied round the shore; waves of enchanted light transfigured the circular isle; the kiss lingered through creation and destruction; days and nights of Brahma, effortlessly traversing the galactic worldlines.

Time resumed. The light began to surge, not in a steady flow but seemingly in chromatic jumps, like a slow glissando. In successive leaps, a touch of scarlet at the upper edge of the horizon brightened to cinnabar, then to vermilion. He began to read to her from his diary, a tribute to Tesla, this stubborn and courageous man of science, words that could only be shared with a handful of his closest friends, words from Tesla's own thoughts, his own words. At that magical instant, Rakoczy almost remembered.

Something borrowed . . . .

"Tesla is with us no more. New Year's afternoon he walked out of the compound into the fresh air and sunshine. It was the first time he had seen the sun and walked on the bare earth since we returned to our own time."

Gerhard had seen him briefly around four o'clock. They spoke briefly. He was fine, he was smiling, and seemed exhilarated at actually setting foot on the earth, breathing the fresh air, inhaling the scents of the desert, and feeling the sun on his face.

As he approached Tikapoo Peak, nearing the five mile radius, the bubble became increasingly visible. Then,

Something blew . . . .

And he was gone. Without a trace.

We all wanted to believe it was really Nikola Tesla, but we were never sure, except for Gerhard. A beautiful, elaborate fantasy. In mere days we were already becoming complacent; the whole scenario was fading into the common light of day. A group hallucination? We all remembered the principle—or the curse—of Maxwell's Demon: if you bend Nature's laws, do so at your own risk. She will bend them back. But she may take her good old time.

With tears in his eyes, Rakoczy took Ludmila gently into his arms and kissed her soft, full lips. "He's really gone. Gone. Nothing left. He will be missed."

She kissed back with force, with passion. It was a sublime kiss.

The eastern horizon was now aflame. Muted violins, bassoons, french horns and double basses intensified; trombones blared in a rising pitch, coda moving towards crescendo. Suddenly the shrill sound of trumpets filled the air, fanfare, as the blazing star, our sun, broke the horizon. Their faces were suddenly illuminated by the gently brilliant rays; morning had broken, a gorgeous day, a desert ready to bloom.

Ludmila whispered gently in his ear. "I love you Sandor. And I have some happy news, joyous, wonderful news for us. For the two of us. Can you guess what it is?"

She smiled wryly.

ABOUT THE AUTHOR

Fred W. deJavanne is a gifted author, theoretician, linguist (six modern languages, three ancient languages), translator and editor – and musician. He has served as professor, vice-chancellor and college president at three major Chinese universities: Tsinghua University, Harbin Medical University, and Harbin University of Commerce.

His wide-ranging interests, besides quantum physics and mathematics, include metaphysics, ancient and medieval cosmology, astronomy, James Joyce, Greek and Chinese philosophy, and psycholinguistics.

His books include, among others, two novels -- *Time Currents (sci-fi)* and *Acid Reign*; *Einstein's Lament* – a collection of epic poems and essays on quantum physics; *Word Power*—a textbook and teaching encyclopedia of English word origins for university students, written in English and Chinese; *Waterlogged Chopstix* -- a travel book and cultural handbook for foreign residents of China; *The Comic Apocalypse*—a study of and guide to James Joyce's *Ulysses*; and original translations, French into English, of *Vertigo of the Void* and *Being and Time* by French philosopher Eugene de Grandry, for which he was awarded the coveted *Grand Prix Humanitaire de France*, for "services rendus aux lettres."

Prof. deJavanne served as Senior Editor *of International Review of the Arts,* and Associate Editor of *Heartland Magazine,* the *Los Alamos Independent* and *The Inkslinger's Review.* A pianist and composer as well, he has two music CD's to his credit: "Live at the Palace" and "The Phantom of the Piano."

He has four grown children who have so far produced eight grandchildren including two sets of twins. Residing in Harbin, China (next door to Siberia), he winters gratefully each year at his other home in Phoenix, Arizona.

{Drmeridian@gmail.com}